A TALE AS OLD AS Time

BY

MYA O'MALLEY

BLUE TULIP
PUBLISHING

A Tale as Old as Time
By Mya O'Malley
Blue Tulip Publishing
www.bluetulippublishing.com

A TALE AS OLD AS TIME
Copyright © 2016 MYA O'MALLEY
ISBN-13: 978-1523941063
ISBN-10: 1523941065
Cover Art by Jena Brignola

For Alexandra, thank you for sharing your love of the paranormal.

To Grandma, your love for Cape May inspired me to write this.

To Mom, Dad and Alan- thank you for your love and support.

CHAPTER
One

Roses. Roses were always said to make things right. Jackson smiled as he formed the plan in his mind. Things had definitely been strained for him and Maria lately, but he was determined to make things right. Driving along the winding road which led up to his house, he hummed along to an old favorite song blasting from the speakers. Fresh, salty air whipped through his truck, lightening his mood.

First, he would give her the roses. Then, he would sweep her in his arms, telling her he still cared. Reservations had been made at one of her favorite steak houses for seven thirty pm. Just enough time to make her remember why they fit, why they were so good together.

Jackson's long hours at the construction site had been unavoidable, but he had secured his promotion to foreman and now life would be easier. He would make more time for Maria and while he was at it, he would put forth more effort to grab a beer after work with Gary, just like old times. Imagining the surprise on Maria's face when he burst through the door gave him a triumphant feeling. Maybe it was even time to start talking about that family he and Maria had dreamed of.

Jackson pulled the truck into his spot, frowning at the other vehicle in the driveway. That was odd. Gary's car was here. Maybe his friend had come around looking for him and had stayed to chat with Maria for a bit. A nagging feeling in his gut reminded Jackson that he and Gary hadn't spoken in a while. Gary also knew the late hours he had been keeping.

With a forced dismissal of the negative vibe that was coming his way, Jackson increased his pace as he headed to the front door. It was locked. Maria usually locked the door when she was home alone, but with Gary here?

He fumbled with his keys, hands shaking slightly. The living room was silent, as was the kitchen. Glancing around, his heart sped up as he swallowed. It felt as if time had stalled, like his steps were rooted in quicksand.

"Maria," he called out, his hand opening the bedroom door. Silently he prayed his active imagination was going into overdrive. The roses hit the floor as his brain processed the scene before him.

"Jackson!" Maria called out, sitting up, clutching the bed sheets in front of her. Her face had gone white, so had Gary's.

"Man, listen. It's not what it looks like," Gary stammered, jumping up to grab his clothes that were strewn across the floor.

He was speechless. His world had been altered in the matter of seconds. *Breathe. One. Two. Three.*

Shock. He must have been in shock. Words couldn't form, his mind was numb. If he had any food in his stomach, he would have been sick right there. Missing his lunch that day had saved him from the embarrassment.

Maria approached him, her mouth open, eyes wide. "Jackson. I'm…we're…"

"Save it." The words finally came. She could save it. Gary could save it. Betrayal tasted foul. Its foul stench resonated from every inch of this house. Jackson's heels stomped on the vibrant red roses, squashing out his past and his future.

That night, he walked out of his house, never to return to Maria or Gary again.

"WHAT YOU NEED IS a diversion," John suggested.

John was an old friend of his from grade school. He was loyal to the core, just what Jackson needed in his life right now. Sitting outside with John and his wife, Jackson smelled the barbeque chicken coming from the grill. He didn't need to think about his problems, he could concentrate solely on the basics; eating, sleeping. Just getting by. Weeks after the horrendous experience of finding his best friend with his wife, the betrayal still stung. At first, he had gone over every fine detail, from the amount of time he had spent at the work site to Maria and Gary's part in the disaster. If only he had spoken with Maria more, communicated. But he had felt secure and trusted her, wasn't that what married couples were all about? Trusting one another?

"I *said*, you need to occupy your time with something else."

Funny John should mention that. Now that he was foreman, he had the extra time to spend at home. Irony hit him hard as he avoided eye contact with his friend. John's wife, Terry, excused herself as she made her way into the house.

"Such as?" It was true, Jackson knew he needed to move on and keep his mind busy.

"I could use some extra help around the pub." John locked his eyes on Jackson.

"What would I even do? I have no experience working in a restaurant," he sighed.

"Come on, you're a quick learner. I need some help around the bar and I'd rather give the job to you than a stranger."

Jackson scratched the back of his head. "I don't know, man." Thinking of the long hours he put in at his job, he figured he would need the downtime. To do what, though? Mope around and feel sorry for himself?

"Tell you what, how about you take some time to think about it and get back to me, say in a few days?"

A few days to mull it over sounded fine. "Sure, but I'm not making any promises."

John winked at him. "Thanks for thinking of me," Jackson offered.

"No problem."

Terry came back outside with some chips and dip, placing

the tray in front of him. He smiled up at her, grateful that he had some friends to lean on.

CHAPTER

Two

$\mathscr{G}$ARY HAD ATTEMPTED TO call him, once some time had gone by. Jackson refused his calls. He didn't owe that man a thing. Same with Maria. At first she had called and texted endlessly, trying to explain how they had all ended up in this situation. Once she realized Jackson didn't wish to speak with her, that he had cut her off, the messages grew nastier and more vicious. It was *his* fault for leaving her alone all the time. What did he expect would happen? He neglected both her and Gary; she claimed it was natural for them to find comfort in each other. *Please.* He knew she was being dramatic, and although he bounced back and forth blaming himself at first, with some distance and time under his belt, he now felt confident that Maria and Gary were cheating, lying, manipulators. Frankly, they deserved one another.

It would be a long time before Jackson ever considered dating again, but his mind had warmed to the idea of working at John's pub. Solitary evenings had been replaced by nights in good company. Jackson figured he was finally at a place where he could take a breath and relax.

$\mathcal{I}$T WAS ONE OF those dark, chilly days that reminded him of childhood. If Jackson were still a child, he may have been outside in the woods or playing in the surf with his brother, or perhaps fiddling around with his dad in the garage. Unfortunately, or fortunately, however one considered it; he was a full-grown adult, working at the pub. The job helped to pay the bills and more, it eased his loneliness. Beyond passing the time, Jackson actually enjoyed the tight knit group of friends he had discovered in the short weeks working as a bartender at Millie's pub. Maria would have abhorred this eclectic group, from Kristen the outspoken waitress who had started right around the time he had, to Andrew the elderly waiter and everyone in between. He supposed that was one of the endless reasons why Maria was now his ex-wife.

"Two dark drafts, white wine and seltzer, make it quick, hot stuff," Kristen drawled, slapping her hands down on the wet, sticky bar. With a swipe of her palms against her apron, Kristen swore. Only Kristen could make a curse come out sounding sweet with her southern twang. Jackson bet the curvy blonde had been a big hit back in Georgia, heck, she was a bigger hit here, and she knew it. Once, and only once, Jackson had entertained the idea of asking the woman for a date back when he first met her. The words had been hanging from the tip of his tongue when her new boyfriend walked right into Millie's and planted an unnecessarily long kiss on her plump lips, as if staking his claim. It was for the best anyway, Jackson rarely went for the outgoing type of woman, he preferred his women adorably shy and mysterious. Problem was, nobody fitting the stated criteria had crossed his path in quite some time.

Winking, he passed the overflowing drinks toward Kristen, whereupon sloshing her with the draft beer. "Excellent, just spectacular," she muttered, flicking some of the amber liquid in his direction. It had been an accident, really, but damn if he couldn't get that smirk off his face.

"Come on, come on," ordered John, who was short on patience on the best of days. "Stop clowning around, you two, we've got paying customers waiting in case you haven't noticed." John had been serious for as long as he'd known him. Chuckling to himself, Jackson recalled his friend's studious behavior in second grade, cozying up to his teachers and abstaining from the typical shenanigans of second grade boys. Adulthood had only made the man more staid and cheap. Yes, the man had his downfalls but Jackson supposed that was one of the reasons why his beachfront pub prospered. All in all, John was one of the good guys, loyal to the bone and that attribute was worth its weight in gold. John was short staffed and Jackson had wondered for some time why he hadn't hired some more help at this point. Shaking his head, Jackson wouldn't be the one to suggest it. Suggesting anything pertaining to the business equated with John becoming offended. The man was one stubborn boss, but Jackson loved him anyway.

After hours of slinging beer and other assorted drinks, Jackson was dead on his feet, but his mind was clear of trouble and worry. John was locking up the bar as the few employees settled in, checking tills, and tips. This was without a doubt Jackson's favorite time of the night. Usually the wait staff sat down after hours and enjoyed some drinks of their own before heading home.

"What'll it be, beautiful?" Jackson stretched his legs, preparing to make Kristen a drink. "Gin and tonic?" It was her favorite drink.

"Sorry to disappoint you, big guy, but I happen to have a date tonight," Kristen flirted, grabbing her car keys.

"Oh," Jackson pouted. He didn't feel like sitting at the bar by himself after hours. John and Andrew were beat and had already announced they were calling it a night. This place could be downright creepy after hours and Jackson never stayed alone, not since hearing from Kristen about the resident spirits that supposedly haunted Millie's Pub and Bed and Breakfast. (Yes, it was advertised in that order) Not one to believe such nonsense, he wasn't naïve enough to admit that unexplained experiences could still scare the heck out of him.

"Come on, I'm sure there are plenty of women that would love to have you beside them, keeping them warm on such a windy night," Kristen chuckled before running back to kiss the top of his head. Damn if he didn't blush, that woman had gumption all right.

"Yeah, our Jackson here would have no problem with the ladies if he would just ask one out on a date already!" Andrew grumbled from across the room. John added nothing to the conversation but a curt nod of his head. Super, so his lack of dating was now the fresh topic of conversation around Millie's.

"It would be great if you all just minded your own business," Jackson mumbled as he prepared his draft in a paper cup to take with him on his walk home. He loved each and every one of his co-workers, but sometimes they seriously needed to stay out of his dating life. He was the last one to leave, so he locked the door behind him, taking one last look at Millie's Pub before heading out into the night. *Ghosts? Spirits? Come on.* It was just a quaint, charming New Jersey Shore pub set in the basement of a beautiful old purple 1800s Victorian monster of a house. With a wave of dismissal, Jackson closed the door behind him, ignoring the chill coursing through his body.

Shuffling his feet across the empty sidewalks, Jackson glanced back at the Victorian home, movement drawing his eyes to a window on the third floor. That was odd because Jackson knew that particular floor was closed for the season. It didn't make sense for the owner of the house to hire a cleaning crew to clean the entire place since business was extremely slow during the fall through spring seasons. Maybe Mike himself was up there just checking things out, but Jackson could have sworn the owner of the property settled into his bedroom on the main level by nine o'clock most evenings, and besides, the elderly man probably didn't take the walk up there unless he had to. Checking his watch, Jackson swore at the late, or rather early morning hour. Again, the chill returned. Kristen and her wild ghost stories were just getting to him; he needed to ignore her when she started spinning local tales of ghosts. What did she know, anyway, being from Georgia? He was the one who was born here in this town, and given that ghost stories held little appeal, even as a small boy, he took the tales with a grain of salt. Although it would be smart to head home to bed, Jackson wasn't feeling very tired. He had too much on his mind, thoughts of Maria and his recent separation wreaked havoc on his sleep these days. How could he have been such a fool? He could almost understand trusting the beautiful brunette and opening his heart to her, plenty of guys fell into a similar trap. What he couldn't believe was that Gary would play such an integral role in destroying his marriage. As if on autopilot, Jackson followed the sound of the ocean. His shoes were off within seconds and the sand was frigid between his toes. Wild wind whipped, whispering his name. How much did he have to drink tonight? Only two beers. Two drinks wouldn't be responsible for the melodic chant he had heard. Pulling his jacket tighter around his body, he plopped himself to the ground, not caring if the sand littered his pants. Sadly, Jackson knew what his future love life consisted of. He would never trust now, it wasn't worth the pain. Right then and there, he swore that no woman would touch his heart again. Placing his head in his hands, he sat, silent. There it was again, that whispering voice, a siren, perhaps calling out to him. Something made him turn his head opposite of the sea, directly to that third floor window of the faraway Victorian, it was too far to see anything, especially in this light, but he made a mental note to ask Kristen a bit more about the local legends of the town that she was so fond of.

THE MEN FROM HIS construction crew did nothing to help his pounding head with all of their loud shouting across the worksite. What was in that drink last night, anyway? Heck, he knew it wasn't the beer, but most likely the lack of sleep and the dream he did manage to have last night when sleep finally arrived. Damn Kristen and her dark stories of spirits and legends. He had seen the most graceful form, classic in appearance, though he couldn't see her face. The figure taunted, teased throughout his sleep. He felt drawn to the female figure, yet fearful, if that made any sense. The most frightening part of all was the setting. Sure, it looked different in his mind, but when he woke, he knew for certain that the female inhabited the third floor of Millie's Victorian. Now, in the light of day, the smart man that he was pieced together the facts; it was the movement in the window last night on the third floor that got his mind working overtime.

"Rough night, boss?" Sam, a young man on the crew punched his shoulder while passing by.

"No... well, yes," Jackson muttered, although the man had

already passed by. Getting through the rest of the day was exhausting and all he could look forward to was a long nap when he finished working. Luckily he wasn't scheduled to bartend tonight. Just as he had turned the block toward his street, his cell phone registered a call coming through. As of late, he felt tightness spread out from the center of his belly. *Please don't let it be Maria or her lawyer, please.* Glancing at the number, he sighed a breath of relief but then figured out what the purpose of the phone call must be.

"Yeah, John," he answered tightly. Jackson squeezed his grip on the steering wheel as he listened to his boss.

"I guess I could, I mean if you don't have anyone else," Jackson bit down on his lip, sighing deeply. Now would be the ideal time to tell John that he really needed to hire some more help, but as usual, he bit his tongue. Perfect. So much for the nap.

"I just finished work, let me swing home and grab a shower and I'll be there within the hour, buddy."

Jackson pressed the end button a bit more forcefully than was necessary. There was no excuse when it came to disappointing John, especially since the men were tight. The extra money would certainly come in handy, since Maria was trying to rob him blind with her alimony attempts. Was she kidding? There were no children involved, thank God. Jackson had once longed to have several children, and, at his young age of thirty- four, he could still swing it, that is if his mind wasn't closed to marrying again. But really, alimony? Claiming that she was used to a certain lifestyle, Maria was on a mission to destroy him financially. He wasn't loaded, and even if he was, he definitely wouldn't share his money with a cheating spouse. Once he was home, he showered, trying to rinse the weariness away. Hoping for a second wind, he jumped in his pick-up truck and drove straight for Millie's. Last night's dream was long forgotten until he pulled into the parking spot next to the giant house. Ridiculously enough, his chest hammered with apprehension, just gazing at the bed and breakfast allowed his dream to come crashing back. *Get a grip, man. You can't be afraid to come to work.* Afraid may not have been the right word, he thought, it was more like an uncomfortable feeling that he couldn't quite put his finger on.

CHAPTER
Three

Every gaze in the place was on her. Jackson wondered if the woman realized just how appealing she was to the opposite sex. Kristen probably got twice the amount of tips that he earned, seeing the customers were predominantly male. It was another long night, although the tourists were mostly absent from the pub, it was a local hang-out of many regulars. Happy hour, post happy hour, you name it; the men flocked to Millie's like John was giving the beer away for free. It was a miracle the men put up with having only one or two servers on the floor at a given time. Let's face it, though, unless it was tourist season, most of the crowd was found at the bar, so most of the stress laid on the bartenders' shoulders.

"Hey, Kristen, are you hanging for a few tonight?" Fingering the bottle of beer in his hand, he swallowed. He wanted to pick her brain about the local legends tonight before his imagination ran wild. John raised his eyebrow, shaking his head, most likely figuring that Jackson was finally making a move with Kristen. If only he knew the true reason for his invitation to stay for a drink.

"Actually, a drink sounds perfect, that is as long as you keep your distance, Romeo," chided Kristen.

"Ooh, Kristen, I'm no Romeo," Jackson winced just thinking about it.

"Well, no, not anymore, but once upon a time, he drove the ladies crazy," John chimed in, gathering all of the bills from the till.

"I knew it!" Jumping up, Kristen narrowed her eyes at him. "What a waste of a perfectly good man. Jackson, with your height and those dark eyes, you could tear up this town."

"Let's not get crazy or anything," John lectured. "It would do you good to remember that you have a boyfriend."

He was a piece of work, that man. "Relax, Dad, I've sworn off women altogether, no worries there." Jackson called out from across the room where he was helping Kristen put the chairs on top of the tables. His retort earned him a sly look from John. Kristen slapped at his arm playfully before grabbing the mop from the back room. It seemed like an eternity before John said good night and closed the door.

The floor was cleaned, tips counted out and the bar wiped down. "Gin and Tonic?" But he was already stirring the drink. If Kristen stayed, it was a gin and tonic. Grabbing another beer for himself, he walked around the bar and settled in beside Kristen. For some reason he found it difficult to begin the conversation about ghosts. He felt foolish. Another beer later, Jackson found the words.

"So, listen. I know you've been trying for a while to tell me these scary ghost stories about Cape Florence, and I know I never appeared interested, but…"

Her hand was on his wrist in an instant. "Wait, back up. Are you trying to ask me to tell you some of my stories? Really?" Her face lit up from within. Oh boy, he might be here for hours.

"Um, yes." That's all it took before she spouted tales of Cape Florence. Nearly an hour later, she was on her third story but she had yet to discuss Millie's Pub and Bed and Breakfast. Rubbing his eyes and stifling a yawn, he figured if he wanted to get any sleep at all tonight, that he should just come right out and ask. "Kristen, not that I'm not intrigued about your story, but I'm particularly interested in finding out more about Millie's. Tell me about the history of this place."

Instead of being insulted, her grin grew wider as she rubbed her hands together. "I thought you'd never ask. This is my favorite, seeing as we work here and everything, but even before I got a job here…"

"Please, Kristen, can you just tell me about this place." He placed a gentle hand over hers. Maria may have been correct about a few things, such as his inability to listen at length to some-one who didn't get right to the point. Hey, he could admit it, he was a man, and he did have flaws.

"Okay, so Millie's dates back to the 1800s. Apparently there was a disaster in Cape Florence and most of the homes on this block burned down, Millie's original house included. There was a huge attempt to rebuild the homes and Millie's received plenty of attention. You see, this house was rebuilt. What was once a home for young women in need of financial assistance, a cheap place to live down here, believe it or not, became this gorgeous, updated Victorian."

"Were the women permitted to come back and stay here once the renovations were complete?" This story captivated his inter-est, right from the start.

"No, but let me finish." Her tone was hushed as she glanced around the pub, shoulders hunched. "There was one fatality in the fire." A chill not unlike the one he had experienced the night before ran through his bones.

"One, only one?" That was awful, just terrible. He couldn't even begin to imagine what the poor person had been through.

"Just one." Taking a deep breath, Kristen continued. "By the time the renovations were complete, the owner, who by the way, wasn't present here the night of the fire, decided to make Millie's an upscale bed and breakfast."

Wait a minute, the owner wasn't at the house? That raised a red flag in Jackson's opinion. Also, the fact that everyone escaped except for one woman was odd. As if she were reading his mind, Kristen nodded.

"I know," she stated, her head hanging low. "There's a lot of information here that just doesn't sit well with me."

Jackson got to thinking about the other women who had fled. "But those other women, the survivors, why couldn't they come back to live in the house?" Most likely it was because the owner wanted to charge an arm and a leg for the rooms.

"Legend has it that some did come back, but they all claimed to see the ghost of the dead woman, and I don't think she was very friendly to the owners, almost as if the ghost blamed the cou-ple. It was very creepy and, as a matter of fact, it seems the wife of the owner had some kind of nervous breakdown, leaving her husband to run the establishment on his own."

Well that was certainly strange, except if the home was truly haunted by a malevolent spirit, he could imagine then it wouldn't be too cozy living here.

"And," Kristen licked her lips before continuing. "I heard that the man disappeared, just took off, without even selling the place."

There was a lot of information to take in and lots of dangling clues for sure. What had been discovered when the police investigated the scene? Surely it seemed possible that some crime may have taken place here. Always a sucker for unsolved mysteries and cold investigations, Jackson got to thinking.

"Oh, I can see the wheels turning already," Kristen gasped, running her hand across his thigh. His eyes darted toward her face, trying to ascertain if Kristen was just being her usual flirty self or if her touch meant more. Her eyes flitted across his face, and he was pretty sure she was just being herself. What a relief, he liked the woman a lot and wouldn't feel good about hurting her feelings. He and Kristen were close friends who walked a close line between flirting and friendship and he was comfortable with the relationship. Most guys would think he was a fool for letting her pass by, she was curvy and sweet but again, not his usual type, and besides, the timing was all wrong. *Maybe in another lifetime, but not this one, sweetheart.* Kristen's eyes lingered a bit too long before she cleared her throat and removed her hand from his thigh.

"I'm curious, very curious about the ghost, the fire. I bet the library or bookstore might have some information on the story." Jackson bit his lip as he planned on visiting some places over the weekend. Suddenly he realized that he had forgotten to ask about the third floor. The third floor intrigued him.

"Well, yeah, there's tons of information at the local bookstore especially. Many authors have researched this town and written books on all the tales. I don't think you'll get more information on this house though, I'm pretty thorough in my research," Kristen shared. He felt sure that she was thorough, but he still wanted to try. All this ghost business was starting to feel good; it took his mind off Maria.

"Hey, do you want to join me on Saturday? I figured I'd check out the two bookstores in town and then maybe hit the library," Jackson inquired.

"Sure, Jackson. Two heads are better than one, right? And I love all the juicy ghost stories." Kristen's eyes met his before she glanced away.

"Great, it's a plan then. Let's head out after breakfast? Or is that too early?"

"Hey, how about we meet at the Cape Diner, grab some breakfast together, and then conduct our research?" Kristen fidgeted in her seat, gazing up at his height.

"Sure, that sounds good. Hey, I almost forgot to ask, do you know anything about the third floor?"

Her brows scrunched, causing her face to look quite adorable. Jackson hoped her boyfriend appreciated Kristen. "No, I don't think I've ever heard of anything peculiar going on up there, why do you ask?"

If he told her she would probably think he was nuts. "I don't know, I thought I saw someone up there last night when I was closing up, but it was probably just Mike wandering around."

Kristen was silent, which was quite unusual for her. "Or it could have just been my imagination, forget I said anything," Jackson added.

"No, you definitely don't have a wild imagination, no offense, Jackson. But I can't see Mike going up to the third floor wandering around. Besides, I like to think I'm pretty in tune with spirits and if I've never seen or heard anything strange going on around here, then maybe all the stories are just stories."

"Well, it could have been a nosy guest from the first floor, maybe someone just decided to investigate the hotel. There's plenty of insomniacs out there, trust me, I should know."

That seemed to give Kristen something to think about. "Hey, if I haven't said it before, I'm sorry about the way things worked out with Maria and Gary and all." Her voice turned to a whisper as she twirled her long blonde hair.

"Thank you, and you've said something before, but I do appreciate it." Silence filled the air now; her words had created an uncomfortable vibe.

"If you ever want to talk about it…" Her hand was back on his thigh.

"No, I don't." He stood up, causing his barstool to tip slightly. "Hey, let's get out of here, huh?"

Kristen waited a beat before standing; her eyes took in Jack-

son's grim face. "You sure you don't want another beer?"
   "Thanks, Kristen, but I'm beat."

CHAPTER

SATURDAY ARRIVED AT LAST; he couldn't wait to research the story of Millie's Pub. As a matter of fact, he didn't even know why it was named Millie's, another detail he was eager to uncover. Rubbing his hands together, he perused the menu while waiting for Kristen to arrive. A cheese omelet with some fresh veggies sounded delicious. Sipping at his piping hot coffee, Jackson mentally reviewed his plan for the day. He decided that Shelby's Books would be a great spot to begin their research, then the library. Depending upon how much information they received, they could either call it a day or hit Seaside Books on their way home. He hadn't been this excited about anything since, well, since he had met Maria. That was a long, long time ago. Normally he would have included Gary on such a mission, but again that was a long time ago.

"Hey there big guy," Kristen drawled. She looked adorable in her jeans and sweater. Sometimes he forgot how young she was, simply because the woman radiated sex appeal even in her unassuming sweater. Kristen was twenty-eight years old, she had her whole life ahead of her. Silly thought, but he felt ancient at age thirty-four.

"Hey Kris." He welcomed her with a hug before sitting back down at the booth. They had a spectacular view of the beach directly across the street. A thought popped into his head, he wondered why neither had considered it before. "Hey, we could stop by the local police department, see if there's any information that was passed down or even the town clerk's office."

"Good thinking, Jackson, you might be on to something there." Kristen scrunched her nose and signaled the waitress for coffee.

"How did you get away from Steve?" He hoped her boyfriend didn't get the wrong idea about their friendship. He wasn't the sort to cause trouble with another man's woman, especially since he had recently been on the receiving end of that situation. Trust, it was so easy to give long ago, now he wouldn't ever trust anyone completely. It still stung to think of it. Kristen's face dropped considerably.

"I'm sorry, did I say something wrong?"

"Nah, it's fine," Kristen glanced at Jackson, stirring her fresh cup of coffee. "I might as well talk about it. Steve and I aren't doing very well. It seems that a younger woman from work is occupying a lot of his time lately."

"A younger woman? How much younger could she be than you?"

"She's twenty-two." Her face dropped again.

Reaching for her hand, he ran his thumb across her palm in circles. "Come on, surely she's not as beautiful as you are." Then the unbelievable happened, Kristen's cheeks flamed a deep red. Shaking his head, he was surprised at her reaction; he didn't think the woman had a shy bone in her body.

"Oh please, you're just being kind. He claims that they're just friends but I feel him pulling away, you know?" Of course, he knew all too well. "I just don't trust him anymore, and, truth be told, I felt him backing away even before *Jenny* came into the picture."

So it seemed that Kristen had trust issues herself. "For what it's worth, I've yet to see a more attractive woman than you in this town, you can do much better, you deserve much better."

Her head tilted as she caught his eye, then she straightened her posture. "Thanks, Jackson, I really needed to hear that today."

It wasn't a lie. Any man would be lucky to have her in his life. Again, another time, another place, drifted thorough his mind.

"What do you say we talk about our plan for today? I got to thinking that with all the glaring red flags, someone must have researched this before. We just need to ask around and maybe someone has already conducted their own research. If we add that to our own work, we might just get some answers," Kristin explained, her jaw set.

"Makes sense. Do you truly believe in ghosts? Do you think it's possible that Millie's is haunted?" Jackson couldn't shake the vision in the window, but his stubborn head told him there were no such things as ghosts.

"Ooh, yes I do, and how cool would it be if Millie's was haunted?" Kristen's eyes glazed over.

"Well, that all depends on the spirit in question, it could be cool or it could be terrifying," Jackson added. Did he just admit to being scared?

"That's kind of sexy, a big guy like you admitting to fear," Kristen chuckled, holding eye contact. There was a moment of awkward silence before the waitress plopped their meals down with a thud.

"Let's eat." Jackson breathed deeply.

SHELBY'S BOOKS OFFERED BASICALLY the same information that Kristen had shared. They were just walking out the door when the teen girl behind the counter called out. "Oh, if you want to come back tomorrow morning, my grandma will be here. She's Shelby, the owner. If anyone would know anything more, it would be her for sure."

Both Jackson and Kristen nodded in agreement at the same moment. "Great, I'll come back tomorrow," Jackson offered.

"Not without me you won't. We're in this together."

That was okay with him, he could sense that Kristen was every bit as invested in solving the mystery as he was.

The library proved to be a waste of time. Jackson was beat from all the walking and was prepared to tell Kristen they should call it a day.

"Let's try the clerk's office and then head back, what do you say?" Kristen's eyes were wide, he hated disappoint her.

"Fine, but then we call it a day. Remember, we're continuing our little tour tomorrow," Jackson reminded her.

"To the clerk's office it is." A smug grin played across Kristen's face.

Luckily the office was open most Saturdays, even though it was a government office. Cape Florence was a small town, after all, and the employees often put in half days to catch up on work and opened up to the public to help out the community. The building was within walking distance from the pedestrian mall, so they set out on foot. Cobblestone streets paved the way to their destination. Jackson closed his eyes for the briefest of moments, allowing himself to step back in time. He imagined the horse and carriages leading the men and women across town, the Victorian homes, and the old-fashioned attire. Compared to life today, it was worlds apart.

"This is it." Kristen led Jackson by the elbow up the tree-lined path to the small but charming building that boasted the office.

"Let's do this."

Upon entering the building, the wooden door creaked, prompting Kristen to wrinkle her nose at Jackson. Jackson saw the humor in the situation too; this little building just might have some of its own ghosts lurking around. An elderly woman peeked her head up from the newspaper she was reading.

"Hello there. May I help you with something?"

"Yes, we're hoping that you can," Kristen gushed. Jackson could never argue the point that the woman was adorable, especially when her cheeks were pink and she had a mission to complete. "Do you know anything about the fire at Millie's Pub and Bed and Breakfast?"

The woman pursed her lips, frowning at the mention of the place. Shaking her head, she cleared her throat and lowered her voice. "I have to tell you, not much, but that particular ghost story gives me the creeps, you know what I mean?" Spinning her head around, the woman glanced to and fro around the office, as if a ghost would suddenly appear.

"Why? Why does that story make you feel that way?" Chills crept up his spine as Jackson leaned in closer.

"I've always sensed that there was a crime involved and somehow that dear woman was the victim."

"What woman? The ghost?" Kristen urged.

"Yes, the ghost. I don't think anyone ever got her name but around here we informally call her Millie, after the name of the pub."

"What do you know? Tell us everything, please." Jackson grabbed his cell from his pocket and fumbled with the screen. "I hope you don't mind if I record you."

With a swipe of her hand, the woman agreed. "No problem, but can I ask why you two are so interested?"

Kristen and Jackson spoke simultaneously, they glanced at each other as Jackson chuckled. "Go ahead, Kris, you first."

Rubbing her hands together, Kristen went ahead. "We both work there and I guess you could say we like a good mystery." Jackson nodded his confirmation.

"Ah, well. I would like to unravel that mystery myself. Say, if you guys ever find out what really happened at Millie's promise you'll come back and share?"

"Absolutely," Jackson promised.

"Your girlfriend is beautiful, by the way. She reminds me of my granddaughter with her little accent." The woman giggled.

Jackson felt the blush starting to build as he fidgeted.

"Oh, we're not together, we're just friends," Kristen grinned as Jackson dropped his head to the floor.

"Oh if you say so. The name's Mary, by the way." Extending her hand, she beamed at them.

After introductions were complete, Mary spun her story, which was exactly the same one that Kristen had shared. Trying his best to hide his disappointment, Jackson stopped the recording on his cell. "Thank you, Mary. It's been a pleasure. There's nothing else? Anything at all?"

Biting down on her lip, Mary's eyes lit up. "Yes, I know. First of all, if you'd like to go in the back and search the records, I think we probably have the floor plan of both the original Millie's and the one standing now." As Mary spoke, Jackson and Kristen locked gazes, nodding silently.

"What else?" Jackson urged.

"Well, I can't believe I almost forgot, but Shelby from Shelby's Books, would know anything there is to know on the subject of ghosts around here. She even does a little trolley ghost tour during the summers and around Halloween."

"Yes, we've been to the shop, she's off today but we're planning on returning tomorrow," Jackson shared.

"Good, good. Well, here are the keys to the back room. Take your time, but just know that we're closing in about two hours. If there's anything else you need, just give a holler."

"Mary, you've been a big help. Thank you," Jackson shook her hand before nodding for Kristen to head toward the back of the building.

"I can't believe she just gave us the keys," whispered Kristen.

"There's a lot of trust around this area, people see the good in one another." As he spoke the words, he caught himself wishing he still held trust in people.

"Trust is a good thing." Kristen caught his eye before moving forward. How could that woman be speaking about trust right now, with everything that was going on with her boyfriend? He knew that she wasn't just spouting words; he could tell that Kristen did trust easily. Well, that made her naive in his opinion and he hoped that she wouldn't get hurt any more than she already had. He made a note to speak with her about that later, now wasn't the time. Drifting dust filled the air as Kristen unlocked the door to the back room. It looked as if this place hadn't been visited in years. Cobwebs clung to the corners of the room.

"Is it me or does…"

"This room gives me the creeps," Kristen stated softly, gazing around.

Now she was finishing his sentences. He supposed they made the perfect team for investigating. A fleeting, humorous thought popped into his head as he imagined the two of them working as detectives together, they would make excellent partners.

"Here, the dates are written on each of the boxes. For such a dusty room, it certainly seems organized." Kristen glanced at the boxes on the shelves. Jackson scanned the boxes, finally zeroing in on a box with the 1800s written in scratchy handwriting. His hand touched Kristen's as they found the box together.

"Go ahead, you can do the honors." Jackson delighted in seeing the glowing, childlike expression on her face. Lifting the top of the box, dust flitted around, causing both of them to cough. Kristen gagged slightly as she rummaged through the papers.

The time period from when Millie's was destroyed and re-built was at their fingertips. Resisting the urge to grab the papers from Kristen's hands, he tapped his foot over and over.

"Relax, I'm getting to it." Smiling down at the papers, Kristen pulled at a file. "This must be it, it has the correct address."

"Is that the only file?"

"It appears that way. Let's move to another room, I can't stand breathing in this dust anymore," Kristen suggested as she clutched the file. He followed her out to the main waiting area.

Glancing up, Mary grinned as she noticed the file in Kristen's hand. "Why don't you two come back here and sit at the table, you can spread out a bit."

"Thanks, Mary." Jackson led the way around the counter and held out a chair for Kristen to sit. They sat in silence, perusing the file. The floor plan for the original house was of most interest to Jackson. Immediately, his eyes jumped to the sketch of the third floor.

"What is this?" The room was large and wide open in the original building. Currently, the third floor consisted of many different suites for guests to stay overnight. It almost looked as if it had been a conference room or maybe a room reserved for parties.

"It was a grand ballroom." Mary stooped over his shoulder, running her wrinkled finger along the paper. "Legend has it that's where the fire began."

His scalp pricked at the mention of the news. "What? Wait, why didn't you mention this before?'

Mary's eyes grew distant. "Didn't I? I apologize; I thought I had mentioned it."

Jackson could see her confusion building; the last thing he intended was to upset the woman. "It's fine, really. Is there anything else you know?"

"No, but again, I think you should speak to Shelby. She's the one who told me the story, I can't recall if there was anything else."

"Okay, thank you, Mary." They stayed for about a half an hour more, taking snapshots of the sketches with their phones. When they had acquired all the information they possibly could, they called it a day and thanked Mary once more.

"It was my pleasure, just don't forget to come back if you solve the crime." Mary waved. Odd choice of words, to mention the word "crime." Actually the word had been on his mind a lot over the past day or so. Was it an accident or a crime? He was determined to find out.

CHAPTER

$\mathcal{B}$RIGHT AND EARLY, AS promised, Kristen knocked on his door. His night had been a whirlwind of thoughts running in every direction. He envisioned ghosts, unsolved mysteries, crime, and that notorious third floor. All in all, he had probably gotten about three hours sleep, tops. Why was it that sleep taunted him, just out of reach, all night long, and now, when he finally fell into a deep sleep, it was time to wake up?

"Coming," Jackson rubbed the sleep from his eyes and winced as the bright sunlight filtered through the room. There stood Kristen with a bag in hand.

"Ouch, someone didn't get much sleep last night." Kristen observed. Dark circles rimmed her eyes as well, Jackson noted, smiling. They were quite the pair.

"Hmm, seems that you had a similar problem."

"I brought some bagels and muffins." Kristen held up the brown bag.

"You're spectacular, thank you. What kept you awake?"

"Ghosts. I couldn't shut my mind off, but I did come away with some interesting theories," Kristen shared as she yawned deeply.

"Hold that thought. I'm going to grab a shower. Help yourself to coffee, just push the button and it's all set."

"Don't mind if I do. How do you like your coffee?" she called out as he walked toward the bathroom.

She was making him coffee now. "Just milk and thanks." It felt good to have a friend. Kristen didn't have the power to hurt him.

"Hey, Kris?' he called out. "How do you like *your* coffee?" Her laughter filled the house.

"Milk and sugar, why?"

He peeked his head around the corner, winking. "Just wondering."

Silly as it seemed, knowing how she drank her coffee was important to him, it made him feel as if they had discovered something new about each other, the bond growing tighter.

He had showered, dressed, and sipped at this coffee while they munched on bagels and cream cheese. Although a few more hours of sleep would have been wonderful, he was pleased they had the whole day in front of them to investigate and gather facts. They decided to walk to the shop since it was a bright sunny day. Many women he had known would have complained about the chilly temperature, but Kristen seemed comfortable as she chatted about her theories regarding the fire.

"One theory is that this woman, the ghost, was an outcast and she started the fire, intending to kill everyone and escape. Somehow she must have been locked in the room and was trapped." Jackson listened, but the story didn't sit right with him. He certainly hoped the ghost wasn't hostile. It would take an evil person to try to kill everyone in the house and he shuddered at the thought of dealing with an evil presence.

"I don't know, I'm not buying into that one. What else do you have?" Jackson shuffled his feet along the cobblestone pathway.

"Okay, fine." She locked arms with him, grinning up at his height. "Try this one. The man who owned the place, what was his name again?"

"Mr. Todd Alcott." They had received the information yesterday at the town clerk's office.

"Yes, Mr. Todd Alcott was secretly running a brothel, and, he and his wife, along with the other women pressured, or forced the ghost into this life. She was angry at the man and all of the women, so she threatened to run and tell the police. They trapped her in the ballroom and killed her."

Kristen nodded her head, looking pretty proud of herself. No, he didn't picture the woman involved in something as tasteless as that. "No, I don't think so, but I give you kudos for trying."

Smacking him playfully, Kristen's jaw dropped. "Okay, wise ass, what's your theory?"

He didn't have one, not yet, but something about that ghost told him that she was good, perhaps even innocent in a way. Sharing his thoughts with Kristen about the subject would be ridiculous because his information was unfounded.

"I don't know. I don't think she's a criminal or crazy or anything. She's just… she's seems curious, but good." His mind was back to that third floor window. Again, it was most likely Mike that night, but if not, he hadn't sensed any danger.

"Ooh, if I didn't know any better, I'd say that someone has a crush on the mysterious ghost," Kristen chided.

"And you are ridiculous." Jackson rubbed the top of her head. They stood before the bookstore. It appeared that it had just opened; the welcome sign was swinging from the inside. Glancing at his watch, Jackson saw that it was nine-thirty. A bell sounded as Kristen opened the door. Several people were already browsing the store. Checking the sign on the door, Jackson noted that the opening time was nine o'clock. The sign was still swinging. *That's odd.* Clearing his thoughts, he followed Kristen's lead to the front counter. An elderly woman who appeared to be in her early eighties greeted them.

"Good morning, may I help you?" His voice creaked with time.

"Yes, we were here yesterday, and your granddaughter mentioned that you would be available to speak with us about ghosts." Kristen jumped right to the point. The woman's eyes opened wide and Jackson was surprised to see that her face seemed at least ten years younger at the mention of ghosts.

"Ghosts, you say? You've come to the right place. I'm Shelby, resident ghost expert, what would you like to know? By the way I run a ghost tour; it should be coming up soon if you're interested." Something about the way Shelby rambled on reminded him of his own sweet grandmother who had passed when he was a child.

"No, I don't think the tour is quite what we're looking for," Jackson interjected. "We work over at Millie's and we'd like any information you have on the ghost stories over there."

"Oh, Millie's?" Something not unlike fear swept over Shelby's face. It was there for the briefest of moments and then it was gone. "That one is interesting. It's a long story and there are plenty of theories, but nothing has ever been solved. If there are any ghosts that I'm intimidated by, it's her."

Great. "Aren't you intimidated by other ghost stories? Why her?" Kristen straightened her back.

"Oh, some ghosts are quite pleasant. Take Amelia, here. She keeps me company, makes me laugh sometimes…"

Jackson spun his head around and saw the sign was still moving. Lifting a finger, he opened his mouth to speak.

"Yup, that's her. She plays tricks all day long; she really does have a sense of humor. Sometimes she flips that sign around during working hours so that customers think I'm closed. Not especially good for business, but funny, nonetheless."

"But…" Jackson was rendered speechless, something that didn't happen very often.

"How do you know her name is Amelia?" There she went again, taking the words out of this mouth. Kristen had her elbows propped up on the counter now.

"Oh, she told me," Shelby stated, her jaw set.

"Great." Jackson turned his head, gazing at the shelves in the bookstore.

"What does she look like? Is she young, beautiful?" Kristen urged, her eyes wide.

"She's quite pretty and does hold some dark secrets. For instance, she told me that Millie is troubled, deeply troubled and that she has revenge on her mind."

"Millie? That's our ghost's name?" Jackson called out.

"Oh yes, Millie's was named after her," Shelby began only to be interrupted by a customer. "Excuse me, I have to ring up this sale. My granddaughter is due any moment and then I can sit and chat."

"I think we're getting somewhere," Kristen whispered.

"I don't know if I like where this is headed. I mean, if I were to buy into this whole ghost story and that's a big *if*, I don't like the fact that she's seeking revenge." He must be losing his mind, the way he was being sucked into all of this, it wasn't like him to believe in such things and if he had he not seen that movement in the window that night, he would be a firm non-believer. Even that swinging sign would cause him to have doubts. That sign... ugh. He was turning into a typical tourist.

"Don't tell me you want to back out now, that you're scared. You're scared, that's it, you're scared." Kristen's mouth hung open in disbelief.

"I am *not* scared," he pronounced a bit too loudly. "It's just that we're investigating a mystery, now we're getting sidetracked with ghost stories."

"You *are* scared," Kristen gasped dramatically. "Don't worry, I'll protect you." She couldn't contain her laughter.

"I hate you, do you know that?" But his own grin escaped as Shelby stared at the two of them from the register.

The granddaughter had to pick today of all days to be late for work. Half an hour later, after watching Shelby ring up purchase after purchase, they finally sat with the woman. Kristen was loaded with questions, firing them off in rapid succession.

"So this Amelia, what time period is she from?"

"Did she personally know our Millie?"

"Was it a brothel?"

Holding his head in his hands, Jackson shook his head. "If you'd just let Shelby speak, you might just get some answers." Kristen glared at him, but held her tongue.

"Amelia is indeed from the 1800s. She doesn't say so much as she speaks in riddles. From what I can gather, Amelia tells me that Millie was the mistress of the owner."

"Todd Alcott," Jackson interjected, feeling pieces of the puzzle start to fit together.

"Yes, Todd Alcott. A slippery man, from all accounts. There was a fire, which was filed away as an accident, but I don't think it was an accident. I think that poor woman was trapped for some reason and won't rest until she sets things right, whether it's revenge or justice." Placing her hands on her lap, Shelby shrugged her shoulders.

"What do you know about the third floor?" Jackson inquired.

A sparkle lit her gaze. "Ah, yes. Well, the third floor housed the grand ballroom, where the fire was said to have started." Shelby shared as she fiddled with her pearl necklace.

"What else?" Jackson could see that she was struggling to remember the facts.

"If I recall, Millie herself was said to have loved dancing the

29

night away in the grand ballroom, guests have claimed to have seen her ghostly image dressed in an elegant modern day red gown, rumor has it she stole it from a guest room, she must have admired it so much."

"Dancing?" Jackson had to admit the sight would startle him.

"Yes, legend has it she's been looking for a partner all these years. Just the right partner, which apparently has been difficult to find after all this time," Shelby mumbled, as if in a trance.

"Could we try to speak with Amelia ourselves? Ask her some questions?" Kristen asked, glancing around the store. *Oh for heaven's sake.*

"Kristen we've taken up enough of Shelby's precious time, I think we should get going." Jackson couldn't believe that she would even suggest trying to speak with this ghost.

Shelby straightened her posture, focused now on Jackson and Kristen. "Oh, it's no problem. I love talking about this ghost business, it's just that I doubt Amelia would speak to you. It took me about seventy years to gain her trust. My parents owned this store before me and I saw her as a child, nobody else did, but I saw her, clear as day. She wouldn't speak to me for years to come, trust is hard to establish with these spirits, apparently."

He could relate to that. Finally, someone was making sense. "Okay, then let's just go," Jackson pleaded.

"Can we just take a look around? We won't be long," Kristen inquired.

"Of course, take your time." Shelby kissed them each on the cheek and wished them luck with their investigation. "Oh and if you find out anything else, be sure to let me know." It seemed that more and more people were becoming invested in finding clues to the mystery.

Shelby turned around, holding her finger in the air. "Oh, how could I have forgotten to tell you? One more thing. Kristen, be careful dear, she doesn't like other women. It's been said that she even pushes women, so I would be careful over there at Millie's."

This was getting creepier by the moment. It was one thing to entertain the existence of ghosts when he felt they were benign spirits, but something different altogether when he wondered if this Millie was not the sweetheart he believed her to be.

CHAPTER

Six

$\mathcal{M}$ILLIE'S WAS QUIET TONIGHT, which was fine with him. He could stand a calm evening, thanks to Millie, Amelia, and all the excitement of ghosts. He didn't have to ask if Kristen was staying after hours tonight, he knew that she couldn't wait to pick his brain about all they had discovered so far. Andrew and John had stayed for a bit and now it was just the two of them.

"Why didn't you want me to mention anything about the ghosts in front of John and Andrew?"

"I don't know, they might think we've lost our minds and besides, I kind of like having this thing all to ourselves." Her gaze wasn't lost on him. She was a stunning woman, but he just wasn't ready. It was important that he was upfront and honest with her, though.

"Kris, how's it going with Steve?"

Fiddling with her long blonde hair, she glanced down. "It's not, I ended it."

"Oh?"

"He admitted to being with his co-worker. He said he didn't want to hurt me but they're in love." Her tough shell appeared to be crumbling as he looked into her misty eyes.

"Oh, sweetie, I'm so sorry." He rubbed her back as she gazed up at him.

"Why can't they all be like you? I mean, you're honest, trustworthy…"

He needed to stop her right there. "Kris, I have plenty of baggage and plenty of issues."

"When are you going to let me in, Jackson? What happened with Maria and Gary?"

His hand dropped from her as he backed away. That was a topic that was strictly off limits. With everyone, including himself. He tucked all of that hurt far back in the deepest part of his mind. If he didn't think about it, it couldn't hurt him, right?

"I'm sorry, I didn't mean to upset you. I just think it would be good for you to talk about it."

"No, Kristen, I'm not talking about it and I would appreciate it if you wouldn't mention it again." He was firm with her, hoping that she got the message loud and clear. Tears spilled from her eyes and he saw the damage he had caused. See? That it just proved that he was far from perfect.

"Kris, don't do that, don't cry." He leaned over just as she gazed up at him, her blue eyes shining with emotion. She pulled at his collar gently, inching closer to him, he didn't stop her. Her lips were inches from his when he closed his eyes. Wrong or right, they were both hurting so much…

Kristen lurched to the side, stumbling to the stone floor as the painting behind the bar collapsed to the ground. *What on Earth?* Shelby's words filled his mind. *She doesn't like women; she's even been known to push them…*

"Oh my God, oh my God." Kristen jumped up, taking in the painting lying on the floor. "Jackson, did you feel that? She pushed me, somebody pushed me!"

It was moments before their lips would have met. What had he been thinking? Perhaps this was a good thing, the timing couldn't have been more perfect. He would have lost Kristen as a friend if he had allowed that kiss to happen.

"Kris, I…"

She could see it in his eyes, he could tell just by looking at her. "Jackson, I'm sorry… I like you."

He silenced her by clasping his hands gently around hers. "Kristen, I like you too. Just not like that, I mean I could if maybe I wasn't so broken."

"You're broken, yes, but you can be fixed, Jackson! Just let me in, talk about your marriage, it will make you feel better." She was pleading with him and he still wouldn't budge.

"No, I'm sorry, I just can't," he whispered. Kristen tore her hands from his and began to walk away.

"You know what? Between the woman haunting this place who just pushed me and your lack of trust in the entire human race, I think I'll call it a night." Kristen sprinted to the door and although he knew that he should try to stop her, he remained glued to the spot, silent. Only after she slammed the door shut did he feel his shoulders relax. Jackson sat, trying to sort through his tangled thoughts. He must have drifted off to sleep; he could have sworn that he heard a gentle whisper in his ear. *Jackson…*

CELL PHONE CLUTCHED IN hand, he was determined to set things right with that stubborn woman. Placing calls to her and texting didn't get results, so that landed him at her front door. He pushed her doorbell for the third time before calling out.

"Kristen!" Nothing. Mumbling, he pressed harder, as if that would change her mind and bring her to the door. Glancing around, he spotted a covered garage. Upon peeking in, he spied her car. So she was home, and she was blatantly ignoring him. Walking back to the front of her house he tried again but received nothing in response. Fine, he would just have to wait until he saw her at work. Figuring it might be a few days before they were on the same schedule, he sighed. He was planning on checking out the police station since he was finished with work for the day and had plenty of time on his hands. Maybe there would be some additional information about Millie's filed away.

He suddenly realized that if he was going to continue this crusade of his, he didn't want to do it alone. Part of the fun and satisfaction of the investigation had been conducting the research with Kristen. It was kind of like watching a favorite movie alone; it was good, just better with someone else. With shoulders hunched, he turned and headed back to his truck.

"Hey," Kristen called out. "Jackson!"

Dressed in workout gear, she was sweaty and cute as hell. He treaded lightly, not speaking until he faced her up close. "Kristen," he began softly. "I...I wanted to tell you that I'm sorry." Watching her stony expression, he wasn't sure what to say next. She had stopped him from leaving, so that was something.

"Sorry for what? Speaking the truth?" Hands placed on her hips, she still looked pissed.

"It's not the truth, I mean it is, but..."

"You're not making any sense, do you know that?"

She was right, he was rambling, and he just wished that somehow she would understand without him having to come out and say everything on his mind. "I know that. Listen, I wasn't lying when I said I like you." Daring a glance at her, he winced as she tapped her foot on the floor and crossed her arms over her chest. "I do and if I were to have a relationship with someone you'd be exactly my type."

Kristen knew him all too well. "That is a lie, you've told me you like quiet, mysterious women."

Did he really share that with her? He was an idiot, a complete fool. Sometimes his honesty was his handicap. "I do like that kind of woman, but I have to be honest here, you're a real special girl and I do find you attractive..." That was no lie.

Placing her hand high in the air between them, she blew out a sigh. "Enough! What is it that you wanted anyway?"

"I wanted to apologize," Jackson began. "I'm sorry if I acted like an ass."

Rolling her eyes upward, Kristen glared at him. "Fine, great, apology accepted. I have to go, I'll see you around."

What else could he do? Figuring that she would be okay in time, he headed for his truck once more. "Hey, by the way." He figured it was worth a shot. "I'm heading over to the police station, you wouldn't want to come with me, would you?"

Hesitating a brief moment, she opened her mouth and then shut it again before speaking. "Fine, but only because I was heading there myself. Come in and wait while I take a quick shower."

She didn't hold the door open for him, as she was already headed for the shower, but he knew they would be okay now.

"Oh and make me a coffee, will you?" Kristen's faraway voice came from down the hallway. "Milk and …"

"Sugar," Jackson mumbled with a grin.

CHAPTER

Seven

"**Y**OU STAYING LATE TONIGHT?" It was a few evenings later, when their shifts coincided again. The visit to the police station proved to be a waste of time, but what was strange was that there was no information at all on possible causes of the fire. Shouldn't police departments hold onto the records or at least pass them down to the clerk's office or something? They had left a message with the young officer to call if any information came up on the subject. Where did they go from here?

"No thank you, I don't appreciate being bullied by a ghost. I can fight, but that fight's just not fair." Kristen hustled away, carrying a tray of drinks to a large group of town workers.

Ridiculous, it wasn't a ghost. But then what was it? He felt the force of Kristen falling the other night. It wasn't like she stumbled though; it felt like she was forcefully pushed away from him. Still, to believe that Millie the ghost was responsible for the push was absurd. He glanced at Kristen gliding across the room with her tray in hand, sporting a large bruise on her upper arm.

"Man, I would give her some space." John stood beside him at the bar. "I just overheard her telling Andrew that she broke up with that Steve character. I never liked that one from the start."

That didn't surprise him. John was extremely overprotective when it came to Kristen, almost as if she were a little sister. Even John's wife, Anne, was enamored with her. It seemed as if Kristen had that effect on quite a few people.

"Yeah, I heard," Jackson mumbled as he grabbed a beer for a man sitting at the bar. Without wanting to go into too much detail, he kept his response short.

"I heard something else, too." John stole a glance at him. This had to be heading in an awkward direction. "I've heard that the two of you are spending a lot of time together." How on earth would he have heard that unless Kristen was talking about the two of them?

"I don't know what she told you, but nothing is going on."

"Don't get all righteous, man. Kristen didn't tell me anything. I'm going to give you a bit of advice. I've known you for a long time and I know you're a good person, that being said, you'll have to answer to me if you hurt her." John's words held a threatening tone.

"John, I wouldn't hurt her, I like her as a friend, that's it."

"Fine, if you say so. Just remember what I said, though. You're in no position to start dating with all that Maria drama still going on." John lifted a bottle of water to his mouth, nodded, and was on his way to greet some customers. Wasn't this the guy that had complained he didn't date anymore?

Where did he get off threatening him? John was only trying to protect Kristen, but it still irritated him.

Who could have possibly said anything about their relation-ship? The list of suspects was slim around here, so Jackson figured that left Andrew. Andrew and Kristen were tight, he supposed it must be him. Jackson planned to give him a piece of his mind later, the man was nice, but he needed to mind his own business.

When closing time came, Kristen glanced at Jackson before grabbing her jacket and her keys. Kristen would probably nev-er stay past closing again. He wasn't afraid of a ghost, though. Ghosts… outlandish. John had settled himself at the end of the bar with a drink in hand while Andrew stretched his arms and headed for the door.

"Hold up a minute, Andrew," he called out. John glanced his way and studied the two men.

"What's up? I'm beat."

"Listen, you didn't happen to say anything about Kristen and me to John, did you?" Jackson was trying to keep his voice down, but the glare on John's face said that he got the gist of the discussion.

"I… um, might have." Andrew's brows turned down. Jackson couldn't be angry with this gentle man.

"Why, Andrew? I mean, we're just friends."

"She doesn't feel the same. I'm sorry, but don't hurt her." Andrew pulled his shoulders back.

"I won't. My God, I won't," Jackson declared as Andrew muttered something to himself, shaking his head.

"Don't, man, don't." Jackson directed his words at John, who surely had something to say on the matter.

Holding up his hands, John was surprisingly silent. Jackson poured a draft for himself and settled in beside John. Changing the subject was probably a good idea. As usual, the focus of his thoughts was on the ghost story.

"Have you ever heard of the legend of the ghost around here?"

John took a swig of his beer before responding. "I suppose I have."

"And?"

"And, it makes for good business."

"So you don't believe any of it? The fire? The woman?"

John shook his head. "I believe there was a fire, there are articles to prove it, but a ghost? Like I said, it's good for business."

Jackson shared his recent adventures with John, explaining further about why he and Kristen were spending so much time together. John nodded here and there, but otherwise remained quiet.

"Also, did you see the bruise on Kristen's arm? I swear, it was like some force pushed her," Jackson exclaimed.

That got a chuckle from John. "Whoa, are you telling me that *you*, Jackson, the man I've known forever, is a believer in the supernatural?"

He supposed he was starting to believe, there was no sense denying it, he didn't know if he believed in ghosts, per se, but he was open to the unexplained.

"I also saw a figure in the third floor window," Jackson admitted, clearing his throat.

John's laughter boomed around him. "Jackson, it was probably your imagination." He was mocking him; his childhood friend was mocking him. "I would maybe lay off the booze when you're here after hours, man." Slapping his shoulder, John stood and turned to leave. Glancing back at Jackson, John raised his hand and chuckled once more. Fine, so now his friend thought he was losing his mind. There was one piece of the conversation that intrigued him, though. The mention of a newspaper article, he had been so annoyed with John that it had slipped his mind to ask where the article had been seen. Of course, they had forgotten one stop on their tour; they had forgotten the local shore museum, which featured antiques of all kinds, including newspaper clippings. It couldn't hurt to take a look.

As he was finishing the last swig of his beer, he heard the door opening. John must have forgotten something. It wasn't John, though, it was a young blonde woman. Why hadn't John locked the door when he left?

"I'm sorry, miss, but we're closed." It was difficult to make out her features in the dim lighting, but as she approached, Jackson sucked in his breath. This blonde haired woman was breathtaking.

"Oh, but I wasn't here to drink, I'm here for the job." The woman's voice flowed like silk. It was difficult to pry his eyes from her face. A job? Did John finally suck it up and offer someone a job? That was welcome news.

"Oh, well…" Where was his tongue? Her green eyes fixed on his face. "I… the boss, my friend, John, already went home for the night." He was surprised John would forget such a thing.

"Okay, well in that case, I'm exhausted. Do you mind if I sit for a few?"

Did he mind? But this was precisely the kind of woman he needed to stay away from. The air between them seemed to hum with electricity. "Um… yeah I guess. Can I get you something to drink?"

Her eyebrows lifted at the offer. "Sounds delightful," she quipped. "What do you have to offer?"

"Beer, wine, gin and tonic?" At the mention of gin and tonic, she flinched and stuck out her tongue. Okay, so she didn't like gin and tonic.

"I'll have a red wine please, if you don't mind."

Her posture and her diction was very proper. He was impressed with her manners. As challenging as it was to look at her for fear of spilling the wine, he took his time and attempted to steady his hands while pouring her drink.

"Thank you. I'm sorry, I didn't get your name," she stated.

"Jackson, I'm Jackson Tomkins. It's nice to meet you." Jackson offered her his hand which was still shaking slightly.

"Emily, nice to meet you too." She giggled then turned her face away.

This spectacular creature was acting just as nervous as he felt. Amazing. "I apologize for my rudeness, I'm just a bit shy is all."

A bit shy? Oh my goodness, this woman was getting to him and she'd only been sitting at the bar for minutes. "Hi Emily, beautiful name by the way." He liked the sound of it rolling off his tongue.

"Thanks." She wasn't much with words, he noticed but it only seemed to make her more mysterious.

"So, are you new to this area?"

"Yes."

"If you don't mind me asking, where did you come from?"

"Oh, not too far."

"Oh," he stated. Fine, so she wasn't up for sharing many details which was okay because he was just a stranger to her.

"I have to go, I'll be back though." She managed as she rose from her seat.

A full glass of red wine remained. "But you didn't even touch your drink."

"It's okay, I don't drink much. It was nice to meet you; I look forward to seeing you again." She was out the door before he could even respond. Gone, but she had left quite an impression on him. Yes, he had a feeling that he would be seeing her again soon.

CHAPTER

SHE STAYED ON HIS mind all night and into the next day. What if she didn't come back, what then? It was as if someone had asked him to share all of the details of the perfect woman, and she had been designed just for him. It was crazy, he didn't even know her, and he certainly wasn't in any shape for a relationship. It didn't matter, his heart was overruling his head here, and he couldn't wait to lay eyes on her again. Love at first sight had seemed like a distant concept, one that writers used to weave elaborate tales of love. It didn't really exist, did it? He couldn't be sure anymore. She was innocence, beauty, and sweetness wrapped in one. He should probably get his head examined, maybe John was right, and all of these ghost stories had gone straight to his head.

"What's on your mind?" Kristen squinted her eyes at him as they approached the museum on the beach.

"Oh, nothing, it's nothing." It was probably not a good idea to share the news of the recent guest at Millie's. He was pretty sure it wouldn't go over well with her.

"Come on, they're open."

Following alongside Kristen, he was concerned about the fallout if Emily did get the job at Millie's. He had sworn that he wouldn't hurt Kristen.

Besides the two of them, the museum was empty of visitors.

Perfect. They could inquire about Millie's and then get on with the day. Kristen wasn't herself, she was uncharacteristically quiet, and he found he missed her chatter. After several attempts to fill the awkward silence, he gave up as he was only given nods and one word responses.

"Hi, welcome to the Museum by the Shore. I don't know if you're familiar with the area, but this town is rich in history. Feel free to look around and ask any questions," the gentleman offered. Jackson figured the man for about eighty years old. It would be great if he could still get up and out the door to volunteer at the man's age.

"Hi, we're here to find out if there's any information on Millie's Pub and Bed and Breakfast. We both work there, and we're interested specifically in the fire from the 1800s and legends of hauntings." Jackson got right to the point since Kristen was still sulking.

"Well, well, it seems you've come to the right place." The man chuckled. "I'm Bill by the way."

"Nice to meet you, Bill. I'm Jackson and this here is Kristen," Jackson replied, shaking the man's hand. Kristen followed, and smiled widely for Bill.

"You two make a fine couple, if I may say so," Bill grinned, allowing his eyes to dart back and forth between the two.

"Oh, we're not a couple," Kristen corrected Bill immediately. Of course she did.

"Are you sure?" Bill's eyes squinted as he gazed at them.

"Oh, I'm sure," Kristen announced.

Clearing his throat, Jackson changed the subject, guiding them back to their focus. "Where should we begin?"

Bill pointed to a showcase in the back of the small room. "There are some clippings of articles written about the fire and the woman who was killed," Bill shared. "Old Millie herself. Actually the poor thing wasn't that old at all, she was only in her early twenties when she passed."

"What else do you know?" Kristen asked, moving closer to Bill.

"Not much, how about you take a look at everything and then if you have any other questions, I'll be right over here, finishing my coffee." Bill ambled back over to the counter. "You'll see that there's a brush and a ladies bag on display that belonged to Millie," Bill added from over his shoulder.

"Wow, would you look at that," Kristen stated as she point-ed to the items. They don't make things like that anymore. Intri-cate patterns were etched on the backside of the brush. Beside the brush sat some faded turquoise decorative combs. The brush, bag, and combs all had hints of the turquoise color.

"She must have liked that color," Jackson added, gazing down at the items. His gaze was drawn to the newspaper clippings in the next showcase. He scanned the article and then went back to read more thoroughly in case he had missed something. "Look, it says here that she loved to dance." Jackson nudged Kristen, who was still entranced with the combs.

"And it gives us a last name. Millie Summers, huh." It seemed a fitting last name for their ghost.

"Are there any photographs?" Kristen finally lifted her head up from the counter.

"No, we have no idea what she looked like," Jackson an-nounced. He would love to see a photo of the woman. In his head he was beginning to form his own image of Millie. He pictured her to be elegant and beautiful.

"She was blonde, a petite thing, quite the striking woman, from what the people who have seen her tell me," Bill interjected from his spot across the room. The man's hearing was certainly intact.

"Who has seen her?" Kristen asked, heading over to Bill.

"My wife for one, but she's not around anymore." Bill's head dropped to the floor.

"I'm sorry to hear that. Did your wife say anything else?" Kristen urged in a gentle voice.

"Just that she was unearthly, surreal. My wife, Tara, her name was, told me that she's seen many ghosts around here but Millie was the saddest of all and the most worrisome."

"Did Tara say why?" Jackson inquired.

"I don't know, she said that she herself wasn't threatened but had heard of the ghost pushing other women, those she felt threatened by," Bill shared, shaking his head. "I'd steer clear of that one if you could."

"How could other women be a threat to her at this point?" Jackson wondered aloud.

"Legend has it that she won't be at peace until she finds her man. God help the man she finds. In order to complete herself and become free of this world, she needs to find her one true love. But it gets worse, she'll have to bring him with her to the afterlife."

"She told your wife this?" Jackson was incredulous.

"Oh not in so many words, but the point got across loud and clear. Luckily she didn't set her sights on me." Bill laughed loudly.

"I don't like this." Jackson felt that all too familiar chill return. Something about this whole story didn't sit right with him. They should probably just let it go.

"Oh no, you're in this with me 'til the bitter end. What? Are you afraid that Millie's got the hots for you?" It was the first time all morning that Jackson had seen her light up. It seemed he was stuck in this investigation of theirs until Kristen grew tired of it.

"Yeah, yeah. Funny girl," Jackson sighed.

"Stranger things have happened; your fellow here is a handsome guy." Bill directed his comment to Kristen.

"He's not…" she began before being interrupted by Bill's laughter.

"I know, I know…" Bill's laughter faded as he sipped his coffee.

"Bill, thank you, you've been a big help," Jackson said, enjoying the banter.

"No problem. I didn't mention this before, it slipped my mind, but I don't think it was an accident, the fire, I mean. I think there was foul play involved," Bill shared.

"I think you're onto something there. We agree and we're trying to expose the crime. Maybe then the poor woman will be at peace," Kristen stated.

"If only it were that simple." Bill sighed as he turned his head away.

YOU DIDN'T TELL ME you were hiring anybody," Jackson began, rinsing the glasses from the bar.

"Huh? Hey, Andrew, we need a mop over here, now!" John cursed as he picked up the broken pieces of glass he had just dropped. John had never dropped a glass before, not that Jackson could recall. *At least it was his own doing,* Jackson thought, *otherwise he and the crew would have heard about it all night.* John hated to waste anything or spend precious time cleaning up a mess.

"What?" John barked in Jackson's direction. Clearly he was in no mood for small talk. Jackson could speak with him later. Where was that woman anyway? He was confident that she would return today, looking for the job.

"I asked you a question," John yelled from his spot at the bar.

"It was nothing, don't worry about it," Jackson grumbled. He swore his friend was different outside of the pub. Shaking his head, John ordered Andrew to hurry. At least John had finally broke down and considered hiring some more help. Closing time came again and Kristen lingered for a bit, despite her apprehension at being in the pub after hours. It was good; she seemed to have lightened up a bit and had even apologized earlier for her silly behavior. He figured she was saving face when she claimed that she wasn't ready for a relationship either. It hurt to see her so vulnerable.

"Gin and tonic?" Jackson held up a glass, moving his eyebrows playfully. It hit him that the beautiful blonde had cringed when he suggested the drink. All night long, his eyes had darted toward the door, hoping to see her again.

"You know what? I think I will." Kristen offered up her bravest smile.

Good, maybe things could get back to normal now. Jackson served up her drink and poured beers for the rest of them. It was a full house tonight after hours, even Cliff, the young chef stayed for a while. With the tension of the day and evening behind them, Jackson and his co-workers let out some steam then cracked some jokes. When John, Andrew, and Cliff called it a night, Jackson didn't feel uncomfortable being alone with Kristen. Whatever awkward moment they had created for themselves had now passed and Jackson was relieved. He wanted to ask her if she was scared being there alone after hours, but didn't wish to rehash the events from the night before.

"You know, I think John is hiring some new help finally," Jackson shared before wishing he could pull the words back.

"Oh? Who is it?"

"I never met her before. She came in last night after you left, stating that she was here to talk to John about a job."

"That's just weird. John would never forget something like that. He wouldn't just leave before the woman came for the interview," Kristen stated.

"I wouldn't think so normally, except for the way he's been talking about the renovations at his house and all. Heck, I was at his place working and it's a gigantic job, I'm sure he's under a tremendous amount of stress." Jackson had been over there on and off helping out the best he could after normal work hours, but they were tied up waiting for an electrician.

"What does she look like?" He should have known that Kristen would ask such a loaded question.

"What does she look like?" He had been told by Maria that it made a man look guilty as hell when they repeated a question like that. Not that he had anything to feel guilty about with Maria. He had never even entertained the idea of straying, something that Maria couldn't lay claim to. Perhaps he should have paid a bit more attention to the way his wife had responded to his questions.

"Yes, that's what I asked. What does she look like?"

Lying was an option, but then if the woman returned, Kristen would see right through his fib. "Oh, she's... pretty."

"Pretty? Go on," Kristen prompted, narrowing her eyes.

"Yes, not my type but pretty I suppose." Jackson coughed, wracking his mind for something, anything to change the subject.

Kristen was on the verge of despising him again so he blurted out the first thing that came to mind. "Want to explore the place? Look for her?"

"For Millie?" Kristen's eyes were wide as she glanced around the room. The distraction had been a success.

"Forget I even mentioned it, we should probably just head home, it's been a long day," Jackson suggested. The thought of actually going up there and exploring gave him the creeps.

"Okay, let's explore!" Kristen practically squealed as she led him by the elbow to the door. Long gone was her fear of Millie, he noticed.

"I don't know if it's a good idea, I mean, we should probably come back when we have flashlights." Jackson attempted to stall Kristen, but she wasn't having any of it.

"You are such a chicken, Jackson. A big strong man like you?" Flipping on her flashlight app on her cell, her smile was evil. She was an evil, wicked woman, and there was no way that he would let her one up him. He was no chicken.

"Fine, Kris, you win. For the record, you were the one who ran out of here the other night white as a sheet."

"Touché," she mumbled.

Disappointment flooded over him as he realized Emily wasn't returning this evening. What if she had gotten another job?

"Ready, hot stuff?" Kristen teased. It felt good to have things back to normal between them, flirting and all.

They closed up and then headed outside to the main entrance. Since it was so late, they remained silent as he opened the front door. Mike kept the main door unlocked for the few autumn guests. "Be quiet so we don't wake anyone," Kristen whispered.

"What?" Jackson whispered back, playing with her. "What was that?"

Jackson felt a smack on his bottom; he then tripped over his own feet in the dim light. Kristen was the first to burst out in laughter, his snickering followed, not unlike the sound of a school boy trying his very best to contain himself in the classroom, knowing he would have to contend with the strict teacher. When they had regained their composure, Jackson led the way to the winding stairway. The house was breathtaking, its presence formal and proud. The creaking steps caused Kristen to start giggling again.

"Stop that, you. " Jackson matched her laughter.

"Where are you going?" Kristen was serious now, tugging at the bottom of his dress shirt. "Stop!" she hissed between clenched teeth.

"If we're going to do this, let's do it the right way," Jackson explained.

"The third floor? Is that where you're going?" She looked pale, even in the darkness.

"No, it's where *we're* going," Jackson corrected, turning to see her expression with delight. She was the one who had taken him up on this offer, one he was certain she would refuse. His smile grew as she clung to the back of his shirt.

"What was that?" Kristen grew still. Jackson strained to hear something but the only thing that met his ears was silence. Deafening silence.

"It's your imagination, let's go." He started. "Or are you too much of a chicken? We could turn around and go home, you know."

"Oh no you don't," Kristen insisted. "I'm not afraid, I was just saying."

Sure. The woman was dead scared, she was just too proud to admit it. Now that he was up here, this close to the third floor, his heart hammered in his chest. Damn if he would admit it, though.

"Follow me," he ordered, grabbing her hand as they reached the top of the staircase. Third floor, top floor, this was it.

Side by side, they walked hand in hand. There was nothing but the sound of their own footsteps and heartbeats. According to the floor plan, this was the floor that housed the grand ballroom. The entire floor had been the ballroom. It would help to have some light here. Where were the light switches? The light from Kristen's cell phone allowed them to see the switch. Fumbling with his hands, he flicked the switch upward. Nothing. "Damn," he muttered. Kristen pulled herself closer to him. Sometimes he wished he were a woman so he could throw his fears out in the open, not disguise them. Maria would say he was stereotyping and that plenty of men showed their fears. He supposed that was true, maybe he was a horrible guy for even thinking such a thing.

"Jackson, I think we've seen enough, I'd rather try to talk with Amelia, in the light of day at the book store," she whispered, clinging to him. Hell, he wanted to cling to her just as badly. There, it was out in the open, he was scared shitless. This place was so creepy, the air held a palpable tension that he couldn't put into words. He took a deep breath. Jackson imagined how glamorous and beautiful this floor must have been as he took it all in, finding it easy to see the arched doorways and cathedral ceiling. Wide windows probably introduced a spacious balcony.

"Jackson, I'm not afraid to admit it, I'm freaked out, okay? Let's get out of here!" Her voice projected in this space.

"Okay, okay. I might have to confess that I'm a bit freaked out myself," he admitted. It was mind over matter, he was sure of it but he just wanted out.

"Good, come on." Kristen guided him forward, close at his heels. He grasped her hand from behind and he led them back to the grand stairway. They were down to the second floor, and he nearly breathed a sigh of relief until he felt it. It was Kristen, behind him.

Spinning around, his jaw dropped. "What are you doing?" Jackson demanded, trying to grasp her. She slipped from his hands, it was of no use, as if she was torn from him, she slipped and stumbled down the stairs. He was helpless to stop it from happening.

"Kristen!" Jackson yelled as she screamed, tumbling further. Oh my God, she was falling, and he was helpless. He sprinted to the spot where she had landed. Kristen was crying in pain.

"Are you okay? Honey, speak to me!" He didn't know if he should touch her or not. "Speak to me, can you move? Does your head or neck hurt?"

Sobbing, Kristen found her words. "It's my ankle, it hurts, Jackson. I can't move it," she cried.

"It's okay, what happened?" He leaned over, cradling her.

"Get me out of here, now, Jackson, please just get me out of here," she sobbed heavily.

Lifting her into his arms, he carried her down the remaining stairs. Retracing the moment when she had fallen, he tried to make sense of it but it didn't make sense. "Shh, you're going to be okay."

When they had made it to the front door and were safely outside, he kept her in his arms.

"It was her, she wants to hurt me, Jackson. She pushed me down the stairs." Kristen gathered her breath and hid her face in his chest. "Take me home."

"Of course, Kris, don't worry." He would have told her that she wasn't in danger, that it was all a coincidence, but his gaze was drawn to the third floor. There it was again, he was sure of it this time. There was movement, he couldn't make out her face but he saw the strands of golden hair, as sure as he saw his hands in front of him, glistening in the moonlit window.

CHAPTER

Nine

KRISTEN NEEDED A FRIEND and she needed company. He had never seen her so upset before. Only after promising her that he would stay the night, on the couch, of course, did he finally see her breathe. Not wishing to spook her any further, he omitted the vision of the blonde on the third floor when they spoke of the incident.

"You think I'm crazy, don't you?" Kristen lay there on the couch while Jackson held the ice pack to her ankle. *No, as a matter of fact, I don't, because I saw the ghost who did it.*

Instead, he bit his tongue and gazed at her shadow-rimmed eyes. "No, Kris, I don't think you're crazy, you've been through a lot, just try to get some sleep."

"But you don't believe me, do you?"

If only she knew. Hell, she probably should know, since she would be returning to work, and she was half of their investigative team. It should be fine now that she was safe and sound at home.

"I believe you," he began.

"You're just saying that, you don't believe me, I can tell."

"I believe you, Kris. I believe you because I saw it again, I saw her at the window tonight."

Kristen's hands covered her mouth in a flash, gasping. "I knew I shouldn't have said anything," Jackson exclaimed. Now she was upset again. He needed to learn when to keep his big mouth shut.

"What?" Kristen's mouth hung open. "Wait... you saw her from the third floor window? Why didn't you tell me?" She shot straight up, wincing as she grabbed for her ankle.

"You're going to hurt yourself, sit back." Glancing at her, he sighed. "I didn't tell you because you were upset, too upset to hear that."

"Well, I guess you're right. Jackson, she has a problem with me. I think she wants to kill me." She spoke so quietly, he strained to hear her voice. He wrapped her gently in his arms.

"Oh, I doubt that." But his own words didn't convince himself. "Come on, we won't go exploring anymore, okay? And if you want, we can drop the whole thing."

Something told him that Kristen wouldn't give up; it was one of the things he admired most about her.

"You know, Jackson, I got to thinking about this whole thing yesterday." Kristen's eyes fixed on his face. "I mean, why are we doing this? Are we getting carried away here?"

He reached for her hand and rubbed circles around and around. "I think... I think it started as just curiosity, normal curiosity, then I suppose because we're both at a lonely place in our lives we took it to another level. What started as a fun way to pass the time became somewhat addictive to me once we really got into it." It was true, her company had eased his pain, and the mission had taken his mind off Maria and Gary.

"Wow. I kind of felt the same way, being with you, and filling my head with all of this spooky stuff has taken me away from all thoughts of my break up with Steve." Kristen turned her face away from his for a moment. "Tell you what, how about we lay off on the exploring but continue to investigate, in safer ways?" Her sweet eyes pleaded with him.

He chuckled as he rubbed her other leg. The girl was determined. "Sure, I wouldn't have it any other way."

"Stay with me?" Her eyes were already closing as he clutched her hand.

"You bet," he whispered, gazing at her face. She was a precious woman, no way around it. He cherished her friendship, and, in a way, he felt closer to her than he ever had with anyone, even Maria at the beginning of their relationship. Leaning over, he kissed her forehead and held her close in his arms as they both slept.

Millie

ACROSS TOWN, SHE DIDN'T sleep. After laying eyes on him, he was all that filled her senses. She felt alive, after all these years her mind had been lulled by the same sights and sounds, darkness settling in all around. Now she was awake, everything vibrant. It hadn't been like this with any of the others, not in all the years she had been looking for the special one, the *one*. As if destined to meet him, she knew that he was at Millie's Pub and Bed and Breakfast for a reason. All she had to do was tread carefully and play her cards right. Loneliness had been weighing on her soul for what seemed like an eternity. It was often better to be alone than with the wrong man, she was finding out through years of tough lessons. Men from her past had bruised her soul, one man in particular. Wishing she could just move on was never enough, she needed love, true love, to ease her soul and make her feel young and free again.

Rocking herself back and forth, her heart soared with hope. Hope. Yes, hope was something that she still believed in. His dark eyes carried mystery and depth, pain even. Two lost souls seeking each other, she imagined what he would feel like, wrapped in her arms, for her only. She could wait, God knows she was well practiced at waiting, but this time she wasn't so patient. There were some minor obstacles in the way, minimum distractions she could easily eradicate. Somewhere along the way, she had hardened herself to others; a part of her soul had grown cold and distant. Thinking back to the innocent child that once occupied her being, Millie longed so hard for that little girl; she even allowed a tear to escape.

"So how do we collect evidence on a crime that took place so long ago?" Kristen asked as Jackson perused the magazines in the waiting room. They were next in line at her urgent care facility to have her ankle examined. The swelling had decreased due to the ice packs that Jackson had persistently applied throughout the night but the bruising was worse and the pain had only increased.

"Hmm?" Jackson tore his eyes from the car magazine.

"How do we prove there was a crime and give consequences to a dead man?' Kristen's latest theory was that the owner, Todd Alcott, was a murderer, and that he had killed Millie and now she couldn't rest until justice was served.

"I've been thinking about this. Obviously there's no punishment for a dead man other than to set the record straight. In the museum on the beach, for instance, there could be a new section naming Todd Alcott as a criminal."

"Okay, I'm following, but how do we prove this theory? I mean, any evidence after all this time would be impossible to find, unless..."Kristen's eyes glazed over. He could see the wheels spinning.

"Unless?"

"We have to try again. *You* have to try again, it's the only way," Kristen begged.

'Wait a minute, why me? Why not *us?*"

"Because, she wants to harm me. I think she likes you, she has never tried to harm you."

It was true, but the thought of traveling that winding staircase to the third floor on his own didn't sit well. At all. "I don't know, Kris," he admitted.

"Think about it. I tell you what; I'll deal with Amelia if you deal with Millie. I'll go over to the book store, try to communicate with her when I'm up to it."

That didn't seem fair at all, except Kristen spoke the truth, that ghost, most likely named Millie, did seem to despise her. "You don't think the playing field is a bit off? I would have to go to an empty floor where I've seen this spirit, who, by the way, is most definitely hostile, while you go to the bookstore in the light of day to try to connect with a prankster ghost who likes to flip open and closed signs and will most likely shy away from you."

"Well... yes," Kristen agreed, smiling at him from her chair with her ankle propped up on a pillow. "You know, you don't have to go there at night, go during the day. Just tell Mike about it, be honest, and I'm sure he'll have no problem with you going up there."

That wasn't a bad idea. Heck, they should have done that first off instead of heading up to the third floor in the middle of the night chasing a ghost.

"Fine, I'll try." Damn that woman got to him, if he said no he would be considered a coward in her eyes, and, for some reason, he wished to remain a hero of sorts. He would be the hero to help uncover this long lost crime and set the ghost free.

"Kristen?" A middle-aged woman called out, file in hand.

"Come on," Kristen said, grabbing at his hand. He steadied her and helped guide her to the examining room. The nurse took her vitals and inquired as to what happened to her ankle.

Jackson listened with delight as Kristen tried to explain herself to the nurse. Fidgeting slightly, Kristen stumbled over her words. "I... fell down the stairs."

The nurse glanced up from her paperwork, adjusting her eyeglasses.

"Excuse me? How exactly did this happen?"

"I... um, just fell." She gazed at Jackson, and he choked back laughter.

"Sir." The nurse pursed her lips at him.

"A ghost pushed her," he blurted, unable to contain himself. Kristen joined in, causing the nurse to glance back and forth, frowning.

"That is not funny," the nurse reprimanded. "I'm sorry, if you'll excuse me. The doctor will be with you in a moment."

"Wonderful, now the nurse thinks I abuse women."

Kristen's eyes met his and the laughter returned. "Ow!" She winced, her eyes misting over. "We must be out of our minds."

"Yes, I'm beginning to think we are," Jackson agreed.

CHAPTER

Ten

KRISTEN'S ANKLE WAS FRACTURED and she wouldn't be allowed to work for at least eight weeks. She would be going stir crazy, needing complete rest for the next few days. She was given painkillers and a cast that required crutches to assist her when walking. With Steve completely out of the picture and her family down south, she was basically on her own. Kristen had a friend or two locally, but most of the women had their own families to attend to, so that left him. Jackson was more than happy to help out, and he promised to stop by to check on her after his day job each afternoon. Typically, he finished up work around four o'clock, giving him plenty of time to check in on her even on the days when he worked at Millie's at night. For the next few evenings, he had offered to stay with her to ensure that she could get plenty of rest and start healing. Glancing at his watch, he figured he should be at her place within the hour, not that she would be awake. Luckily, John's niece was filling in. Cassie was in her late teens and on a hiatus from college. She wanted to "find herself," according to John. Although he wouldn't be happy as her parent, the timing was great. What had ever happened to that woman, Emily? John was in no mood to approach as the place was bustling with late diners.

When at last the pub had quieted down, Jackson decided to grab a quick beer to unwind before heading to Kristen's place.

"Lock up, huh? You're on your own tonight, I promised the wife I'd take Cassie home," John said. Andrew was already nodding goodbye, and Cliff had taken off about a half an hour ago when the kitchen had closed.

"Sure, no problem," Jackson called out, waving to Cassie. It wasn't that he was afraid to be alone, but it was a bit unnerving. Okay, he could at least admit it to himself; he didn't want to be here alone. Taking a last pull of his beer, he wiped the counter down and grabbed his keys.

"Hi, Jackson, right?" He recognized her voice before he saw her.

"Emily," he cried out. His chest was pounding; she was more beautiful than he had remembered.

"I hope you don't mind, but I just got off my other shift, and I figured you'd be open." She spoke so softly, her words melting.

"I... uh, sure. What happened? You never came back for the job," Jackson inquired.

"Oh, yes, the job. I got a job closer to my house."

He could feel the disappointment. "Sorry to hear that, I think you would have made a nice addition here."

"Thanks, that's quite sweet of you, but this is better, I'm sure of it."

"Where are you working, if you don't mind me asking?"

"Audrey's," she managed.

"Audrey's? I've never heard of it."

"Oh, that place across town, the one that looks like an old ship," she answered, twirling her waist length blonde locks.

"The Jetty?" The Jetty was an okay place but it didn't get nearly the amount of customers that Millie's packed in.

"Yes, that's it, The Jetty." Emily smiled brightly, fidgeting. "Slipped my mind there for a moment." Laughing easily, she tugged on his sleeve. Was Emily flirting with him? It certainly seemed that way.

"Can I get you a drink?"

"Water, please."

"Right, you don't really drink much." Jackson recalled the fact she had shared.

"Good memory," she stated, her eyes taking in her surroundings.

"Take a seat, please." Jackson settled on water himself, hoping that Kristen was asleep and pain free.

"I'm so sorry, is there somewhere you need to be? How presumptuous of me!" she exclaimed, standing up suddenly.

"Don't be ridiculous, sit, please," he instructed. She had been on his mind since he had first met her. "Don't leave."

"Are you absolutely sure?"

What was it about her voice? Was that an accent he heard? "Is that some kind of accent I detect?" When he had first met her she stated that she hadn't grown up far from Cape Florence.

"Accent? No, I don't think so."

Maybe it was just because she was so well spoken. He didn't know what to say to her. Before he had met Maria, he had never found himself tongue-tied with women. Either Maria had done a number on him or this woman was getting to him. Most likely a combination of both, he considered. After some preliminary small talk, he got to wondering if Emily had ever heard of the legend of Millie's.

"I know you're fairly new to town, but have you heard that Cape Florence is rich with the legends of ghosts?"

Emily's mouth opened with surprise and then she was silent.

"This place in particular, has a resident ghost named Millie," he shared.

"Millie, you say? Interesting, no, I haven't heard much except that there were some local ghost stories, but you know how it is, every town has their own."

"There's more to this, I believe. You see, there was a fire and one woman, Millie, that is, died. Everyone else escaped, don't you find that odd?"

Emily shifted in her seat. Was he scaring her? Making her uncomfortable? There he went again with his big mouth.

"I find it peculiar, yes. Has anyone looked into the crime?"

"Well, that's just it, funny you should call it a crime because most people just call it an accident."

"Are you researching this story or something? You seem quite interested."

"I'm sorry, am I scaring you? I can stop talking about this if you want, I tend to ramble on about the subject."

"No, quite the contrary, ramble on, please. You've piqued my interest," Emily added.

She was amazing, this beautiful creature actually wished to

sit here and listen to his stories. He continued until almost all of the facts were presented. One thing he purposely left out was the sighting in the window the other night. He didn't wish to scare her away.

Emily bit her lip, appearing to be taking this all in. Nodding forcefully, she spoke, "I like it, I like the way you've gone out of your way to try to piece together this mystery. All of the tourists around here must think it's all a big joke, something to get caught up in on vacation, a small thrill, if you will."

For someone who didn't have information on the topic until minutes ago, she was certainly showing some passion for the subject. A thought struck him, with Kristen tied up for the next few weeks; Emily here might just make the perfect partner in crime, so to speak.

"I'm sorry to hear about your friend, Kristen, is it? That must have been awful for your girlfriend to have gone through."

"Kristen? No, she's not my girlfriend, we're just good friends, that's all." He emphasized the fact.

There she went again, twirling her hair, biting her lip.

"You seem very interested in this story; you wouldn't be interested in joining me in my investigation, would you? I mean, now that Kristen is laid up and all."

Emily stood, smoothing her blouse. "I... no, I don't think so. Listen, I didn't realize how late it was, I'll see you around?"

"Hey, Emily? Can I call you or something?" He stood, arms extended, but she was walking away. Emily stopped and stood motionless while Jackson felt his chest pound. Faster than he would have thought possible, they met halfway, as if drawn together. She pressed her lips to his, the unassuming shy girl. He must have figured her wrong, but it didn't matter, not when she was in his arms, kissing him like he'd never been kissed before.

Time passed as he tasted her soft lips, savoring the sweetness. He was lost in her, he was a goner. "Jackson, I'll see you," she whispered before placing one last kiss to his hungry lips.

"Wait. Emily, wait," he begged. She spun around, taking one last look before leaving.

He had no idea how long he had been standing there. How was it possible that he missed her already?

Millie

SO THEY WERE SEARCHING her out. Many people before had attempted to uncover the truth, but their interest had been a passing fancy, merely an interest in the history of the town and the ghosts that still inhabited Cape Florence. The folks were correct in thinking this town was rich in ghosts and spirits, if only they knew the half of it. If only they could see what lurked in the darkness as they slept. Giggling softly, Millie was certain the majority of visitors would run, never to return. These two were different, however, especially Jackson. He intrigued her and she hadn't felt any emotion other than boredom, sadness, and hopelessness until he had come around. Jackson might just have the perseverance to uncover the dark secrets of this house. The girl, Kristen, was another story. She hadn't meant to hurt her, not really, but if the woman hadn't been frightened enough after she pushed her in the pub, she clearly needed a bigger hint. Tossing the woman down the stairs should have done the trick. Sure, she supposed she could have killed her, but Kristen should really learn to mind her business and keep her hands off Jackson. Why on earth would Jackson want to kiss *her*, she wasn't his type at all. The only problem now was that he was waiting on her, hand and foot. Not much that she could do to rectify that situation, but now she needed to bring out the big guns and lay some pressure on Jackson. He might just be the man she was destined to spend all eternity with.

Shaking her head, Millie knew her mother wouldn't be pleased; she had been raised better than to think of her own selfish needs. *That was a long time ago, mother, and this girl needs some peace.* With the grace of a dancer, Millie glided down the hallway, closing her eyes. If she tried hard enough, she could just about make out the grand ballroom this floor used to hold. Music filled her head, yes; she could hear the music again. Now all she needed was her partner.

$\mathcal{I}$T WAS A GOOD thing that Kristen had been sleeping soundly when he had arrived back at her place the night before. He wasn't in the mood for answering questions and he also wasn't a very good liar. Kristen was starting to know him well enough and she would have most likely read the high emotions all over his face. Was Emily just going to pop in and out of Millie's like some kind of mysterious angel from his dreams? He needed to see her again. Visiting the woman at her workplace, The Jetty, was a possibility but he pegged her for a quiet, private person, and didn't want to ruin this by being too pushy. Patience, man, slow down and do this right. Her kiss convinced him that she felt the same way, he was sure of it.

Breakfast dishes had been cleaned, Kristen was sleeping again, and he had the day off. There was no time like the present to head back to Millie's and the third floor. Not sure what he was expecting, Jackson figured he'd just go with it. It was highly unlikely the ghost would just spill the details, give him all the answers, but maybe she'd leave clues. He was hoping that Mike was around; he felt funny snooping around without the owner's permission. Mike was a good guy, he was sure he'd understand, but he'd feel better if he spoke with the man. Placing his truck in park, he shielded his eyes from the sun. It was the first time he had viewed the third floor in broad daylight, now it just appeared to be an ordinary building, nothing funny here.

"Mike," he called out upon entering the main floor entrance. "You here?" Heading toward the main desk, Jackson thought he heard him. Sure enough, Mike's nose was in a stack of paperwork. He signaled for Jackson to wait. Tapping his foot on the hardwood floor, Jackson's eyes averted to the winding staircase.

"What brings you here, Jackson? Relatives coming to town?" Mike inquired as he restacked his paperwork.

"No, I'm here because, well, it sounds crazy, but I'd like to check out the third floor."

Mike's hands were flat on his desk, back straightening. "Well, why would you want to do something like that? The floor is closed until the spring."

"I have reason to believe…"

"There's a ghost here, haunting the third floor." Mike finished his sentence.

"Among other rooms here, yes. How did you know?"

"I live here." Mike studied him eerily, tapping at his desk with a pen.

"Have you seen her?" Jackson urged, leaning on Mike's desk.

"Sort of, more like the vision of her. She's stunning, actually. Flowing blonde hair, tiny little thing. I would recommend keeping your distance, she's been known to be spiteful, and she's got an axe to grind."

"I know, I know all about it. As a matter of fact, she's taken an extreme disliking to Kristen."

"That's crazy, what has she done?"

Jackson filled Mike in on the course of events, up to and including Kristen's fall. Mike shook his head as if he wasn't surprised. "I don't think it's a good idea to open the third floor this year, I also don't think you should go up there ghost hunting."

"Not open the third floor? But every summer you're jam packed. You would lose too much business, besides, I don't think she would harm the guests, she has this personal thing for Kristen it seems," Jackson explained.

"I don't know, I have to think all of this through. I've heard legends that she has pushed women in the past, women she feels threatened by."

Why would she feel threatened by Kristen? The other part of the legend states that she's looking for her true love. Could it be that she feels Kristen is in the way? That she harbors feelings for him? No, that would be awful, horrible. Ridiculous.

"I'm sure your guests will be safe, they have been for years." Jackson pointed out. He hoped so, God he hoped so.

Mike threw his hands up in the air, "If you want to go up there, be my guest, you've already ventured up there at night, what could be worse than that?"

"Thank you." Jackson pumped Mike's hand.

"Be sure to tell me if you find anything," Mike called out.

"No problem." Add Mike to the growing list of curious towns-people. Taking two steps at a time, he willed himself not to think of Kristen's experience that occurred the last time he was here. He was upon the third floor in a flash, his heart racing from the cardio activity as well as from the unknown. The air was still and dusty up here, sunlight filtering through. Everything seemed normal in the light of day. Okay, this was going to be easy, he would look around, see if he could find anything out of place and he would be out of there. No problem.

His searching proved to be futile today, nothing was amiss. It was time to call it a day. Maybe there was nothing else to un-cover, maybe Millie was comfortable this way. He headed back to the staircase just as he heard the music. Soft at first, the melody increased in volume until it was filling his head with the most incredibly sad music he had ever heard.

"Hello?" He thought he heard a woman's voice, calling out his name. There it was again, louder.

"Jackson? Are you there?"

The voice was achingly familiar, right there on the edge of his memory, so close.

"Jackson!" Emily exclaimed, glancing around the suite.

"Oh my God, Emily! You nearly scared the crap out of me." Jackson gulped back his fear, trying to steady his pounding chest. "What are you doing here?"

"What is that? Where is the music coming from?" Emily cocked her head to the side, lips parted. Her lips were moist and plump, close enough to kiss. The question flew from his mind; he was caught up in a spell, as if hypnotized.

"I... I don't know." Jackson couldn't pry his eyes from her mouth, he drew closer and closer still.

"I think she wants us to dance." Emily's voice matched the melody, soft, sad, and smooth. His lips crashed down, and she wrapped her tiny arms around him, reaching up for his kiss. He swayed with her, feeling her, feeling the music in his very soul. He was in a trance, back in time, when he opened his eyes he wasn't afraid. The small suite had been transformed into a grand old ballroom. He and Emily had the place to themselves. The beat changed to an upbeat number. Reaching for her, he lifted her, twirling her as she shrieked in joy. Placing her down on the ground once more, they kissed again, this time with serious intent. He didn't wish to go back to his world; he was meant to be here with Emily in this magical place. It was gradually consuming him.

"Stop!" Jackson cried out, waking out of the trance. "Not like this." Emily and he both appeared to be wrapped in the spell. As suddenly as he cried out, the music had stopped and they were once again standing in the suite of the third floor. He and Emily had been so close to taking their relationship to a whole other level. He barely knew this woman and the passion he felt for her was both gripping and frightening. He had nearly lost control back there, yes he had come to his senses at the last possible moment, but he didn't like feeling this way.

"Wow, Jackson, wow," she breathed, glancing around the room. "What happened back there?"

"I don't know, as exhilarating as it was, it scared the crap out me."

"Me too, come on." She grabbed him by the hand and led him to the staircase. Neither spoke until they were clear of the third floor, back on the main level.

"Want to grab a cup of coffee or something?" Jackson rubbed his eyes, still unable to believe what had just happened up there.

Emily shifted her feet, grasping at her long hair. "No, I think I need to rest, it's been quite a day."

"Yeah, same here. That's not a bad idea. Can I give you a ride home?" As tired as he was, he still didn't want to leave her. The otherworldly experience he had shared with her upstairs had been surreal, and a bond had been formed in his mind. Gone was the theory of the ghost being in love with him, if that were true she would have every reason to harm Emily, and, so far, the woman remained off limits for Millie.

"I have someone picking me up soon."

"Oh? I could wait with you here if you'd like."

"No thank you. I appreciate the offer, Jackson, but I'd like some alone time here before my ride comes."

"Sure, that's fine. Do you mind me asking who's picking you up?"

Her gaze faltered, she looked down at the floor. "Just a friend, just a friend."

The knot in his stomach tightened. Was this jealousy he was feeling? How could Emily be interested in anyone else when she had just held him and kissed him like he was the only man alive? Just a friend, he had heard that before, but what choice did he have but to trust Emily? He didn't know why, but he did feel as if he could trust her.

"Will you come back to see me?"

"Are you working tonight?" she asked shyly.

"No, but I could be here," he answered too quickly. He was acting like a sucker and he needed to take a step back. This woman had him, and she was calling all the shots. Was it the challenge that was keeping him interested or was it her innocent beauty?

"Be here then," she ordered. Leaning over, she placed the sweetest kiss on his lips, leaving him wanting more.

CHAPTER
Eleven

Millie

*I*F ONLY HE COULD see her for what she was, for how she truly felt about him. It was ridiculous to think that a mortal woman would be a threat, but she wasn't taking any chances. Each time she saw him, she fell harder for him. She would wait for him tonight at the pub. It was so difficult to see him, so close, hurting from his own pain, without reaching out and telling him they were meant to be. Her own memories were still so raw, even after all this time. Focusing her mind on Jackson made it better, washed the awful memories from her mind momentarily. Right now, though, she allowed her mind to wander to the year 1871. It was a joyous year and it was a horrifying one.

He was handsome all right, even her sister, Sammy, would approve. He must be new in town. The man turned his head while crossing the cobblestone street, catching her eye just at the moment a horse and carriage came from around the corner, on his blind side.

"Sir! Watch out!" she cried. He jumped back, stumbling on a rock but missing the carriage, only by a fraction. Her heart went out to him; he blushed a deep red, dusting the dirt from his otherwise bright white dress shirt and vest.

Edging closer to him, she felt her pulse race. He was not only handsome but he exuded class and manners. His long dark locks touched upon his boyish face. "Ma'am, I thank you for the warning."

She gulped, choosing her words carefully as if he would be grading her on her grammar like a school teacher. "You're... you're welcome, sir."

Casting his eyes upon her, it was her turn to blush. Maybe it was her imagination, perhaps he wasn't judging her, just appreciating her. If only, she thought. She knew that her looks were okay, but she could never compete for a man like him.

"I'm Todd Alcott. It's a pleasure to meet you." He leaned for her hand, kissed it, and waited for her introduction. She gave him her name, did a bit of a curtsy, and stood speechless, like a fool.

"It would be my pleasure to repay you, I'm in your debt, dear lady. You probably saved my life."

She highly doubted that, he was being most dramatic, but it pleased her so to hear him speak so kindly when most distinguished gentlemen wouldn't lay their eyes on her kind. Growing up poor had done a number on her confidence; she knew she was at a disadvantage to the beautiful, wealthy women in town. Sometimes she daydreamed about having started life differently. Where would she be now? Barely into her twenties and here she was, well on her way to becoming an old maid, right there with Sammy. Sammy had her share of suitors, as she had too, but both women were head strong about not settling down until they found true love. Mother scolded them constantly, claiming they would miss out, that they were too picky. "There's no such thing as being picky when it comes to matters of the heart, mother," she would say. "I will find that man, my one true love and I will be complete, mark my words."

"I would love to take you out tonight to repay you for your kindness. Where should I pick you up?" His hat was off in respect to her, to her! Where should he pick her up? She didn't want Mother or Sammy to see this gentleman, he was her secret. She didn't wish to spoil this feeling with warnings that he wasn't her kind and that he would only bring trouble. What was she thinking? It wasn't as if he were pursuing her romantically. Mr. Alcott had certainly not insinuated such a thing,

"How about I meet you right here this evening?" She smiled at him, hoping he would accept the response with no questions asked. Of course, such a man would be too smart to have the wool pulled over his eyes.

"Oh, so secretive? You wouldn't be sneaking out on your husband now, would you?" His gaze fell upon her naked ring finger.

"Dear no!" She clutched her chest, feeling heat rise to her cheeks. Her own eyes attempted to find his ring finger, but his hands were *covered in gloves. "And you? Would you happen to be hiding from a wife?" How very brazen of her! She hoped she hadn't turned him away, gone too far. Normally quite reserved, she didn't know what was coming over her. Men from her past seemed like immature boys compared to this gentleman.*

"Me? Married? Of course not." He swept down and laid the sweetest kiss upon her bare hand. "I'll see you here, at this very spot, say, right before sundown?"

"Yes, I'll be here."

And that was the day it had all started.

"**H**OW ARE YOU FEELING today?" Several days had passed since the ballroom incident and Kristen was starting to feel better. The pain was less intense and she didn't require painkillers round the clock.

"I'm okay. I think I'm starting to feel much better."

"Well, you still need to take it easy, Kris," he added.

"I'd like to get out today, take a walk, what do you say, maybe we can stop by Millie's to say hello and have some lunch," she suggested.

Wheels turned in his head. That might not be the best idea. He hadn't worked up the courage to tell Kristen about his experience in the ballroom. She might even think he had lost his mind if he shared and how could he tell her that he was falling in love with a girl named Emily that he had only just met days ago?

"I don't know, how about we take a walk on the boardwalk, get you some of that taffy you love so much and grab lunch at the pedestrian mall?"

"What's wrong with Millie's? I wanted to stop by and say hi to John and Andrew," she asked.

"I don't know, I mean, wouldn't you like a break from Millie's with all that's happened?"

Her mouth fell open and she touched his face. "You're adorable, you know that? Are you trying to protect me from Millie? I don't think she would bother me in broad daylight with other people around."

Don't bet on it, he wanted to say. "Yeah, but still…"

"Tell you what, you can bring me during the day when it's safe or I'll find a way there myself tonight if you refuse." Kristen's gaze hit him directly, challenging him. Tonight? No way, Emily would be there, she had promised to stop by again. Kristen could be so stubborn at times.

"Fine, we'll do it your way, but you need to take it easy. It's a beautiful day, we'll start on the boardwalk and then head to Millie's." It was a spectacular day, unusually warm for autumn. Would Emily be spending the day outdoors before heading to her shift at The Jetty today? He had promised Emily that he wouldn't visit her at work; she claimed her boss got irritated when friends stopped by and engaged her in conversation. What he didn't tell her was that he had driven by, looking in the window the other day as he passed. He thought he had caught a glimpse of her, tray in hand, hustling the floor. It was too bad that she hadn't gotten a job at Millie's. Then again, he doubted that she and Kristen would get along. Sometimes it was better to keep parts of one's life separate.

They headed out, breathing the fresh air. Last night he had dreamed of the ballroom and Emily's breathtaking beauty as he held her in his arms. This time, when he had kissed her, she turned to bones, a skeleton in his arms, but she still wanted to kiss him. He was convinced that all this ghost hunting was responsible for his macabre dream. Meanwhile, Emily didn't even have a cell phone. In this day and age he couldn't fathom being without it, but he supposed some people liked to keep things simple. The way he saw it, it just added to her mystery. Although, he had to admit, it would be awesome if he could text her and hear her voice during the day. True to her word, Emily had been stopping by each evening after closing. She wasn't ready to meet John or Andrew at this point and that was just fine with him, he didn't need his relationship with Emily getting back to Kristen right now. When Kristen was feeling better, he figured he'd tell her, there was no sense in telling her now.

"This is beautiful." Kristen gazed up at the sky, breathing

deeply. Jackson pushed her in the wheelchair they had rented for outings such as this. With Kristen, he felt a comfort unlike no other relationship he had ever had. When she was back on her feet, he knew it was only a matter of time before she was swept away by some guy. Would the new boyfriend understand and accept his relationship with Kristen? He hoped so; he had grown close to her and didn't want to lose their friendship. It wouldn't be the same though, it couldn't. He would also need to be honest with Emily about his relationship with Kristen. Some women would have a problem with the fact that his best friend was a beautiful, sexy, smart, intelligent woman. He could continue listing her attributes, but it made him melancholy to think of the possibility of losing her.

"Jackson?" She craned her head around. Smoothing the top of her head, he breathed deeply.

"Just admiring the beautiful day," he lied.

"Oh, do you think any of the stores will be open on the board-walk?"

"Morgan's Candy Shoppe will be open, don't worry." They passed the small arcade, still up and running after all these years. When he was a child, he, John, and Gary had spent endless hours here, playing the old classic video games. As teens they had stood, macho, chests puffed out, trying to talk to the tourist girls that were here for just a week or so on vacation. Even the thought of childhood memories involving him and Gary stung so deeply.

"Your cell, Jackson, your phone is ringing." Kristen spun around, her brows scrunched.

"Hello," he answered after viewing the blocked number.

"You've been served the papers and you need to sign them, Jackson." It was Maria. She wasn't even supposed to be calling him. If she hadn't been playing games such as blocking her number, he never would have picked up.

"Listen to me, you are *not* supposed to be contacting me, do you hear?" He glanced at Kristen, who turned to look away. There was no reason to subject her to this conversation.

"Excuse me for a second." He placed the chair in a safe spot near the arcade and walked down the boardwalk a bit. Seagulls shrieked, reminding him of his ex-wife. Counting to ten, he resumed the call.

"I am *not* agreeing to the alimony, get rid of it, and you'll be free of me." He clenched his jaw.

"No, I've grown accustomed to a certain style of living, you have *two* excellent jobs, and I'm entitled to continuing the life you promised me when we married," she whined.

"Wait a minute, Maria. I'm working the second job to take my mind off you and all this bull I have to deal with. I didn't have that job when I met you, and you're not entitled to crap!" His hands shook and he tried to steady his breathing.

"We're not legally divorced yet, so we'll see about that, and don't even think about lying and taking any income off the books because if I suspect you're doing that I will have my lawyer conduct a full investigation on Millie's bookkeeping!"

"You wouldn't dare! Leave me alone, you have my best friend, why don't the two of you just leave me the hell alone!" He was aware that his voice carried because he saw the pain on Kristen's face as she caught his eye.

"Gary and I want to get on with our lives; we want to move in together, so we need you to just sign..."

"What did you just say?" Steam was coming from him as he felt his chest pound harder and harder.

"I *said* we are moving in together, there, you might as well know."

Was this some kind of joke? It wasn't a very funny one, but he knew that she wasn't kidding, she was moving in with the man that was once his best friend, the man who had been like a brother, the man who was his own best man when he married Maria. Nothing he would say would be pretty, so he did what he thought was the best possible option; he ended the call and stood gazing out at the ocean. How did it come to this? He was certain that part of the appeal Gary held was his bad boy charm and his money. So why couldn't they just leave him alone? Why take his money when Gary made twice the amount? What did they say about rich people? Sometimes they were the cheapest around.

She was there sitting in her wheelchair beside him. At one point she reached for his hand and he held it, the two of them just looking out at the sea.

"Jackson?" she called after minutes had gone by.

He turned his attention to Kristen. "How about that taffy?" Kristen's eyes were misty as she nodded her head. She was exactly what he needed in a friend right now.

*J*UST WHEN HE THOUGHT his day couldn't be worse, he was prov-en wrong. Kristen had just ordered a burger and salad for lunch, and he was placing his own order, which was same except for French fries instead of the salad. John was commenting on how much better she appeared when she reached over and touched Jackson's arm.

"If it wasn't for Jackson here, taking such good care of me, I wouldn't be where I am now. He's been such a sweetheart, staying over each night, making me breakfast before he leaves for work each morning." Kristen gushed. John glanced between the two, raising his brows. This was exactly when it had happened.

The lights dimmed, causing people to gasp, and then the framed painting above Kristen's head came loose, landing right on top of her head. It wouldn't have been so bad if it hadn't been so heavy. Jackson was on his feet in an instant, calling out for her.

"Kristen!" Jackson yelled, rushing for her. Kristen lay silent for a moment at an odd angle before slightly righting herself and opening her eyes. He nodded at her; they both knew what had happened here.

"Get an ice pack!" Jackson ordered John, who stood with his mouth hanging open. "Kris, honey, can you move your head? How do you feel?"

Tears sprang from her blue eyes, and it touched him to the core. What did this ghost have against Kristen and when would she stop? Intuitively, Jackson knew that Millie would stop at nothing to hurt or even kill Kristen. What had started as a daring push, progressed to the stairs and now this. Who knew what would happen next? It was simple. Kristen was no longer safe here and from the look etched across her face, she wouldn't deny it, not this time.

"Kris, we have to get you out of here, it's not safe any longer,"

Jackson ordered, gently lifting her and placing her back in her wheelchair. She should have just stayed in her wheelchair and not insisted upon sitting at the table where the frame was located directly over her head. Who was he kidding? Millie would have just devised another plan of destruction for Kristen.

"I know, Jackson, I didn't think... I should have listened to you." She cried hard, holding the ice pack John had just given her to her head.

"What's all this?" John inquired, trying to follow the pieces of their conversation.

"*This* is about the resident ghost, Millie. She pushed her down the stairs and now this! It's not safe here, not for her, hell, I'm not sure it's safe for anyone here," Jackson barked. John's eyes went wide, but he didn't speak.

"Let's go, Kristen, let's get the hell out of here!"

Once they were outside, his eyes were drawn to the third floor. He shouldn't have looked, but he was powerless not to. Flowing blonde hair appeared, and, just when he thought he could try to make out her features, she closed the curtain, leaving it swinging.

Go to hell, Millie, go to hell.

Jackson had a new problem, besides trying to solve a cold crime and free the spirit of a ghost; he would now make it his top priority to keep Kristen safe from harm. No more investigating for her, no way. Heck, he wasn't sure it was smart for him to continue. Things were going to change, he could feel it, maybe it was time to drop this whole investigation and leave Millie's. As much as he loved working there, the unsettled feeling he had left him terrified.

CHAPTER

Twelve

*H*E WAS PISSED. Plain and simple. The latest encounter with Millie had left him more than frightened; it had left him filled with fury at the thought that this ghost of a woman had Kristen in her sights. He would keep Kristen safe at all costs.

The only highlight of his day was looking forward to seeing Emily later. If the woman had carried a cell phone, he would have told her that they needed to meet elsewhere. He was scared to return to Millie's, but there was no other way. He couldn't risk losing Emily, especially after the day he'd experienced. Going to The Jetty was not going to work, her shift was ending soon, and Jackson had just gotten back from taking Kristen back to the doctor's office. The doctor claimed she had been lucky, that it could have been much worse. He prescribed some more painkillers and instructed Jackson to keep an eye on her for any signs of a concussion.

"Are you sure you'll be okay while I'm gone?" Jackson was secretly thrilled that Kristen's friend had offered to spend the night to give Jackson a break. Under normal circumstances, he would have been fine staying here with Kris, but he had to see Emily, he needed to tell her about what had happened today at Millie's. They needed to find a new meeting spot.

Jackson's mind started wandering. Emily's mystery could be wrapped in lies. As much as he wanted to trust her, which he felt strongly about, pieces of her just didn't fit. She was acting as if she were a married woman or something, the way she claimed she had no cell phone, wouldn't give him her house number, tell him where she lived, nothing. Heck, he couldn't take her out in public, and he wasn't permitted to visit her at work. Something was up, and he needed to find out what it was. He needed to unravel the mystery of Emily. Tonight.

THROUGHOUT THE EVENING HE glanced around the pub, trying to see if anything was amiss, but it was business as usual. John still wasn't convinced that foul play had been involved with either incident, but he hadn't seen the ghost in the window and he hadn't felt the pull as Kristen was thrown down the stairs. He also didn't know what it felt like to be alone with Emily, dancing in a haunted ballroom from another time and place.

"John, I'm just giving you a heads up, I'm not sure if I can continue to work here any longer, with all that's happened. I'll work until you find a replacement, but that's it." It seemed like a fair trade-off. Glancing around the pub, he half wished that he and Kristen had never gotten it into their heads to go exploring. He would miss Millie's Pub.

"But Kristen's coming back, I mean after the cast is off, right?" John peered at him.

"Are you crazy? No, she is not coming back here, ever. The ghost is trying to kill her, John. I'm not going to let that happen." John just didn't get it. He supposed he wouldn't understand either, unless he had experienced it firsthand.

"Well, I'll see about that. Kristen is one of the best waitresses I've ever had. Cassie can't fill in indefinitely, you know."

"John, don't you dare make her feel bad about this, if you care about her, you'll let her go. I don't have time for this now; we'll worry about it later." Jackson poured the drinks that Andrew was waiting for. Andrew was silent, shaking his head at the exchange between the men.

"That's right, you have work to do," ordered John as he walked off.

Closing time. It had been a tiring evening, both mentally and physically. John, was obviously pissed that he had given notice, and gave him the cold shoulder for the reminder of the evening.

"For someone who's so afraid of ghosts, you certainly spend a lot of time here after hours lately. What is it that you do here alone, Jackson?" Jackson could understand John's curiosity. Never before had Jackson stayed when the rest of the crew left for the night.

"I'm stressed, the quiet gives me time to think," Jackson answered, hoping his friend would accept his response. John nodded, placing his hand on Jackson's shoulder.

"Sorry, man. With all this talk of nonsense around here; I forgot you're still dealing with all the stress from Maria."

The man did have a heart. "Thanks, John."

When the doors closed, Jackson was on high alert for signs of Millie and waiting for Emily to come walking through the door. Nothing from Millie, that was a relief. Like clockwork, minutes after John and Cassie had left; Emily brightened the dim room with her smile. She was something else. Jackson stood, watching her every move until she was upon him. Opening her mouth to speak, Jackson clamped his palm over her mouth.

"Get over here," he muttered, laying a kiss on her mouth. The kiss was about longing, passion, and everything in between. Jackson let his emotions of the day get lost in that kiss until Emily broke free.

"Whoa, I guess you missed me as much as I missed you," she whispered sweetly.

"Oh my God, yes." He couldn't help it, his fingers roamed from her hair, to her face, and to her neck.

"Jackson, you naughty boy," she teased.

He was caught up in her and he needed to remember his goal for this evening. "Emily, we need to talk."

Her eyes darted over his face, brows creased with worry. "Oh, Jackson, no…"

She was worried, as if he would ever hurt her. "No, sweetie, it's nothing like that." Her shoulders dropped and the smile returned to her face as she waited for him to continue.

"I've had a really awful day, beyond stressful. It got me think-ing about a lot of things in my life…"

"Oh? What happened today? Tell me." Her hands magically caressed his face; he felt a pleasant chill spread through his body. He hadn't intended to tell her about his day, that would just open up the whole Maria situation, which he didn't want to talk about. Now, though, as her hands worked their magic, he found himself eager to share things with this woman, things about Maria that he had never shared with anyone, even Kristen and John.

"Want to get out of here? Take a walk on the beach? It's so beautiful out tonight," Emily suggested in her serene voice. Nod-ding, he allowed her to guide him out the door to the moonlit beach. The third floor window was the furthest thing from his mind right now. Emily found a cozy spot near the sand dunes, and he helped guide her down to sit beside him. After kissing her once more, the story of his life with Maria began.

Emily was an excellent listener, asking questions at times but for the most part was silent as Jackson got near the end, the hard-est part of his story, the part he shared with no one.

"Go on," she prompted, twirling her elegant fingers through his hair.

"As I said, Gary was my best friend; we grew up together here at the Cape. I trusted him with my life. I thought he would give me the same in return." Drawing a breath, Jackson continued. "If I had paid more attention, I would have noticed that Maria had started backing away, spending more time outside of the house. She claimed she was spending time with her friends, and I took her word for it."

"You were a good husband, building a life for the both of you." That's right, Emily got it, she understood.

"Yes, that's what I was doing, but part of me knows that I wasn't as attentive during those months. She claims I neglected her, I suppose I did to a certain extent, but never intentionally."

"Of course not," Emily whispered, placing soft kisses on his forehead.

"What I didn't notice was that my relationship with Gary was suffering too. I mean, I used to talk to the guy several times a week, we'd grab dinner together, but looking back, I saw that we barely spoke during that time. The killer is, I was too busy to even notice." Emily placed small kisses on his cheek.

"Not your fault, she was selfish, you were doing it all for her, for the future of your family."

He hadn't thought of it like that before, but Emily had a point. Just by speaking with her, he felt a weight being lifted, one that had crushed him for so long. He felt he was falling in love with this woman, right here and now. He wouldn't speak of it for fear of scaring her away, but damn, he was falling hard for her.

"Yes, I suppose I was. One day I came home early. The contract was taking up all my time, but I'd finally gotten the promotion. She didn't expect me home, why would she when midnight was the usual time I got home the past few weeks." This part was the hardest. He'd come this far, for his own sanity he needed to get the rest of the story out.

"I...I had flowers, a dozen red roses, Maria loved roses. I saw Gary's car in the driveway. I opened the door to the house and it was silent..." Jackson struggled to continue the awful tale.

He stopped, fighting back tears, not wanting to finish. It was like reliving the night all over again. "You're doing just fine, trust me." Emily breathed into his neck.

Jackson shared more.

"Let it go," she urged, "You're almost there."

At last, he finished speaking.

He hadn't realized his eyes were shut tight until he opened them. Emily was holding him close, he was pressed against her soft body. "That was good, it felt good, right?" He nodded as she pulled him closer, he was losing himself in her inescapable kiss.

He sat with her on the dark, sandy beach and thought about her, how right if felt to sit beside her, sharing his darkest secrets. Emily's mouth turned down, she faced away from him she focused on the sea.

"What's the matter, Emily? You look sad," he asked, rubbing her back. Was his story about Maria too deep, too intense?

Her eyes filled with tears. "It's nothing, I'm just thinking is all."

He was alarmed; the last thing he wanted was to scare her away with his baggage. "Was it me? Did I do something wrong?"

Facing him, she sighed. "No, quite the opposite."

It touched him that she felt so much for him that it would bring her to tears. On the verge of telling her that he was in love with her, he bit down hard. As much as he felt for this woman, it was too soon to tell her his true feelings. What was this feeling coming over him? It was a losing battle, his heart and mind was tangled up in Emily. But they needed to spend time getting to know one another, learning all the quirks, good and bad. It reminded him that he needed to speak with her about their own relationship, he had almost forgotten.

"Emily?" He picked up a piece of her glittering locks, fascinated by the beauty of her.

She still looked sad, too sad. He hesitated before continuing, but this was important. "Your turn. I like the fact that you're mysterious and all, but I want more from you, I need more from you."

Shaking her head firmly, she looked away. "Emily, please." He placed a gentle hand on her cheek, turning her to him.

"I need this, please."

"Fine. What is it that you need to know?" Emily locked her eyes on him.

"Well, for starters, why no phone? Why can't I go to your house, see you at work?"

Her eyes darted back and forth and she hesitated before speaking. "Damn you, Jackson, why can't you leave it alone? Take my word for it, it's not safe, for either of us."

"What are you talking about? What's not safe? I can't go on this way, you have to open up to me," he begged. He could see how hard this was for her. "Emily, are you married?"

Her laugh was bitter. She turned from him once more and then gazed back at him. "Yes, Jackson, I am." His heart dropped. Did he just hear her correctly?

"Excuse me? Did you just say that you're married?"

"Now settle down, Jackson, it's not what you think. I didn't want to tell you because it could be dangerous for you."

"Say it, Emily, what could be dangerous?" He was on edge, what had happened to her?

"My husband, he hurts me, badly." Her eyes clouded over as she told her own dejected tale. Clasping her hands, tightly, he nodded for her to continue.

"My story began much like yours, a couple in love, getting married. At first it only happened when he drank, I tried to leave but he would cry and beg me for forgiveness. For weeks afterward, he would behave and it would almost be like it was in the beginning, you know?" Emily managed. He didn't know, God, he couldn't begin to imagine. He held onto her hand and nodded.

"Then it got worse after several years, much worse. Drinking or not, at least twice a week I needed to be punished. He's a police officer, and he's rotten and crooked, like in the novels," she cried out, rocking in place. Sorrow was quickly replaced with anger, frustration. How could any man hurt a woman?

"You don't have to continue… I think I understand," Jackson said, rubbing at her back.

"No, I want to, it feels right. I ran away, I've been hiding ever since."

"He hit you?" He was outraged, a police officer of all people?

"Yes and he will do it again and worse if he finds me. I don't have phones, I can't tell anyone where I live, and I have to work at a job I hate. I'm afraid to go out in public, I'm just a mess."

Wow. It was no wonder she was afraid to tell him. He wouldn't give her secret away; she could trust him with her life. "I won't tell a soul. I'm so sorry you had to go through that sweetheart. Come here." Jackson pulled her close until her sobs subsided. It all made sense, the pieces of Emily were finally fitting together, and he loved her even more.

CHAPTER
Thirteen

Millie

THAT VERY FIRST NIGHT Todd met her, looking dapper and more handsome than hours before. Giggling like a schoolgirl, she allowed him to kiss her hand. She hoped he was as smitten as she was. Ridiculous, this feeling she had. Was this the thing people called love at first sight? Perhaps this is what she had been holding out for. Mother would be thrilled. As they walked, Todd dropped her hand, to her dismay. No matter, what did she expect? They walked off the cobblestone path, toward the beach. Something about the beach in the waning light made her feel romantic. He led her to a remote spot near the dunes. Waiting there for them was a blanket and picnic basket, how surprising!

"Wow! How did you arrange this?" He must have planned so carefully. It was romantic, charming of him. This man certainly appeared to know how to treat a woman. It was refreshing to see that even a man like Todd, who appeared to have money, would forgo the fancy restaurants and come up with such a creative idea to thank her.

"Let's just say that I have my ways." He had been staring at her for the entire walk, but now he gazed at her with such intensity. Guiding her down to the soft, red and blue blanket, she shivered a bit in reaction to her own emotions. So he was secretive, she liked that, it gave his character some depth. Most likely because she was such a romantic, she lost herself in novels. Jane Austen's stories were her favorite. She and her mother *would spend countless hours reading and discussing the characters to-gether. Her favorite quotes were taken directly from the woman. "She was stronger alone...," taken from "Sense and Sensibility" was one of the most meaningful. Whenever her mother reprimanded her for being so picky, she quoted Jane Austen, smiling fiercely. How could her mother attempt to argue with that?*

"How is it that a beautiful thing like you isn't betrothed to anoth-er?" Todd reached for her hand, kissing it gently. Butterflies coursed through her belly as she blushed lightly.

"I...I guess the proper man hasn't come around yet?" It was a ques-tion rather than a statement.

"Nice. Does the man necessarily have to be proper?" He winked, edging closer to her. This sassy man was playing with her.

"I... uh," she stammered, blushing deeper now. How could a lady properly respond to that type of question? As if sensing that perhaps he had carried it a bit too far, Todd backtracked.

"I'm kidding. Just kidding, beautiful woman."

"Oh, well, I knew that," she muttered, glancing around the beach. "It will be dark soon."

"Why yes, it will. Does that frighten you? Being alone on a mostly deserted beach with a complete stranger?"

When he put it like that, maybe she should reconsider this little thank you picnic. The man was utterly gorgeous but quite brazen.

"There I go again, scaring you. This happens whenever I run into beautiful women, you'll have to excuse me."

"Oh, okay. How often does that happen? Running into beautiful ladies, I mean." Perhaps it was time to give a little jab back to this man.

"Got me there, you did." He pointed a finger, laughing. "I like your spunk, but I'll go ahead and answer your question. Not very often, until I saw you."

"Smooth, Mr. Alcott, I'll give you that. Smooth and full of malar-key." She giggled loudly, covering her mouth at the pitch of her own laughter.

"I guess you caught me." His gaze grew serious as he stopped talking. The silence unnerved her a bit. He fixed his stare on the ocean next, still quiet.

"The ocean speaks volumes, do you know that? It's been around since the dawn of time, if only it could speak to us, what tales would it tell?"

It was a profound statement. She liked this part of him and could see herself courting a man who matched her intellectually. It perplexed her that the ocean and the land had stood, well before she had ever been born. It would still stand far after she was gone.

"I suppose it would tell a tale as old as time," she offered, gazing up at him. For a moment, he moved forward, was it her imagination, or was he about to kiss her? As suddenly as he leaned in, he was now sitting back, reaching into the picnic basket. She readjusted her hoop skirt and cleared her throat.

"A tale as old as time, you say? I rather like that." He seemed to ponder over that concept as the sky grew colorful, as if it wished to create the perfect ambience, just for the two of them. Nodding her head, she waited as he turned his attention to the egg sandwiches, prepared on biscuits, fruit, and tea.

"This looks delightful, you really shouldn't have gone through the trouble." It was a simple picnic, no splendid affair, but she considered it perfect.

"But you saved my life, surely I will be repaying you in many different ways, this is just the start."

There he went, making her blush once more. "There's no need, really…"

"Nonsense, now let's eat before the food spoils," he stated, biting into his sandwich.

The sandwich was the best she had tasted, but there was the possibility that her senses were on high alert, being here with this charming gentleman. After they ate to their fill, she glanced at the darkening night. She would need to return soon or mother would worry.

"I'll return you home soon, I promise. First, I want to know all about you. What are your dreams?"

Her dreams? Nobody had ever inquired as to what her dreams were. It was a simple life she led, helping mother around the house, passing the time with her sister, and reading her books. Quite unromantic, actually, but she was a dreamer and yes, she had dreams.

"My dream, my dream is to become a writer," she shared. It felt special, sitting here with this man, sharing her most private dream. Her own mother knew nothing of this dream; she would only laugh if she were privy to the news. Same with Sammy, although Sammy had her own mind, she was wrapped up in finding a man, the man of her dreams. Inspirations of becoming a writer would seem like a ridiculous waste of time to her.

"A writer?" Was he surprised? Disappointed? It was hard to tell, *she waited silently for him to offer more. "Like that woman?"*

"Jane Austen," she filled in, smiling proudly.

"Yes, that's the one. I haven't the pleasure of meeting a woman who had such high aspirations."

Was he mocking her? Did he think her foolish? It was a mistake to tell him, this stranger sitting beside her. She cleared her throat, picking at her fingernails. This nervous habit was a clear giveaway of her worries.

"I'm giving you a compliment, my dear. I'm quite impressed. Most women I've encountered are seeking to grab a man, hold on tight and never let go. All dreams vanished, poof, once there's a man to take care of her."

"Oh, well. Thank you." She had misunderstood. Jane Austen would be proud of her, sitting here with this man who admired her dreams. This man didn't even ask her how she, a woman of low income, had learned to write. She was lucky to have parents who valued education, aspired for their children to become more educated than they had been. It wasn't easy, though, hours were part time, and chores must be completed each day. Luckily, she had caught right on to her studies, a quick learner, her teacher had praised.

"You're very welcome, and I hope all your dreams come true." Todd Alcott leaned over, closing the space between them. He was going to kiss her and she was going to let him. She closed her eyes for the impending kiss, leaning in slightly to meet him. His lips touched hers with sweetness, passion. Oh my, this was like nothing she had experienced.

"I've wanted to do that from the moment you saved me," he breathed, eyes alight.

"I've wanted the same." She liked the way he mentioned that she had saved him, it made her feel important in his eyes.

CHAPTER

$\mathcal{D}$AYS LATER, HE FELT strange, now that he had admitted to himself that he loved Emily, it terrified him. When he was with Emily, he felt her love so strongly, as if captured in a web of love and attraction. With distance, he wondered if he was getting too close to her, too serious. This woman, who by all rights should no longer seem mysterious, but was more baffling than ever. He had never met such a woman; she was wrapped in mystery and innocence, all in one beautiful package. Now that she had opened up to him about all of her secrets, there was something that didn't feel right, as if she was still holding back. What else could there possibly be to say? Why did she always have to see him at Millie's, never venturing further from the house and the beach near the property? So she didn't feel comfortable in public, he had never thought to ask before, but certainly his house should feel safe to her? Maybe he would even offer to take her away overnight, to another town. But there was that feeling again, the apprehension that he was getting too serious, too fast. Why did it take falling in love with her to make him aware that he was getting into something serious here, something with the power to hurt him? Wishing that Kristen were a man so that he could speak with her about this relationship of his, he held back, not wanting to create tension in their friendship. Kristen would never understand when he had just recently shared he wasn't ready for dating. For dating? Geez, he thought he was in love. It seemed that he was helpless to slow things down, even when he was away from her, though feeling clearer, he felt the undeniable pull, the urge to see her, touch her face. Wasn't that love, though?

Kristen had called moments earlier, asking for company today while she visited Shelby's Books to attempt communication with Amelia. After all that she had been through, Kristen should be running as far as possible from any thoughts of Millie, but there she was, back to work on solving the mystery. Fine, she could gather her facts outside of Millie's all she wanted, but there was no way he was allowing her to set foot in Millie's again. John had still not found a replacement for him at the pub, times were tough with Kristen being out, so Jackson agreed that he would continue to work for the time being, unless some other incident occurred, that is. Besides, Millie's was still Emily's favorite meeting spot after hours, when it was just the two of them. He couldn't deny that he enjoyed their special moments together as well.

Heading over to pick up Kristen, he found himself looking forward to spending time with her again. He was back at his own place as Kristen was better able to get around now on her own and her head was feeling better. As long as she stayed away from Millie's she should be fine, he figured, with a sigh. Even with her broken ankle and recent head injury, the woman was all smiles, a trooper.

"Ready to go, ghost hunter?" Jackson watched a grin light up her face as she grabbed her crutches.

"Ready as I'll ever be," she stated.

"You don't want to grab the wheelchair? You might be tired later." He knew that over the past few days she had steered away from the use of the wheelchair, claiming that the fastest road to recovery would be to tough it out a bit, get her muscles in action.

"Nope, I'm good." With a bright smile, she stood beside him. "See?"

"All right, but I'm parking in a handicapped spot," he explained. They would grab her handicapped sign from her car on the way out.

He doubted that Kristen had really thought this through, this plan about speaking with Amelia. At least this ghost didn't have it out for her... God, he hoped not.

When they arrived at the store, his eyes were peeled on the

welcome sign, which was still for the moment. Normally he would think that was a good sign, but considering that they were there to speak with the ghost, maybe it wasn't a good sign. He laughed to himself at the slight pun. About to share his wit with Kristen, he glanced up, finding Shelby there to greet them.

"Back again, huh? Somehow I knew the two of you would return." Shelby grinned. "My, my, what happened to you, dear?"

"Let's just say she had some encounters with the other side," Jackson announced.

"Oh? What happened, did you find anything out yet?"

"Only that Millie does indeed exist and that she wants to kill me," offered Kristen, nodding her head toward her crutches.

"Dear, dear. It's not a good idea to go messing around with hostile forces, never a good idea," Shelby muttered, her voice fading.

"We're finding that out the hard way," Jackson added. "But our Millie seems to have a personal beef with Kristen, what it is, we just don't know yet."

"She hasn't tried hurting you?" Shelby pushed her glasses down her nose, gazing at Jackson.

"No she hasn't, it's odd, isn't it?" Jackson inquired.

"Not really, not from what we know about her, Millie, that is. In all the history that I've followed, it's the women that she threatens."

"So we've heard," Kristen mumbled, glancing around. "Let's just hope Amelia here is a bit kinder toward females."

After filling Shelby in about everything that had happened, (minus the ballroom incident) Shelby stood, taking it all in. "I don't like it, not one little bit. You're in danger, my dear, and you'd best be smart about this and keep your distance."

"I agree with you. I believe she does wish to harm me, and I won't be naïve about it anymore. The only thing is that I'll be forced to find another job once I'm able to work again. I'll miss Millie's, all my friends, and customers. I just wish there was some way..."

"There just might be, Kristen, don't give up hope, but for now, stay far, far away from that place. Jackson, I think you'll be okay, but don't go tempting fate, you hear?" Shelby warned.

"Can we try to speak with Amelia, please?" Jackson asked, taking in the old walls. If walls could speak, he thought. There must be quite a bit of history here.

"Like I told you before, she won't talk to either of you," Shelby reminded them. Kristen met Jackson's gaze, she was as disappointed as he was.

"Me, however, she just might enlighten *me* on your troubles," Shelby added, a sparkle in her watery eyes.

"What do we need to do, just tell us," Jackson urged, stepping closer.

"I think it would help to have your presence around for this. Come, my granddaughter can handle the floor for a bit, let's go to the back." Leading the way to the deserted back room, there was a noticeable shift, a change in the air. Kristen's mouth fell open, glancing at Jackson. She was frightened and he didn't blame her.

"Say the word." He offered her this last chance to back out now.

"No, no." Shaking her head, Kristen hobbled along as close to Jackson as she could manage with her crutches.

Once they were all tucked away in the back room, Shelby closed the door, muttering softly. Jackson didn't ask her to repeat herself, he was pretty sure he didn't want to know what the woman had been saying. She even appeared nervous, which did nothing to ease his own tension.

"Amelia, we ask you to join us," Shelby began. Was she kidding? He was pretty sure the ghost had joined them already.

"We have two souls here, one in extreme danger at the hands of Millie." Kristen edged closer, grabbing Jackson's hand. "Bring us to an understanding, what does the spirit want? Why is she trying to bring harm to this young lady?"

The door opened slightly, then wider. Jackson still couldn't believe his eyes; the temperature in the small room must have decreased by at least twenty degrees. The door slammed shut with such force; it caused the books on the table to tumble to the floor. Tugging on Jackson's shirt, Kristen's eyes went wide with fear. Jackson stilled her, bringing her close to his chest. "I've got you," he whispered.

"I want to leave, please, Jackson."

"Shh! Quiet, the both of you!" Shelby boomed with such force that Jackson shrank back. The woman's voice had changed, this wasn't Shelby's sweet voice any more. My God, what had they asked this poor woman to do? If he had known…

"You brought me here for a reason, now pay attention! You are Kristen, I presume?" Shaking a wrinkled finger at her, Kristen nodded.

"You've gotten in the way; you need to be taken out. She's tried it the nice way, tried to use her manners, but you won't leave him alone, will you?" The female voice bellowed.

"Jackson, I'm leaving," Kristen wept, preparing her crutches.

"I'm with you," Jackson agreed, guiding Kristen to the door. It wouldn't budge, the door wouldn't open.

"Silence! You've come for help?" She barked, the window panes trembling.

All Jackson could do was turn his head and face this ghost that had taken over Shelby's body. "Yes."

"If it's true love she's meant to find, this one must be left far behind. But beware, for there it does not end, she's meant to find him and both their stories will then end."

"What? What are you trying to say here?" Jackson took a step forward, with Kristen pulling at him to stay with her. He was curious now, he needed to know what Amelia had been saying. Shelby had mentioned that she spoke in riddles of sorts, he needed to remember what she had said and figure it out. She needed to say more.

Shelby sat, taking a deep breath. Her face was flushed and sweaty, despite the chilly temperature in the room. Not a word was spoken as Jackson was trying to ascertain if Amelia had left them. He was at Shelby's side despite the chance that she may not quite be herself yet. "Shelby, talk to me."

"Please, both of you. I'm asking you to stay out of here. Go, please and don't ever ask me about any of this again." Shelby managed through ragged breaths.

"I'm sorry, we never thought..." Kristen's eyes welled with tears as she approached the elderly woman.

"Neither did I. You're in danger, and I think I was wrong about this whole thing. It's not just Kristen, it's you too, Jackson. Stay away from Millie, she's pure evil now. Amelia's very being turned cold just by attempting to make a connection with her."

"Has that ever happened before?" Jackson felt awful about putting Shelby through such a horrifying experience. It could have killed a woman her age.

"Never and I don't think I could survive another experience

88

like that, please, for everyone's sake, take the message and be safe."

"Yes, yes of course. Again, I'm sorry." Jackson didn't want to admit that he hadn't figured out the message yet but their time here was up. Turning to leave, he let Kristen exit the room first.

"Jackson," Shelby cried out. He spun around instantly at the sound of her voice.

"What, Shelby? What is it?"

"I believe you're in even more danger than Kristen. It's you she wants." Shelby warned, her breath finally catching up.

"What?"

"Go!" she yelled, this time the voice was her own.

CHAPTER

Millie

THE MAN WAS COURTING her; he was actually courting a girl like her. She couldn't be happier, more filled with life. Her senses heightened, the world was a vivid canvas of colors, hers for the taking. Oh, if Mother knew the truth. Claiming that her suitor was a humble young man, her own age, her mother was pleased at first, but as the weeks went by, she mentioned on more than one occasion that the man must not have been brought up with manners or he would pick her up at the house, like a proper gentleman. Millie worried that it was only a matter of time before Father became involved. If that happened, he would forbid Millie from seeing Todd. She called him Todd now, yes, no longer Mr. Alcott, as they were courting. Why couldn't he pick her up, though, such a distinguished man, her parents would be proud to see her in such fine company. As sheltered as her life was in her humble home, she had never heard of Todd Alcott before. Now she was aware of his growing social status in town, he had just bought up several magnificent homes in town, all for the purpose of helping poor young women. He provided rooms at little charge and held fancy functions to solicit donations so that these women had a place to call home. He was also buying up land and business properties in town. Now that she was tuned into his name, *at times, she could hear conversations on the street, focused on Todd Alcott and all of the good he was doing to build up the town. Her one disappointment throughout all of this time of happiness was the fact that she still couldn't meet his mother, his brother, even see where he lived. Todd claimed that he was embarrassed that at his age of twenty-five, he was still living at home, helping his elderly mother tend to the family property. She found it selfless of Todd that he would put his own needs last to attend to his ailing mother.*

"What are you thinking of, my love?" He was running his hand through her hair which was adorned with a stunning turquoise comb, a gift he had recently given her. She had worn that comb every single day, surprising her mother, who complained that she never used to wear her long blonde hair up. It used to flow free... not anymore. She doubted she would ever remove this generous gift.

"My love? I don't recall you using those words before, Todd," she teased, although her chest hammered at his very words. Love?

"I have something for you, my dear." His hand went into his coat pocket. Pressing her hand down on his, she wasn't about to let him get away with ignoring her last comment.

"Wait. Why did you call me your love?"

"If you would please let me give you your gift, my goodness, you love to talk," Todd stated, smiling.

From inside his pocket, he produced a unique brush. It was etched in the most magnificent pattern with turquoise color blended throughout. Her hands reached to cover her mouth from squealing. "Todd Alcott!" She would spend hours running the bristles through her hair.

"And, my darling, I have something to tell you." It couldn't get any better than this, a matching brush to complete the set! It didn't matter what the man had said only moments before. Nothing mattered as she gazed at the precious brush. With brush in hand, she raised her arms to unfasten the comb. She brushed her smooth locks, drawing attention from Alcott.

"I was going to tell you that I love you."

That caught her attention indeed. Stopping the brush in the middle of her head, she stared at him. "Did you just say...?"

"I love you," he repeated, louder this time.

She was in his arms without hesitation; her little world had just gotten a bit more colorful. All of her dreams were coming true. "I love you too, Todd Alcott."

*T*HAT NIGHT AT HOME, *she wrote. Ever since she met him, he brought words to her pages. Her vision of becoming a writer was coming to life before her eyes. She wouldn't share this book with anyone until Todd saw the finished product. Dipping her quill in the dark, dark ink, her words flowed smoothly. This book was for him, it was to be dedicated to Todd Alcott. It was to be a love story, and it was well on its way. Todd would be pleased to know that it was actually their love story. Each night when she returned from his arms, she wrote. Not quite a diary, she considered it more a diary brought to life written as a novel. Oh he would be so proud, and, who knew, perhaps with his wide reach into the community, he could help her share her story once it was finished. She could become Cape Florence's own version of Jane Austen, perhaps purchase a better home for her parents to live in. Oh yes, she certainly had her dreams. She never considered them to be so far out of reach that they were unattainable. She would complete this book and she would put forth so much effort to share it with others, it simply must come to light!*

*T*HINKING BACK TO HIS earlier visit to the bookstore, Jackson sighed. If Amelia was correct, Millie had set her sights on him. What did that mean? How could a ghost want him and why? True love, Amelia had spoken of true love, but how did he fit into this theory? How could this ghost of a woman bring harm to him in the name of love? It was all conjecture at this point and nobody said that Amelia had all the right answers. Right now he had other things on his mind.

"I had an idea that I think may sit well with you." Jackson was leaning against one of the booths that gave him and Emily plenty of room to sit and stretch out together. He was savoring a red wine for a change, and, as usual, Emily had water by her side that sat untouched.

"What is it?" Emily turned her gaze on him; he drank in the depths of her green eyes. Gone was the notion of slowing things down again, it was incredible, really, that this woman had so much power over his thoughts and actions.

"How about we head over to my place? Surely your ex-husband couldn't track you down there," he offered. It made sense, unless the man was following Emily, which he highly doubted, she would be safe. It also might help him to gain some perspective since the vibe around Millie's was so mysterious. Perhaps having Emily in his own home would give him the home team advantage, he may think more clearly and even the playing ground. In his relationships, he craved an equal give and take. With Emily, she was clearly taking the reins and he bet that she knew it too, therefore, it left him feeling unsettled.

"No, I don't like the idea of putting you in danger, Jackson. I just found you and I won't let anything happen to you."

"First of all, *I'm* supposed to be doing the protecting, and it's just absurd to think he... by the way what's his name anyway?" Jackson had never even asked.

"His first name is Arthur, that's all you need to know and, no, I won't budge on this, take it or leave it, we meet here and the beach, that's it." Crossing her arms around herself, she pouted.

How could she be so stubborn, unyielding? How long was this nonsense going to continue? She seemed to read his mind and it bothered him. "As long as it takes, for as long as I need this in order to feel safe." Emily twirled her long, blonde locks, spinning her hair in her hands. He went to speak but shut his mouth, it was of no use, she would win as usual.

"Your hair, it looks so pretty that way, it elongates your neck," he whispered, unable to take his eyes from her. Nibbling on her neck, she froze, body stiff and rigid.

"Stop it, I don't like my hair up, take your hands off me please," she ordered firmly.

What had gotten into her? In all the times they had met, he had yet to see her stressed or irritable. He removed his hands instantly. "Sorry, I didn't mean to offend you."

Taking a noticeable breath, she faced him while she smoothed out her long locks. "It's fine, please, just don't do it again." With that she was back to the sweet, innocent Emily, leaning on him once more.

"I don't like the way you're stressed about Maria," she blurted, running her fingers through her own hair again. "It upsets me."

"Well, I appreciate the concern, but I can handle it." He was touched that Emily had given the subject such thought. It showed that she was a kind person.

"Why don't you have her and that Gary character here for drinks one night and try to talk some sense into them?" Emily's green eyes turned dark.

How peculiar an idea. Why on earth would he want them here, at his workplace? "Whoa, the two of them, here?"

"Think about it, having a conversation in a place that feels comfortable to you might make you feel more confident, they just might finally listen to you, Jackson." Emily spoke with the softness of an angel, but she was totally off base, here. The idea was preposterous.

"With all due respect, Emily, no. There's no way I would even entertain that idea, but thank you for thinking of me." Hoping her feelings weren't hurt, he closed his hand around hers.

"But if you change your mind, tell me."

It was a funny thing to say, but then again, a lot of things were offbeat about Emily. Her quirkiness intrigued him. "Sure," he stated. They remained silent, he enjoyed the feel of her beside him. His lids felt heavy as he tried to fight the fatigue, he had been under so much stress lately. It felt nice to drift off.

Her hands were on his face as he glanced around the pub. Raucous laughter filled his ears as he took in the room. Men and women of the Victorian age filled the pub. Taking in the ladies and gentlemen of the era, he was out of place in his jeans and T-shirt. Emily was beside him, dressed in her own jeans and sweater. "Emily…"

She appeared as frightened as he did, glancing around, mouth open wide. Nobody seemed to take notice of the pair as they sat in their booth, which was actually now a round table. He was speechless, gazing at a man whose smile radiated wealth and social status. He was handing out drinks, grabbing at a woman who smacked his bottom. This dark haired woman was thin, young, and attractive. Emily watched as the man kissed the raven-haired beauty hard, creating cheers from the patrons of the pub. This was Millie's Pub, it had to be. Millie's Pub from another time. He wasn't frightened as much as curious at this moment; it was amazing to be sitting here in this state of timelessness. "Kiss me, Jackson, right here, right now." She didn't give him much choice as she leaned over, grabbing him. There he was again, lost in Emily. He could think of nowhere he'd rather be than here with her in this pub from the 1800s. He breathed her powdery scent, swearing that he would never want another woman as long as he lived. The heck with Maria and Gary, there were no troubles here in this room with the most beautiful woman he had seen.

"Let's stay here," she chuckled softly, placing kisses across his eyes and cheek. "We're both so much happier here, away from all of the stress. No more Arthur, no more Maria, Gary, alimony payments…"

"Yes, I would…" He didn't wish to break the beauty of the moment. Nobody would know where he went, nobody could find him here. There would be no Maria, no lawyers. No Kristen. Wait, no Kristen, the girl who was fast becoming his best friend would slip away, forgotten. "No, Emily!" He sat up straight, blinking his eyes, snapping suddenly into the present.

"What was that?" Emily cried, clinging onto Jackson's arm for support.

"I don't know, I have no idea," he muttered, coming out of his daze. The vision felt to right, so tempting. He had been so close to just giving up and giving in to that other world. What would have happened if Kristen hadn't popped into his mind? Would he have been trapped in another time with Emily? It had felt surreal, so right somehow, as if he belonged there with Emily and this pub from another place in time.

CHAPTER

"Kris, it was so crazy, I was there, actually sitting at Millie's Pub, it had to be in the 1800s, I could tell by the clothing, and I'm pretty sure I saw our Mr. Todd Alcott, giving drinks away, dancing, kissing a young woman." Jackson gushed, unable to slow down.

"Jackson, slow down. I swear you're not making any sense," Kristen cried out. She was grabbing his face, shaking him.

"I know it sounds crazy, but there's so much I haven't told you, so much I was afraid to share." It was time. Time to tell Kristen about the ballroom, the 1800s pub, even Emily. It didn't feel right to keep everything from her, he probably should have opened up much sooner, and he was sorry that he hadn't. Even when it came to the subject of Emily. Hiding his relationship with Emily was bound to backfire; if she witnessed the two of them together she'd never understand.

"What is it, Jackson? What haven't you shared? Tell me," Kristen urged. "I mean, I can't believe you would hide anything from me at this point."

Sitting down, he knew that he would need to remain calm in order explain everything, for Kristen to grasp all that had happened. Grabbing onto her hand, he sat beside her on the couch. He took a few steadied breaths before continuing.

"Okay, so you need to keep an open mind, hear me out." How

did he even begin? He supposed he should start with Emily. "One night, a while back, I was closing down Millie's when this woman walked in, the one I told you about, she was looking for a job."

Kristen blew out a breath. "The *pretty* one."

This wasn't going to be an easy conversation, he could feel it already. "Yes, Kristen, that's the one. Anyway, this is the hard part."

"Go on," Kristen muttered, fiddling with her fingernails.

"Emily, that's her name. She kept coming in and I'm not even sure how, but we became close," he admitted.

"Close? What do you mean by close? How close are we talking here?" Her eyes were on him.

Oh boy, he didn't want to hurt her, this part would kill him. "Close, Kristen, and I'm sorry…"

She struggled to sit up straighter and moved several inches from him. "Why would you be sorry, Jackson? We're friends, isn't that what you had said, *friends*?" Kristen spat, edging against the couch.

"Listen, I'm coming to you with this because there's more to it and you need to know about Emily in order to truly understand. I love you, Kristen as a friend and I don't want to hurt you, which is why I'm telling you all of this." He could imagine where her mind was headed with the news, she was probably wondering what Emily had that she didn't. Hell, he had wondered the same and it was on the tip of his tongue to tell her that before Emily had come around, he believed he was starting to feel something deeper for Kristen. Once he had met Emily, it was as if the woman's presence was so strong that Kristen didn't have a chance anymore. It wouldn't be wise to explain his thoughts to Kristen on that one.

Tears pooled in Kristen's eyes as he reached for her hand. She didn't pull back, but her eyes remained fixed on the ceiling.

He told her about the ballroom, watching her expression change from pissed to hurt, finally settling on shock. "Jackson, this must mean something," she whispered. "And she didn't attempt to hurt this woman, like she did me?"

"Not at all."

"Is there more?" Kristen was all business, but at least she was talking to him.

"Yes, there's more. Emily is very secretive. We only meet at Millie's and the beach right in front of the pub, just the two of us.

She doesn't want to meet any of my friends yet."

"What? Wait a minute. Doesn't that seem odd to you? What kind of girl are you involved with here?"

It did sound bizarre, that is until you knew the full story. "She's on the run from an abusive husband," he shared. Raking his hands through his hair, the stress of this conversation was getting to him.

"Are you out of your mind? You're going to take on a woman with huge issues and baggage right now? So let's see, you've got your own divorce to go through, dealing with the loss of your best friend, and chasing down a ghost who wants to kill me, oh yes, she wants to harm you too, according to Amelia. That's not enough to satisfy you?" When she laid out all the facts, it did seem ridiculous, he must be crazy.

"You're right, God Kristen, you're right, but I can't seem to stop seeing her. She has this power over me…"

Kristen's brows rose. "Really? Come on, Jackson, listen to yourself. You told me, and, let me add, not so long ago, that you were not ready for a relationship. Now you're very close to this strange woman, who by the way, can't go out in public and won't meet any people close to you. *Come on, wake up!*"

She was upset, for many reasons he believed. If Kristen were still involved with Steve he doubted she would be this upset. What she said made sense but it hit him that her pride was bruised as well. He needed to tread carefully here.

"Please, just hear me out. I'm not finished, there's more. I started telling you about Millie's and going back in time. When I was there, it was amazing, I felt like all of my troubles had vanished. I wanted to stay there, with Emily. I felt as if it was where I belonged, does that make any sense?"

"Not really, but don't you see? This entire experience and the one in the ballroom is tied into Millie. She *wants* you to feel that way for a reason. We just need to figure out why. We need to figure out what she's up to and fast. I'm tired of hiding. I've been thinking, Jackson, a lot. If we run, we not only lose our work place, but we leave her open to doing this again. She wants peace, closure, we have to find a way to give it to her without getting hurt or killed in the process."

Millie did want closure, he could feel it all around him but it was disturbing to think about what closure meant to the ghost, at what cost would they bring her peace?

"Kristen, come here." He opened his arms to her, offering a place of comfort for them both. "You said something before, about all of my baggage?" He held her close, smoothing her long blonde hair through his fingers.

"Yeah?" She chuckled softly. He was getting her back, they would make it through this, come out friends still.

"Well, you had one thing wrong," he mentioned, gazing at her face. "I didn't lose my best friend, she's right here." He kissed the top of her head as she clung to him.

WHY COULDN'T HE GIVE his heart to a kind woman that wasn't weighed down by baggage? It didn't make any sense why he was so smitten with Emily, but here he was again, meeting her on the beach, this time in the cloak of darkness. Was it possible that each time they met, he was falling deeper for her? Neither spoke as he wrapped his arms around her. After minutes ticked by, he placed the softest kiss on her lips. Each time they kissed, he felt that sense of peace, similar to his experience in the ballroom and pub. It was love, it must be love, there was no other explanation.

"Tell me more about you, Jackson Tomkins. I want to know everything, your dreams, your childhood. What were you like as a small boy?" He laughed as she rambled on. He spoke of his childhood friends, even Gary, upon which time she squeezed his hand tight for support. He spoke of his dreams to have children one day, a nice big family. Emily turned away, her gaze directed on the vast ocean.

"You want children? Funny, I never considered that you would," she mumbled.

"Well of course I do. Don't you someday?"

Her eyes grew distant and she pulled away from him, wrapping her arms tight around herself. "I suppose I used to."

"Used to? You're what, twenty-two, twenty-three?"

"Something like that," she answered with a faraway look in her eyes.

Something was wrong, he had hit a sore spot. Suddenly he wondered if she wasn't able to have children. "Emily, if I'm getting too personal here, stop me. Can you have children? Is something wrong?"

Weeping softly, her green eyes misted in the moonlight. "Jackson, I can't have children. Arthur and I tried, went to doctors and I'm infertile. It caused a lot of stress between us. I understand if you don't wish to pursue this any longer." Her voice trailed off, her sadness rubbing off on him. Was she serious? He couldn't leave her if he tried.

"Emily, I'm so sorry." Cradling her, he kissed the top of her head. "And I'm not going anywhere, don't you even worry about that."

He needed to change the subject to cheer her up. "Your turn, what are your dreams? What did you dream of when you were a girl?" He wished he had known her then. She was probably adorable with her sweet smile and blonde hair.

He was met with silence, then a curt response. "I don't have dreams, not anymore." It was heartbreaking, this melancholy side to Emily. Was she in a bad mood or did she harbor a chronic, deep sadness behind those beautiful green eyes?

"Oh, come on now, Emily. Everyone has dreams."

"I *said* I don't dream anymore," she snipped.

First the hair and now this, she had some secrets she wasn't willing to share still. "Listen, honey, I know you've been through hell and back…"

"You have no idea," she muttered, eyes straight ahead.

"You're right, but it's all in the past, right? Look to the future, you and I met, isn't that something to be positive about?"

"Jackson, it's not in the past, every day, every *single* day I have to bear the weight of the abuse, the betrayal, it's never going to be over." Still, her eyes were fixed on a distant point.

How could he get through to her? He was damaged too and he could still see brighter things in his future. "Emily, I make you this promise, right here, right now that I will never hurt you, nor will I let any man ever hurt you again. If you stay by my side I will protect you as long as you'll let me."

"Promises? I've heard them all before, empty promises that don't mean a thing," she exclaimed.

She had such a darkness about her right now, he figured no matter what he said or did she wouldn't come out of the black mood she was in until she was ready. Saying nothing more, he sighed, pulling back to give Emily her space. He had known she carried a past, but what else wasn't she saying?

"I'm sorry for upsetting you, Jackson. It was wrong of me to bring you down with all my troubles. I just get a bit melodramatic at times, I guess." Her hand was back in his and he was relieved the storm had passed. "I want you to tell me about Maria now, tell me something you've never told another living soul."

Thinking hard, he bit his lip before deciding to continue. With Emily, it was safe to share his darkest secrets. "At first, when I found them, there was a part of me, so deep inside of me, that wished them harm. I wanted revenge. I wanted to hurt them both. Of course I got hold of myself, but it scares me to think that I could have such darkness in my soul, it was like it was hidden, but always there waiting, you know?'

"I know, and it's not anything to worry about, it's human nature, you pulled back and never acted on your thoughts, that's what matters."

"I guess, but it scared me still. Then I reached a point where I didn't even care about myself much, I was in such a state of sorrow that I never thought I could crawl out of the hole I dug for myself."

"But you did," she soothed. "I was there, in the same place as you and, sometimes, unfortunately I still find myself in that place, but since I met you, it's becoming less and less, does that make any sense?

It made perfect sense to him. Each and every word she said relieved such pressure on his mind, his soul. Was it still too early to tell her he loved her? It didn't matter; he didn't care about how it would sound. He was pretty sure she felt the same. "Emily, I have something I want to share with you." His beating heart assured him he was doing the right thing by telling her. "I love you. I love you like I never thought I could." Tears fell from his eyes as he huddled with her, keeping her warm. It didn't matter where he saw her, be it a haunted pub or a cold beach at night, he just wanted to be happy again, and, with her, he could feel alive once more.

"Oh Jackson, I've waited to hear those words. I love you too, and it scares me more than you'll ever know."

CHAPTER

Seventeen

Millie

JACKSON WAS A LOT kinder than she had originally bargained for. It would have made her job much easier to swallow if he wasn't such an upstanding guy. But then she supposed, she wouldn't have fallen for him as hard and, therefore, would still be searching for her partner to help her finally find peace. Her criteria for finding the right man included a bit more than just falling in love. It was him all right, there was no doubt in her mind, Jackson was the one she had been seeking since that fateful night in 1871. She would have to find a way for her to rationalize her actions from this point on. It would be difficult, for she was really coming to care for the man, but at least they would spend eternity together.

Sammy swept past her, knocking into her with the wooden spoon. They were helping mother by preparing supper so that she could attend to the sewing duties. "Sammy, what is the matter?" *She couldn't bear the cold silence and thumping around any longer.*

"You know very well, and I'm surprised such a smart girl like you would carry on in such a way with a man who clearly disrespects this family."

"What are you talking about? He doesn't." She had been speaking to Todd again about meeting her parents, he had agreed to, but each

time the opportunity arose, he had another excuse. It wasn't that he was embarrassed by her upbringing, she didn't think so, but then again she couldn't be certain as his actions betrayed his words.

"Oh? You know he does and I'm warning you, I heard Mother and Father speaking just last night, and they are going to put an end to this, they're tired of the disrespect, it's been going on far too long."

"Put an end to it? I won't allow such a thing!" Millie exclaimed, clutching her apron tight in her hands. Her very being was shaken to the core. With a hammering chest, she placed her palm on Sammy's arm.

"Then do something about it, now. I don't wish to see you thrown out on your bottom, sister, I love you too much. Wake up!" Sammy begged, pulling her close. "Don't leave me here without you. I couldn't bear to lose you."

She could see why Sammy was so distraught. The sisters were quite close and she would feel the same way if Sammy left, for whatever reason. But Todd had her acting completely irrational lately, behaving like a woman in love. Yes, she was in love and wouldn't let anyone tear them apart. He was making promises now, promises to take her away and give her a proper house that belonged to the both of them. He would make a move when he was more settled with his Mother, when she didn't need him to care for her. She would speak to him again, tonight by the beach, and insist that he must visit her house, sooner rather than later. Mixing the soup, she bit her lip.

"It's okay, Sammy, I promise you I will speak with him," she stated, picking at her fingernails.

Dinner had been a horrendous stress, knowing that Mother and Father had such decisive plans. She knew that her own mother had been thrown from her home when she had met Father. Her grandfather didn't approve of their relationship and made her mother choose: her suitor or her home. Mother had chosen her suitor and told the tale that it made her grow up, become a better person. As much as Mother loved her, she would side with her Father and speak of growing up and becoming a woman. Oh, it was too much to bear. If she had her proper house, she would feel differently, but the house Todd spoke of wasn't in their immediate future, not yet.

Later, at the beach, she spared Todd the drama, but focused on the importance of meeting with her parents and spending time getting to know them.

"Silly, silly girl. I told you I would, the time just hasn't been right yet. You need to relax, everything will work out, I promise you."

"Yes, Todd, you have promised such for weeks, but as of yet, I haven't seen it happen." She didn't wish to be firm with him, but he needed to see the importance of the issue.

"Have I mentioned that I love you today?" He brushed sweet kisses along her neck, creating the most delightful shivers. How is it that the man always managed to make her forget why she was cross with him? As his hands moved further, she stopped him. This was getting to be a regular situation the past few times she had seen Todd. She considered herself a good girl and that meant she would wait until marriage.

"No, Todd, I told you," she muttered as she removed his hands from her body. She could predict the deep sigh before she heard it. He was upset with her and that was fine, but she wouldn't budge, not when it came to something as crucial as her values.

"Dear girl, we've been through this before, I've made a promise to you, correct?"

Nodding, she decided whatever carefully chosen words he would use, she would stand her ground.

"Yes, Todd, you have promised but I have told you that until I see the ring on my finger, wait a moment, let me restate that, until you and I become Mr. and Mrs. Todd Alcott, that part of our relationship will have to wait. I love you, you claim to love me, show me by being patient."

"You're a silly girl, do you know that? Do you not believe me when I tell you that you will become my wife?"

That wasn't the point, and he knew it. She did believe him and appreciated that he cared for his sick mother so lovingly. *"I believe you, Todd, but these are my values we're speaking of here and they won't be compromised."*

"You know, I was going to wait for a more romantic moment, but you give me no choice." Fumbling his hands into his pocket, his large hands gripped a small, shiny object.

Her hands flew to her mouth in surprise. It was a small, tasteful diamond. It was perfect because it was from Todd. *"Is that...?"*

Getting down on one knee, Todd glanced upward, into her eyes. *"Will you marry me?"* Waiting a beat, she thought he would continue, have more to say, but that was fine with her.

"Oh yes, Todd, yes!" She pulled him up and allowed him to twirl her around.

He leaned over, kissing her until the heat was too much to bear. *"Todd, please."*

"But we're properly betrothed now, surely this will be okay with

you now."

"Didn't you hear me? Not until we're married. Now let's not ruin this beautiful moment, come, let's take a walk." She couldn't wait until she arrived home to add this to her story. Now that they had definite plans for marriage, he was certain to meet her parents soon. A nagging thought in the back of her mind surfaced; proper tradition included the suitor asking the father for the daughter's hand in marriage. Her father would be furious. Would he approve, say yes? Determined not to lose this man, she decided that if her father disapproved, she would marry Todd anyway.

HE FELT LIGHTER THAN he had in years. Regardless of what Kristen had to say, he knew that Emily was good for him. Despite how their relationship would play out, he knew that she was there for him at a time when he needed her most. Concern over her fragile state of being with her ex-husband filled his mind. She was good for him, but was he good enough to help chase Emily's demons away?

Kristen's ankle was well on the mend, and she was preparing to go back to work. Right now she knew better than to appear back at Millie's and it infuriated him that Millie was winning. Kristen mentioned looking at The Jetty for some temporary work, just until they solved this mystery with Millie, hopefully, therefore releasing her spirit. Jackson had nearly pounced on her, telling her The Jetty would be an awful choice for employment. Kristen seemed to accept his story about it being slow during the off-season there, but the look in her eyes told him that she thought he was probably strung a bit too tight. He had agreed that the stress of everything was getting to him. The last thing he needed was Kristen and Emily working together. It was a breath of relief that Kristen had averted her attention to looking for a job on the pedestrian mall.

"Jackson, I've been meaning to speak with you about something," Kristen began, fingering her hair. He had a feeling this wasn't going to be good.

"About?"

"Okay, hear me out. Please just promise me that you'll keep an open mind," she asked.

"I can't promise that I will, but go ahead." He held his breath, waiting.

"So this Emily…"

"Here we go, Kristen, would you please just accept her in my life because she's not going anywhere." If this continued, he would lose his patience. For the past few weeks, Kristen had successfully avoided any mention of Emily, but she had been a bit distant. It wasn't difficult to guess what had been on her mind.

"I've been thinking that her story doesn't quite make sense, you know? I mean if she had an ex-husband who was really trying to hurt her, she could at least bring you to her home, or for God's sake, your house at the very least. She should still be able to meet your friends," she exclaimed.

"Kristen, I don't like what you're insinuating here. The woman is protecting me and herself. What are you getting at, that she's still with her husband? That we're carrying on an affair, and she's been feeding me a line of bull this whole time?"

"No, I mean, maybe…" she stammered.

"Kristen, I don't appreciate this. I like Emily, no, scratch that, I'm in *love* with Emily, and I won't have you bringing us down." His breathing had intensified. He should have known that a friendship between a man and a woman would never work.

"I'm not finished. I've been asking around town, nobody's ever heard of a woman named Emily, and I searched her first name on the internet, nothing shows up! How did you say she makes a living?" Kristen was pacing his living room.

"Kristen, you've crossed the line here!" How could she go sneaking around behind his back, asking questions?

"Don't you see? I did it because I care for you, Jackson. She's bad news. I feel it in my bones. She's either a con woman of some kind or maybe she is having an affair…"

Cutting her off, he'd had about all he could take. "With all due respect, stay out of my business. You're fabricating stories about Emily because you don't like her, you never did!"

"How could I possibly like her, Jackson? I never met her; *no-body's* ever met her, wake up!" Kristen boomed, standing right before him. He looked down at her and clenched his fists, he was so upset with her right now, he wanted to punch the wall. Just as he had practiced deep breathing when he first experienced the betrayal of Maria and Gary, he slowly counted to ten once more.

"I know her, I trust her, and that's the bottom line, take it or leave it," Jackson ordered, stepping to his front door. "If you value our friendship at all and want to see it last, don't ever bring up Emily's name around me again." He opened the door and stepped out into the chilly night, leaving Kristen alone in his house.

He would walk to Millie's Pub tonight to meet Emily. He needed to blow off some steam. It was difficult to clear his head of the accusations Kristen had thrown around. In his mind he was already making excuses for Emily. So maybe Emily wasn't her real name, so what? Plenty of people on the run changed their name for the sake of security. He didn't give a crap if her name was Bob or Billy Joe, he still loved the woman. It was sad the way this whole thing was playing out with Kristen, if she continued on this little tirade of hers there would need to be some changes made in their relationship.

CHAPTER

Millie

SHE WOULD NEED TO hide her diamond ring until she could convince Todd to stop by to meet her parents. He had promised it would be tomorrow night, and she hoped he kept his word. This wasn't merely courtship now, this was serious business. The man was to become her husband, her family. Tucking the ring deep inside of her dresser drawer, she peeked over her shoulder at Sammy, who was sleeping soundly. By candlelight she would write on her precious paper, adding the events of the evening to her love story.

When all the words spilled form her heart, she sighed and prepared for sleep. Sammy was sound asleep; otherwise she would have loved to share her news. No, that wasn't the plan, though. Until Todd was physically in her home, meeting with her mother and father, the secret would be locked close in her heart. With heavy eyes, she found sleep.

Upon waking, she spied Sammy opening her dresser drawer. Darn, she had forgotten how lazy the girl could be. She must be out of clothing again. Sometimes it was unfortunate to have a sister that was essentially the same size. She couldn't recall a time when she had borrowed any clothing from Sammy, though.

"Sam! Get out of there!"

Spinning around, Sammy's mouth fell open. "Well somebody is very out of sorts this morning."

"I mean it, get out of there!" Springing to her feet, she shoved the drawer shut tight, almost closing Sammy's hand in it. Her heart was hammering in her chest, if her sister got wind of this now, there would surely be trouble.

"What are you hiding?" Sammy hissed.

Her hand was on her sister's mouth in an instant. "Shh! What is the matter with you?"

"What is it that you're not telling me?" Sammy stood her ground, hands planted on her tiny hips. Her sister was a stubborn one and she doubted that she would let this go. It was clear she had no choice, besides, part of her was spilling over, anxious to share the news.

Grabbing her sister by the hand, she led her to her bed. "Now, you have to promise me that you will be quiet about this. Can I trust you to keep a secret?" She did trust her sister, and she knew that regardless of how Sammy felt about this, she wouldn't betray her.

"Yes, of course I can, I've only done it about a thousand times before," Sammy reminded her. But those had been matters of trivial concern; this was the secret of all secrets.

"Are you sure? It's a big one, sister."

Clasping her hands around Sammy's, she took a deep breath and prepared to speak. Instead, she sprang to her feet, making her way over to her dresser drawer. Slowly, as if to prolong the moment of suspense, she reached back until she felt the tiny object.

"Don't peek, close your eyes until I tell you to it's okay."

"Come on, hurry!" Sammy cried out.

"Quiet! Mother and Father will hear you." Placing the ring on her left ring finger, she inhaled deeply, exhaling just as deeply, she spun around, holding her diamond ring high in the air.

"Is that what I think it is?" Sammy sprung to her feet, shrieking. What was the matter with the girl? Didn't she just tell her to be quiet! Her hand was on Sammy's mouth once more.

"Do you realize how loud you are? You're going to draw attention to us!"

"I…I'm sorry, but are you actually going to accept that?" Sammy exclaimed, her mouth open wide.

"Of course I'm going to accept it! Why wouldn't I? I'm in love with the man!" Why couldn't her sister be happy for her? Her own sister! She hadn't even realized she had been yelling until she heard the approaching footsteps.

"Oh my God! What have I done?" Clamping her hand down on

her own mouth now, she locked eyes with Sammy, her heart pounding furiously.

The door opened and her father was there, a scowl etched onto his face. "What is this all about?" He boomed, taking in the sisters. His eyes scanned her face, as she gulped, moving both hands behind her back. It was a stupid move, too obvious.

"What do you have behind your back there?" He edged closer as she backed up into her dresser. Praying silently, she dared to look up at her Father's confused face.

"I... nothing, it's nothing. Sammy and I were just arguing about something, I'm sorry Father, for raising my voice and disturbing you." Her voice was shaking, a clear giveaway that she was lying. Lying was forbidden, but then again so was sneaking around and allowing a gentleman to give her a diamond ring without her father's permission. Please Father, just believe this one lie, and I swear Todd will be here today, just as he'd promised. She would make sure of it now; she had come too close to ruining everything.

"Show me your hands," he ordered.

"Father, I..." she stammered, sweat clinging to her nightgown. Stealing a glance at Sammy who was shrinking back into the corner of the room, she knew she was caught. There was a slight chance he wouldn't see the ring, wasn't there?

"Show me your hands!" Her father's voice rose to a tone she seldom heard, but when she did, it always made her cringe.

Throwing her hand up quickly, she spun around to show him there was nothing there, nothing on the floor, nothing. Her father walked around, searching the floor, eyes scanning all around. "There's nothing here."

"No, there's not, Father, nothing at all." But in her nervousness, she had forgotten that when she became nervous or excited, she often used her hands when she spoke. With her hands in midair, she realized her mistake as her father's eyes zoomed in on the sparkling diamond.

Red rage registered on his face as he drew closer, prying her fingers apart. Sweat formed on his forehead. "Father! I'm sorry, he's going to..."

With a swift hand, her father swiped her belongings from her dresser; bottles flew, her brush, and clip were next. "Father!" Sammy wept from the corner, rocking herself.

Finally, his tirade ended and her father appeared to have caught his breath. This was good, right? Now maybe she could make him understand. Todd hadn't meant any disrespect, he was just a busy man tend-ing to his mother.

"Get out," her father spoke so calmly that it frightened her more than his yelling had.

"But Father, please!" Begging wasn't beyond her, she needed to make him listen.

"If you think for one moment that I would allow a man who had never showed your mother and I respect by even introducing himself, let alone asking my daughter to marry without my permission, you've got to be out of your mind."

"But I love him, Father, I love him!" Crying out, she was near hysteria.

"Love? Little girl, you have no idea what love is. I said get out. You are no longer welcome in this house, ever again. You've got an hour to pack your bags and say your goodbyes."

"But I can't, I have nowhere to go!" What would she do, roam the streets? The house Todd had promised her was nowhere in their immediate future, it would be a while, she had no money.

"I'm sure you and your future husband will figure it out, it's not my problem, not anymore." With his hands thrown up in disgust, he walked from the room where Mother could be heard sobbing from the hallway.

"Mother!" She rushed at her mother, straight into her arms. "Mother, I'm so sorry! I want to stay," she wept into her mother's shoulder.

"That's no longer in my control, dear. I will be heartbroken, truly crushed, but you made up your mind here, you dishonored your father and me."

"But Mother, he's coming to meet you today or tonight, I was going to tell you." The lame attempt did nothing for her case. She knew it wasn't her mother's choice, once her father decided something, that was it.

"Where is she going to live?" Sammy cried out, moving toward the women. "Please Mother, talk some sense into Father, please!"

"She will live with her suitor." Her mother cringed as she spoke. "He will take care of her now."

"I can't Mother, he's not ready for me. He lives at home taking care of his ailing mother." Gut wrenching sobs tore from her mouth. If only she could go back in time and change the course of events.

"Well, that's something you two will need to figure out. I'm sure he'll make room for you at his mother's home." Tears fell from her mother's eyes as she ran her hands through her daughter's hair.

"But he won't, he won't..." An endless stream of tears fell; she squeezed her mother's hands tight.

"It seems you have more than just the problem of where to live, now doesn't it then?" Her mother's words were sad, but she didn't quite understand what her mother was getting at. She wasn't speaking clearly.

"Mother?" Swiping at her runny nose, she swallowed.

"Gather your things and I'll see you out in a bit." With that her mother was gone. She and Sammy clung to one another until her father's footsteps sounded once more, reminding her that her time here was almost up. She needed to pack her few belongings, which she found could be contained into one cloth case.

'I love you sister. I will never forget you, Sammy. You'll always be my best friend." Clinging to her sister's shoulder, she didn't know how this had all turned so bad, so fast.

"I can't let you go, it was my fault. If only I didn't insist upon sneaking through your things, asking what you were hiding..."

"It's not your fault," she cried out, taking her sister's face in her shaking hands. "It's my fault; it's been my fault from the very beginning." It was all true, she should have insisted that Todd court her in a proper manner.

"Sister?" Sammy's eyes pooled with fresh tears. "Be happy and never forget me."

Wrapping her arms tightly around Sammy, she breathed in her powdery scent. She would remember that smell and think of it when she became lonely. Sammy was a fine sister and a better friend. This feeling in her gut felt as if she were being ripped apart from the inside. "Always be as sweet as you are, Sammy. I'm proud of the woman you've become. I love you." Turning on her heels, she didn't look back, she couldn't, or she would never survive the hurt.

Saying goodbye to her Mother nearly ripped her heart out for the second time. Father had left, gone out on an errand. Mother had stated this was killing him, tearing him apart. He had a funny way of showing it. Memories of herself, Sammy and her mother, baking together, filling their time with laughter, filled her senses as she took in the kitchen one last time. She would never see her mother's fine handiwork adorning the walls, each stitch telling its own story. There would be no more family breakfasts, dinners. No more birthday celebrations, no more anything. A thought popped into her head, what if she was to give Todd Alcott up? Would Father permit her to stay then? She highly doubted it and, besides, she was a grown woman now, a grown woman in love.

"Take this, dear, don't ever tell your father I gave it to you." Her mother placed a sack in her hands. It was heavy. "It's some food and supplies, dear. Enough to get you started. Now, go, please, before he gets back." Rubbing her fingers over her daughter's face, she cried loudly. "Oh, why did you ever have to get involved with that horrid man?"

"Mother, I'm sorry, for everything," she wept, clinging to her mother's dress. She wasn't ready for this, what would she do out in the world on her own? Not wishing to frighten her mother, she wouldn't voice her fears; she would keep them tucked safely inside.

"You're a good girl, always have been. Of all the people I've known in my life, you're among the kindest, most selfless…" Her mother couldn't continue, nor could she. Without another word, she bravely separated herself from her weeping mother, a woman now, out to make her way in the world.

_I_T HAD BEEN HOURS, and she was still on her feet. Where was Todd? Glancing around the beach, she realized he wasn't due to meet her for a while. She found a spot in the dunes to spread out. Opening her sack, she grabbed at a biscuit and some tea which her mother had supplied. What would she do if Todd wouldn't have her? Twirling the diamond on her finger, she allowed herself to weep deeply now. She would most likely never lay eyes on her family again. As angry as she was with her father, she knew she would miss him too. A man with his pride wounded was an angry man indeed; she couldn't completely place the blame on her father. She knew the terms of their family, and she had to pay the price for her betrayal. Todd loved her, though, and she felt confident that he would do right by her, take her home, and marry her, sooner rather than later.

"Darling!" Todd's voice registered. She must have nodded off. She felt someone shaking her, waking her. Opening her eyes, it all came back, the horrendous events of the day and all of the heartache that followed.

"Oh Todd!" she cried out, clinging to him fiercely. "Thank God you've come!" Without another word of formality, she spilled the entire story, from start to finish. She was relieved to take the pressure off and lay in his arms when the story was complete. He would help her now; she was safe in his strong arms.

Todd was unnaturally silent, causing her to peek up at his handsome face. "Todd?" Running her fingers through his thick dark hair, she waited.

"Well, um. This is most unfortunate," Todd stated, clearing his throat.

"Unfortunate? Well, yes, that would be correct. It's horrible, but now that I'm safe with you…"

Righting himself, he turned to look out at the beach beyond. His silence was unnerving, what was he thinking? "Todd, what is it?"

"You can't come home with me, Mother…" he began.

"What?" She shot straight up, pulling away from him.

"Mother, she's worse than ever, I can't, I'm sorry." Todd bit his lip, turning away.

"You're just going to leave me here, homeless on the beach? Todd, I have nowhere to go, no money, only you!" she cried out, unable to believe what she was hearing. "What would your mother have against me? I don't care, tell her I'm a friend, tell her anything!" The pitch of her voice was rising to near hysteria.

"Calm down, now, let me just think," Todd stated calmly. He rose to his feet, pacing the dunes, over and over until she thought she would go mad with the silence.

"Stop! Stop walking around like that and tell me what you're thinking! How could you ask for my hand in marriage and then leave me here, all alone?" This was a nightmare of the worst kind. She would be a homeless woman, dirty, begging for food and drink in the streets, groveling.

"Okay, okay. I've got it! Here me out. Tonight, we can head right on over, and I can get you a room. I have room in one of my places for women. It's a spacious enough room with a bath on the floor to share, of course, and a kitchen downstairs."

"What? You're going to put me in one of your homes for the disadvantaged?" It was too much to bear. Didn't this man love her anymore?

"Now keep an open mind here. It will just be temporary until the situation with Mother is settled. It shouldn't be long."

"What is it with your mother? Marry me and surely she wouldn't be upset if you brought me home," she pleaded. What kind of mother was this?

"No, she's very ill and doesn't take change well. It would be unkind of me to disrupt her now. Back to the room, the more I think about it, the better it sounds. We can be alone there, just you and me."

Figures that's what he would focus on. But having a place to be with Todd, away from the beach, would be good. They never did anything besides take long walks on the beach, it was getting to be a tired situation. "How long?"

"Just until Mother passes or my brother comes to help out. Not long."

"Why hasn't your brother been helping out all along? My goodness, you've been caring for her on your own when you've had a perfectly capable brother to share the responsibilities this entire time!" This was absurd! "And why can't we ever go out? Have a proper dinner in a restaurant?"

"Why all of these sudden demands? You know that I'm saving money right now, for our future," he explained, running his hands through his hair.

"Why couldn't you have just come to meet my parents? Asked my father for his permission? None of this would have ever happened!" she cried out.

"Are you saying this is my fault?" He turned, eyes squinting at her. She didn't need him angry with her too, where would she go then?

"No, Todd. I'm sorry. It's just after all that's happened…"

"Fine, fine then. We have our plan and it will most likely work out better this way for us. We'll get to spend much more time together, how does that sound?" He was back, filling up the space between them.

"That part sounds wonderful," she admitted, glancing up at Todd's dark eyes. He was so very handsome and he was all hers, she needed to keep things in perspective.

"It's settled then, we'll leave shortly." Closing the deal, he placed a lingering kiss on her lips. She could breathe a sigh of relief, he would take care of her, things were starting to look up now.

CHAPTER
Nineteen

THE COLD AIR SLAPPED at his face. Pulling his jacket tighter around him, he pulled Emily close. She shivered slightly, but the cold didn't seem to affect her much. She never complained about being cold on their walks out to the beach. Most women he had known, including Maria, would have refused to even set foot on the beach this time of year. "You okay?" Jackson asked, placing a kiss on her head.

"Yes, better than I have been in some time, as a matter of fact."

"Emily? When do you think we'll be able to do normal things?" Some of Kristen's words had apparently sunk in.

"Normal things?" Emily peered up at him.

"Yes, like meeting my friends, coming to my house, you know."

"I'm not in a normal situation, and if you have a problem, speak now." Her clipped tone told him she was upset.

"I'm sorry, I'm just kind of looking for a time frame here," he explained.

"A time frame? Let's see, how can I put a time frame on how long it will take for me to stop being afraid of my crazy husband." Emily dropped her head, shaking it back and forth.

"I won't let anything happen to you, I promise you that." If she would only let him, he would keep her so close.

"That's rather kind of you, but nobody can keep me safe, not from him. I hope I don't lose you, but I'm growing rather tired of the same conversations, sometimes I wonder if you and I should have ever started this."

He should have kept his mouth shut, it was Kristen, she had gotten into his head with all of her doubts. "I have something I want to speak with you about. That woman, my friend, Kristen, I told you about her," he began.

"Kristen?" Emily repeated her name slowly.

"Yes. I'd like you to at least meet her. It's safe, nothing could happen."

"No way," Emily stated firmly. "It's not going to happen."

"But why? She's been asking lots of questions about you, wondering why I've kept you hidden away. She's beginning to wonder if we're having an affair." Jackson laughed. He felt it would be good for the women to meet at this point, help to establish a friendship, possibly, that is, if either woman would allow it.

"Jackson, exactly what is it that you don't understand? It's a huge feat that I've let you into my life. I haven't gotten this close to anyone in years. Now, if you prefer to keep that friendship of yours going with Kristen, maybe it's best that we just part ways now."

What? How had this conversation gotten so messy? This wasn't what he had imagined when he brought up the topic of meeting Kristen. "No, Emily, God no. I'm sorry, again, for upsetting you. I guess I couldn't possibly understand the hell you've been through to make you this worried."

"I'm not trying to mess with your head or anything, but if this Kristen was any kind of friend, she'd back off and give you space here, not demand things. If she truly cared she would want you to be happy."

"Yes, but she does want me to be happy, she just wants to make sure I'm not going to get hurt in the process." He didn't need Emily thinking that Kristen was some sort of manipulative woman.

"Oh please, Jackson. Men are so naïve when it comes to women and how they operate. It's crystal clear, to me at least, that this friend of yours has her own reasons for being concerned, let me spell it out for you. She wants you for herself, Jackson."

But that was ridiculous. Actually, it wasn't, but he wasn't about to admit to Emily that before she had come along, he and

Kristen may have very well tried their hand at dating, it had only been a matter of time before he was ready to date.

"I don't know what to say to you right now except that I'm with you and I only want to be with you."

"So then this Kristen, she won't be a problem any longer?" Emily inquired, picking at her fingernails.

He didn't realize that she was a problem to begin with. Besides this conversation, which in his mind, didn't equate with a problem really, he was surprised to hear Emily's opinion.

"She's a friend, a good friend, and she's not going to come between us, I promise."

"Huh! Let's hope not, Jackson. If I were you, I'd start keeping her at arm's length, that is, if you value our relationship."

Was that a threat? He didn't like this jealous side she was displaying, it didn't suit her, but because he knew the woman had been through so much, he let it pass. He noted that he and Kristen had already started spending less time together and he found that he missed her. Moments later, as Emily laid back into his arms and kissed him, he felt younger and more carefree once more. She had that overwhelming ability to draw him in. Kristen and his worries were far from his mind.

Millie

From where she stood, there was nothing else she could do to keep Jackson away from her. Unless Kristen had the guts to come back to the house, she couldn't reach her. But she could reach Jackson and so far he seemed to be open and receptive to her mind games. A willing participate was always the easiest and let's face it, part of the reason she had chosen him in the first place was because of his vulnerability, that being one of several reasons. Jackson was one of those men that cared so deeply, too deeply in this case. It was not a bad thing, not for her. She didn't know what she was waiting for. Impatience and patience bound together in her mind. She could take care of this now or she could play a bit more, she had all the time in the world, after all. The problem with watching and playing was that, for the first time in so long, she was doubting herself, questioning her motives with him. It wasn't that he was the wrong man, quite the contrary. Jackson was special in so many ways, familiar even though she had known him for a short time, it was destined. Jackson was her one true love, but he had so many dreams of his own, left unfound. She had no idea that he had wanted children, a family. Each time her wall cracked a bit, she would need to focus on Todd Alcott among others, remember how cruel men could be, that should make her job easier to do. Who knew, maybe in time, the man would even thank her for taking him from all of his misery. Maria and that Gary fellow had caused him such heartache; she would do him a favor so that all he saw was her.

*I*T WAS A MONTH *later, and she was still in that boarding house. At first she was unhappy, she didn't belong there, not with these women. Sure, she had been brought up with little privileges, but these women came from battered homes and worse. Todd claimed it would be any day now. Her writing was suffering as her love story was becoming cold and monotonous; she had less and less to report of her own romance. Todd came by each evening, but no more walks on the beach. Now they only stayed in her room, and each night was a repeat of the night before. Most evenings he would bring her the most glorious leftovers, meals from his mother's home. She would eat alone as he nibbled on her neck, attempting to bed her. It wasn't going to happen, she wanted to scream from the top of her lungs! She had begged him at first to get her out of this place but now she was slowly starting to become part of this unlikely sisterhood. She had friends, for the first time in her life she had real friends. Perhaps*

missing Sammy had pushed her to pursue other friendships, ones that she had shied away from before. She wasn't quite as timid as she'd been with other women in the past. She was now coming out of her shell. Most of these poor women had never attended school, they couldn't read or write. She almost felt motherly to some of these young women, especially at nighttime. Each evening, they would all gather downstairs in the formal room and she would read her cherished Jane Austen stories, ones that Todd had purchased for her. She took up dancing as the top floor housed a huge formal ballroom. She was a natural, every once in a while, Todd would hold a ball, most likely to keep her happy. He would never attend, claiming that he had business to attend to, but he would supply the music and food for the women. No men, just the women dancing the night away. A few times, after hours when all the other women were sleeping, she would come up here by herself and turn the music on. Todd had joined her a handful of times, holding her close, pressing against her, asking her body for more than she was willing to give. When? She would ask, again and again about marriage. Soon, he would tell her. It was always the same response. Would he ever treat her better? Fulfill his promises? She was seriously starting to have her doubts.

Twisting her ring on her finger, there was a soft knock on her door. It was too early for Todd to arrive. "Be right there," she called out.

"Marilyn, it's wonderful of you to stop by." Marilyn was one of her closest friends here at the house, just a year or so younger than herself. Marilyn had been acting odd lately, staring at her when she thought she didn't see her.

"I was wondering something," Marilyn began, wringing her hands together.

The poor girl looked so nervous. "Yes, sure," she urged Marilyn to continue. Leading the way to the small seating area in the center of the room, she sat first, waiting for Marilyn to follow.

"What is it, Marilyn, you look so serious." She hoped that everything was okay with her.

"I love your story time, every night it's the highlight of my day, just looking forward to it, you know."

"Well, thank you, Marilyn, I'm pleased you feel that way."

"What I wanted to ask was if you could, that is, if you wouldn't mind and you have the time…" she stammered, still twisting her hands.

"Marilyn, please." Leaning over, she took the young woman's hands in hers. "Go on," she prompted.

"Will you teach me to read?" Marilyn blurted out, flushing a deep red. She was taken aback by the woman's question. Tears pooled in her eyes, she had never felt more special than at that very moment. Even the moment when Todd had first claimed his love for her dimmed in comparison.

It took a moment for her to compose herself. This must be what it felt like to be a teacher. "Marilyn, it would be my pleasure to teach you to read." Marilyn jumped up, throwing arms around her.

"When can we get started? I'm sorry, I apologize, I'm just so excited is all!" Marilyn gushed. It felt good to smile. She had come to find that the feeling of happiness had been fleeting for the past month or so. Without even realizing, she must have been turning her ring, a new habit that she had picked up since wearing it.

"I'm excited too. How about we start tomorrow, perhaps in the afternoon?"

"Oh yes! I can't thank you enough."

"It will be a wonderful experience for me, thank you for asking." This would be the moment she knew she would remember as the turning point here at the house, she was one of the family now, and she couldn't be happier. No need to beg Todd for his attention and promises, she was slowly losing patience and knew she had a lot of thinking ahead of her.

"I hope you don't mind me asking, but the girls and I have been wondering. You wear a ring, but there's no mention of a suitor, no sight of him and if you don't mind me saying, you look so sad."

She was ashamed that it had been so obvious. "Thanks to you girls, I feel at home like I haven't in quite some time. I think this place and all of you, have forced me to grow up and become a better person for it. As for my suitor, I honestly don't know anymore, I suppose time will tell."

CHAPTER
Twenty

"I'M GOING UPSTAIRS," he called out to Kristen from his cell. He got to thinking after last night with Emily that he had been neglecting Kristen and their friendship lately, especially after their recent argument. He didn't need to announce the time he spent with either woman, and he certainly wasn't about to give up on his friendship with Kristen or his relationship with Emily. Both women were behaving in a jealous way, and, while he was flattered to a certain extent, he felt torn between the two.

"I wish I could be there with you, Jackson." Kristen's voice sounded from his cell. That was a joke.

"No you don't."

"You're right, I don't." Kristen chuckled. This was what he had missed, the give and take that only he and Kris seemed to share. Emily was different, more serious, and easy to speak with, which was fine, he supposed that's why he craved both women in his life.

"Listen, let me go but I'll stop by in say, an hour or so to fill you in."

"Okay, what if you don't find anything?" Kristen asked.

"Feel like a late lunch?" His stomach had started to let him know it had been hours since he had last eaten.

"Sounds great, see you then. Oh, Jackson?" She called out.

"Yes, Kris?"

"Be careful, she can be a real witch when she feels like it."

That got a laugh from him. "I will and yes, she certainly can be." And worse, Jackson figured. If they could just find a way to help her, everything could go back to normal. Placing his cell in the back pocket of his jeans, he crept up the giant staircase. Once more he felt himself being pulled back to another time, this time it was his own doing. He found it impossible not to feel it when being in this house.

If only there were still some clues left, that way he wouldn't need to go lurking around the haunted top floor of this place. Once he was up there, he breathed deeply and closed his eyes. Nothing except that odd feeling. He had his cell opened to his photos and selected the one of the original floor plan from the clerk's office. This was the ballroom, but of course he knew that, what he was looking for was the balcony that used to be attached to the room. Finding it in the diagram, he walked forward. Yes, this was the window that he had seen Millie occupy each time he had glanced up. How sad it must be for her to be trapped here, all alone. No wonder she was so bitter. But still, it wasn't right that she had hurt Kristen and wished her harm. If he listened carefully enough, he could just about make out a faint voice in the distance. It sounded as if a woman was weeping, softly at first but then louder until the noise took up so much space in his head that he thought it would burst. His head was pounding, the worst headache he had ever had. Gripping his head in his hands, he cried out for her to stop. The pain lessened, but he felt faint as he experienced the most amazing vision. He wasn't sure what was happening, but he saw flashes of a man, he was handsome and from what he could tell, this man appeared to be Todd Alcott. Yes, he recognized him from the old photos in the shore museum and the visions from the pub. Todd Alcott leaning over, as if he would kiss him. He realized with a chill that what he was seeing must be through Millie's eyes. It was if he were there, experiencing life though her perspective. Pleasant at first, there was a flash of a beach, picnics, laughter. But then in his soul he experienced such sadness, he was now in a dark place as a young blonde girl clung to him, sobbing. An angry man, pointing his finger toward the door. He felt such loneliness he wasn't sure he could stand it. Then he was wrapped in an older woman's arms, clinging to her until he felt himself pulling away. Next, he wandered the streets, alone and empty. He felt as if he would go mad, this darkness was dragging him to a dangerous place. Holding his head tightly, he forced himself to the present. Oddly enough, it was Kristen's face that gave him the strength to move the sadness from his mind. "Millie! Stop!"

The sudden light hit his eyes, causing him to squint, but the horrendous pain in his head was gone. It took him a moment to make sense of what had just happened, his mind flashing back to the images. My God, she was telling him her story. He no longer felt anger for her, how could he when she had just shared the most intimate emotions one could possibly share with another. If he wasn't sure of it then, he was now. Millie was reaching out, trying her best to tell him her story. She had been wronged, he was sure of it now. "Millie," he cried out, his hand reaching forward into the filtering dust. "Tell me what happened to you, you poor woman." He needed to know, but wasn't sure he could take any more visions. "Is there another way? I can't bear the pain." He wasn't just referring to the physical pain his headache had caused, but also the emotional pain of what she had experienced. Sitting down where the balcony once stood, he placed his head in his hands, tears fell softly. One thing had become clear as a result of his vision, he knew there was more to setting Millie free than just solving the mystery. The ghost was so tangled up in her past, in all of the raw emotions that he had experienced firsthand. She needed to let go of her anger and hurt or she would never be set free. *Millie, I'm not leaving you. I won't let you down.*

Millie

SHE WEPT ALONGSIDE HIM, sorry to have caused him pain. This man had a kindness unlike any other man she had ever met. Why couldn't it have been him, all those years ago that had captured her heart? If Jackson had lived during her time, they could have been happy, raised that family he had spoken of. She had motherhood stolen from her, among many other things. Millie had always wished for a little girl to share her dreams with or a boy to hold close and love. She could see she had hurt Jackson and it consumed her soul. If there was another way, she would have done it. What would it do to him when the visions became worse? This was the only way, the only way to free herself; she needed to stay strong. The only problem was that the more she got to know Jackson, the harder she fell. She was in love with him, no doubt, but there was so much more to her relationship with him, it was becoming quite complicated, even for a tough, bitter soul like her.

GUIDING HER FINGERS UNDER the row of words, she could see the excitement on Marilyn's face. After several weeks of reading lessons, she wondered if today might be the day when things clicked for Marilyn. It wasn't that she lacked the ability to blend the sounds together, it was more that Marilyn had no foundation. She had started at the beginning, introducing letters and sounds, Marilyn had been an eager student, and she saw the potential the girl had for learning. Word had quickly gotten out about the reading sessions, which meant that most of her time was occupied by her new hobby. Not only did she meet with Marilyn almost every day, but her days were also filled with several other women who wished to learn.

"You might just be able to take over story hour before you know it," she gushed, causing Marilyn to blush a soft pink color.

"I don't know about that, but I think I'm starting to get it, I think I'm getting there. Thank you." Marilyn beamed, throwing her arms around her neck.

"Yes, I think you're well on your way, and it's my pleasure, it really is." A warmth spread through her body, creating a peaceful feeling.

"Have you ever considered teaching?" Marilyn released her, wiping away her tears of joy. "You're a natural."

Teaching? Well, she wasn't sure what the requirements even were, but she had heard that some testing was in order. She wondered if it were something that she could pass. She had also thought teachers weren't permitted to marry, but she didn't know if that was even a concern at this point. The last few times she had seen Todd, she had brushed away his advances. Todd had appeared hurt but it didn't stop him from being persistent. Her new role as the teacher of these women (yes, she could feel comfortable in the title of that role) had given her strength. She felt as if she were being used when it came to Todd lately. As a matter of fact, looking back at her evolving relationship with him, she was beginning to wonder if she were being used the entire time. What was it? Was she not pretty enough, educated enough, fancy enough to bring around in public? Todd was due to arrive with her dinner shortly and she was prepared to have a little conversation with the man.

Taking special attention with her appearance, she wished him to see her in her best light. If Todd had been using her for his own selfish reasons, she was prepared to let him go and show him just what he was missing. As of late, he would arrive later and later, as if this were the last stop on his full schedule of activities. The only activities that she got to enjoy with Todd were the occasional dance in the grand ballroom. Just last week, she had heard of a splendid affair he was planning this month located on one of his other properties, he had arranged a ball for donations to his charities. All of the finest people were due to attend. She would ask him tonight if she could attend with him. Her heart sank as she imagined all of his excuses. Perhaps his sick mother might attend and spot her, God forbid. Perhaps it would cost too much for her to accompany him. His excuses tired her, making her feel down and low about herself as if she were an embarrassing secret to hide away. It was a good thing she had Marilyn and the other young women of the house. The house with no name, that is what this place had become for her. Todd had yet to give the property a name as he did with some of his other properties. Mary's Victorian, Anna's on the Sea, Beatrice by the Beach and more. She had wanted to know where these women's names had come from, he had informed her that Mary was his mother, Anna, a niece of his, and, Beatrice, his grandmother on his father's side. For reasons beyond her comprehension, it irritated her that this house had no name. It was a symptom of a bigger problem, as if this property was not as important as the others in his mind, therefore, somehow she wondered if she were not important to him as well.

Almost an hour after he should have arrived, he stumbled in. Had the man been drinking? She had seen it before, more and more lately, the stench of whiskey made her withdraw from his touch.

"Come here, darling, oh how I've missed you." Planting a wet, sloppy kiss on her lips, she turned, backing away once more. It might make for a difficult conversation if he was in such a state.

"Todd, I want you to sit, we need to talk," she began, picking at her nails.

"Oh? You sound so serious! You're especially beautiful when you're so serious!" Todd chuckled, taking a seat in her tiny seating area.

"Todd, I want to go the ball." She figured she would start with the request and follow the conversation from there.

"The ball? What ball?" He frowned, casting his eyes upon the dark wood floor.

"The ball! Surely you didn't forget. It's all anyone has been talking about. Over at Anna's on the Sea." Twisting her diamond, she steeled herself for the excuses.

"Oh, that one! Silly me, I've forgotten about it because I won't be attending. I have a rather important business meeting to attend that evening."

It was a lie, it had to be. "But that's ridiculous! Why would you schedule an event as important as the ball on a night you're already committed to?"

"See, I didn't know that when I planned the event, but what does it even matter?"

"Fine, so you're not going. I'd still like an invitation to attend." She crossed her arms over her chest, pouting.

"Are you mad? I can't have you showing up with another man." Sweat trickled from his forehead.

"Well, couldn't I go with my friends?"

His eyes were wide, registering disbelief. "Friends? You have friends now, since when?"

What was that comment supposed to imply? "Yes, the women from the house, I've grown quite close with several of them. I could even bring Sammy." She and Sammy had been secretly meeting in town after a chance encounter several weeks ago. It had been good to see her again, but Sammy was so fearful that Father would find out and that she, too, would be thrown from the house. Perhaps Sammy wasn't the best idea.

"The women of the house? This house? Are you mad? You can't bring these women to such an affair!"

"And what is wrong with these women? Aren't they one of your *biggest causes?" He sounded terribly cruel right now, a side of him she was unaware of.*

"Um, yes, they are, but bringing them to a function such as this? It's of no matter anyway, you cannot show up at the ball without a date, and I forbid you to find one,"

He forbid her? Who was he, her father? The ball was pushed from her mind for the moment as she felt her heart racing; she needed to discuss other matters of even more importance than the ball. The ball was merely one of the numerous problems that had been festering for so long. Was this true love? If so, she wasn't sure she wanted any part of it. This couldn't possibly be what love was all about.

"Forget about the ball, I'll dance by myself as usual. We need to talk, Todd. What are we doing here? Where is this relationship going? We never do anything together, ever! I'm in this room forever waiting on you, and all you wish to do is something that I will not even consider until after marriage. Are you ever planning to marry me or are you going to leave me rotting away in this house with no name!" *Her hands were shaking, she curled them into tight little fists and paced the seating area.*

"Well, my goodness. Somebody woke up on the wrong side of the bed this morning!" *Todd exclaimed, rising from his seat. He closed in on her, grasping her hands in his.* "I think you owe me an apology, dear. I feel as if I'm being attacked here."

Leave it to Todd to turn the tables so smoothly. "I won't apologize unless I get some answers, and even then I'm not sure." *Pulling her hands out of his reach, she turned to face the window. The beach was so beautiful from up here. She found she missed those first meetings of theirs, the picnics on the beach.*

"I have never seen you in such a mood. But fine, you'll get your answers and then I'll get my apology. As for the ball, the answer remains no."

She sighed, bit her lip, but permitted him to continue. "As for our impending marriage, it will happen sooner rather than later. I will apologize for one thing, for not being here as often as I should be. For not taking you out and treating you like the queen you are. Mother's condition has deteriorated quite rapidly, and I'm spending most of my time at her bedside."

Oh. Feeling guilty for giving him such a hard time when his mother was so ill, she wondered what he must think of her. "I'm sorry, Todd. I had no idea things had gotten to this point."

"Wait, there's more." *He came upon her, placing a gentle kiss on the tip of her nose. "Lastly, as for me not keeping my hands off of you, I admit I'm guilty there. You're so beautiful, I find it such a challenge not to sweep you up and have my way with you." He kissed both of her hands, gazing down at her.*

"Oh yes, and one more thing. The house with no name, as you so gently put it, will have a name as of now. What shall we call it? You decide."

"Me?" She was on the spot, left feeling like a fool for all of her nagging. She was still left confused about her conflicting emotions regarding this man, but she felt sadness for his mother.

"Yes, what shall we call it?"

"I...I don't know. It's your place, you name it, but call it something special, something grand."

"Yes, something special. Oh, I have the perfect name for it." Giggling softly, he whispered in her ear. It was a start, she supposed as she allowed Todd to kiss her once more.

CHAPTER
Twenty-One

"IT WAS ALL CONSUMING, she filled my mind, my senses with her pain. The heartache was so intense that I almost couldn't bear it, my head felt as if it would explode," he whispered as he sat across from Kristen in their window seat at the Cape Diner.

"My God, Jackson, I can't even imagine what it must have been like for you to experience that. I'm so sorry," she exclaimed, reaching out to grab his hands.

"Don't be sorry for me, be sorry for her." He would never be able to forget Millie's pain and emotions; it would haunt him as long as he lived. He already planned on having a restless night tonight, there was no way he could possibly sleep, not after the day he had. He'd be lucky if he slept at all this week.

"You want me to feel sorry for her? After she nearly killed me, twice?" Kristen sat back, her mouth open. "You've got to be kidding me."

"No, I'm actually not kidding. Kris, if you could have been there, if you could have experienced the pain." It was hard to think about, even now when he had distance from Millie's Pub and Bed and Breakfast.

"I don't care. I have a difficult time feeling anything for that ghost except anger and fear." Gazing out the window, she remained silent. He knew that Millie had hurt Kristen, but now that he was inside of Millie's head, he could easily see how she had slipped from pain to madness. Biting into his juicy burger, he figured it was a waste of time to try to convince Kristen that Millie was acting out of a place of sorrow. Sorrow for loss of such a young life with so much hope for happiness.

"Fine, you can continue to despise the woman for all I care, I'm just not going to agree with you. Boy, this burger is phenomenal."

Kristen's eyes sparked, something he'd missed seeing in her. "First of all…" She pointed a ketchup smeared finger at him, "… she's not a woman, she's a ghost."

"Call her what you will, she's still a woman, and she's still got a soul, I saw it, Kris, I was there."

"Okay, so you feel sorry for her, I just don't know why you're taking her side. Did you forget how much she despises me?"

"It's not you she despises, it's something else. How could she hate you?" He brought his mind back to the image of Todd Alcott, the picnic on the beach, the kiss, everything. At first he thought Millie must miss Todd, recalling sweet memories, but no, there was a sense of darkness, even over the fonder memories. What was it that Amelia had said about Millie wanting him? That he was in danger? If Amelia was correct, and that was all circumstantial at this point, but if it were remotely true… "You're in the way, that's it, you're in the way!" He laughed, slapping his leg. It felt so good to place some of the pieces of this mess together.

"What does that even mean?" Kristen's eyes narrowed as she placed her burger down.

"That must be it! It has to be," he continued, smiling broadly at Kristen.

"*What* must be it? Are you going to tell me or are you going to sit there like a fool?" Kristen demanded.

"*You* are a threat to Millie. Why didn't I see this before? Follow me here, listen. Amelia claims that she wants me, that I'm in more danger than you. She muttered something about true love. What if she feels threatened by you?"

Kristen shook her head firmly. "I'm flattered, Jackson, that I would be considered a threat, but your theory has some rather large gaps in it."

"How so?" Jackson thought it made perfect sense. Kristen and he were friends, best of friends. Kristen was a stunning, sexy woman… but Kristen was right, it didn't fit.

"Emily!" They both announced simultaneously.

"Yes, you're right. Emily doesn't fit into this puzzle smoothly, does she?" Jackson was stumped. If the ghost was threatened by another woman getting in the way, then why not cause harm to Emily?

"It was a good theory, Jackson, but it doesn't hold water. Let's face it, Millie has a personal vendetta against me, for whatever reason." Kristen sighed as she picked up her soda and sipped at it.

"I agree that Emily doesn't fit here, but I still think I'm on to something." He had to be, he felt it in his bones. Maybe this ghost was smarter than he realized, could she sense that perhaps Kristen would be more important in his life than Emily?

FOR SOME REASON, HE felt anxious to see Emily tonight, more so than usual. If he was right about Kristen becoming more important in his life than Emily, he felt unease at the idea of Emily losing importance in his life. He was being ridiculous, though, how could a ghost predict his love life? Feeling a bit brighter, his heart still leaped in his chest when Emily walked in. She smiled warmly as she rushed to meet him. When he embraced her, she held on tightly. She smelled of fresh powdery perfume, which instantly lightened his mood.

"It is so good to see you, Emily." With her in his arms, he was no longer concerned.

"It's great to see you too." There was sadness in her eyes today; he longed to wipe it from her face.

"You okay?" Running a finger along her cheekbones, she smiled up at him. "Yes, I'm fine."

She didn't look fine, but he knew when to back off and give her space. Changing the subject, he told her about his experience with Millie earlier in the day.

"You must be terrified. I'm sorry you had to go through that.

What do you think she was trying to tell you?" She eyed him carefully.

"I think she was telling me the beginning of her story, and I think there's a lot more to her story. I don't think I've seen the end of it."

"I don't think you have, either," she muttered, her eyes darting around the room.

"It was so odd, seeing everything from her perspective. I wish I could see *her*, you know? I often wonder what she looks like. My guess is that she's beautiful, a classic beauty, you know?" Jackson shared.

"But sad," Emily added. "So very sad. She must be with all she's been through."

"Yes, I'm sure she is sad. I got a new perspective on her today and I've decided that no matter what happens, I'll be there for her until we figure this out."

"We?" Emily ventured, picking at her fingernails.

"Well, sure. Kristen and I have been in this together, right from the start. As a matter of fact, she's the one who got me started on all this. Kristen knows all of the local legends around here. When I saw the figure in the window, I went to her and we decided right then and there to solve this crime."

"She sounds like a lovely woman, determined, beautiful." Emily's voice trailed off.

"You've seen her?"

"No, it's just the way you speak about her, I can tell."

"That's neither here nor there, we're friends, that's it. You don't need to worry about her, I told you that." He wondered why she would comment on Kristen's appearance.

"If you say so." The sadness was back in her eyes. "She sounds like she's been a good friend to you though, that's good." He saw concern in her eyes but it passed.

It got him thinking if she worried about their relationship as well. "Emily, do you ever think about where all of this is heading with us?"

A strange look came over her as she cleared her throat and began to speak. "I try not to think about it, Jackson."

What did that mean? "Well, why not, I mean, do you think we're going somewhere with this? Do you see a future for us?"

"Didn't we speak of this? I function best in the here and now.

I don't enjoy spending time worrying about what may or may not come to be."

"I get that and I'm sorry, but I've hoped that I could brighten your life, you know, since you've brightened mine. I hate to think that I don't make you a happier person."

She reached across the table and held onto his hands. "Jackson, I can't even begin to tell you how very happy you have made me."

Then why did she appear so sad? "I'm glad to hear that, I am, but can you at least tell me if you want to stay with me? Do you see us together in the future?"

Tears spilled from her green eyes, she looked tortured. "Yes, Jackson, I see us together for a very, very long time."

Millie

*N*OT MUCH HAD CHANGED *since their talk a few weeks ago. She was trying her best to be a patient woman. Her heart and head collided with one another, creating confusion. Marilyn and the other girls had been great friends, listening to her go on about it. The one fact that she didn't share was Todd's name. Todd had insisted upon privacy when he brought her here months ago. Stating that other women might feel resentful at her position here, she agreed and kept their little secret. It was of no use to mention her troubles to Sammy, she could tell from the empathetic glances that her sister knew she wasn't happy and that her plans weren't working out the way she had hoped.*

It was the night of the grand ball and the first time that Todd had told her he wouldn't be stopping by with supper or afterwards. He claimed his meeting would run half into the night, so he would see her the following day. Making her way down to the kitchen, she heated up some leftover soup for herself. She wasn't in the mood to eat, but knew she should have something. Her mood had been all over the place the past few weeks. Marilyn had finally taken over the story time one night a week, and several other girls were following in her footsteps. It made her proud and delighted to see the success of her girls. On the other hand, it was becoming quite clear as Marilyn had pointed out so wisely, that if Todd's mother were truly this ill for so long, chances are she would have passed already. Marilyn had never heard such nonsense of hiding a future bride away because the mother was ill. She figured the truth was just too ugly. Todd must be embarrassed to bring her home to a mother who wouldn't approve of a low class girl such as she. When the mother eventually passed, then maybe Todd would finally wed her. For all she knew, the mother may not even be ill. She was tired, dead tired of the lies and the neglect. She deserved more. If only she could pull herself out of this relationship with Todd and make a life for herself, she would be fine.

"What has put you in such a mood?" Marilyn walked into the kitchen, stirring the soup. "I never thought I'd see the day when you came down for supper."

"Get used to it, I have a feeling you'll be seeing much more of me around here at suppertime."

"Well I'm glad." Marilyn reached over and patted the top of her head. "Now what's with the sour mood?"

"Oh, it's just man troubles, that's all." Choosing her words carefully, she proceeded to tell her that her man refused to take her to the ball. Realizing too late that only the middle to upper class would be attending, she hoped that part of the story had gone unnoticed.

"How would you even get an invitation? Please don't take this the wrong way, but girls like us are not likely to be invited to such an event."

"Oh, I know I'm being silly, but he has this friend who works with one of the people who put the affair together," she lied. It sounded like a ridiculous cover up.

"Oh? Who does he know? Todd Alcott or his wife?" Marilyn stood with her hand lingering over the pot of soup, preparing to stir it when she felt her world go black.

"**S**WEETHEART, ARE YOU OKAY? *Wake up?*" *Cold water was the first thing that registered in her mind, that, and Marilyn shaking her, over and over.*

"*Stop that, Marilyn!*" *Sitting up, she had nearly forgotten the news she had just learned of. Placing her head in her hands, she cried out. How could he? That liar! After all this time she had been such a fool to believe the lies that spouted from his mouth over and over.*

"*What is it? Are you ill?*"

"*I'm all right,*" *she began, prepared to spill the entire story with her friend. After thinking it through, she decided to wait until she saw it with her own eyes. Yes, she knew exactly where the scheming liar of a man was headed tonight. How could she get into the ballroom though? She needed to find a way and she needed to find one quickly. Steadying herself as she rose, Marilyn's arms were around her.*

"*I'm going upstairs, I don't feel very well.*"

Marilyn stood, head nodding toward the stove. "*What about the soup?*"

"*You can have it, suddenly I'm not very hungry.*"

"*But, I can help you if you need assistance walking up the stairs,*" *Marilyn offered, eyes wide. The woman must think she had lost her mind. At this rate, she was well on her way.*

"*Thank you, but I can manage on my own,*" *she answered. Stopping to gather herself before climbing the winding staircase, she thought she would be sick right here. Could there possibly be an explanation? Was Marilyn mistaken? She must be thinking of one of the other men involved with the properties. But it was Todd who owned the houses and it was he who was running the affair. She had no idea how she finally made it to the top of the never-ending staircase, but somehow she managed. With force, she pulled open the door to her room, racing to her closet. Todd had bestowed her with plenty of gifts as of late, he bought dresses in beautiful shades of turquoise, since he so admired her in that color. She danced the night away in those dresses, by herself in the ballroom after the women had gone to sleep countless nights. Sad, melancholy tunes that matched her recent shift of mood. Why did he even bother? All to shut her up and stop the questions, no doubt. What had been his ultimate plan? To hide her away forever? He would until he grew tired of her no doubt, hoping to break her will and bed her with his stupid diamond ring!*

Scanning her closet, she laughed heartily as she spied the mature red gown in the back. She had told him how she had admired the dress in a shop window in town recently; it was divine, low cut and screamed for attention. It wasn't her style at all, but it had pulled at her. To her delight, he had actually purchased the "horror of a red gown" as he had called it, most likely to buy himself more time and quiet her nagging. He hated the color red, said it was for tramps and such. She thought it was stunning. It was absolutely perfect for this occasion. Never again would she wear his favored turquoise. Turning to stare at the turquoise brush and comb set on her dresser that she had once loved, she had no choice but to use them until she could afford another.

Slipping into the slinky red number, she carefully applied her most elegant makeup, and she made her way upstairs to the ballroom. She was early, so she would let off some steam and dance on her own until the ball began. Figuring she had little over an hour left until the start of the ball, she lost herself in the desolation of the music.

So lost in the sad melody, she had almost forgotten the time. If she didn't hurry, she would lose her nerve. With her head held, high she walked down the stairway, her mind focused on her plan of action. The walk to Anna's on the Sea took only minutes as it was not a big town. Her thumping heartbeat gave away her strong façade. She would need all of her courage to make it through the evening.

The upbeat music and laughter could be heard from several streets over, causing her bleak mood to go from bad to worse. It should be her at that party, dancing by Todd's side. Instead, she was alone and destitute in the streets. Where would she go from here? How could she possibly stay in a home that the deceitful man owned? She had too much pride to stay on, she had already decided. How she would miss those women in the house that she would always refer to as the house with no name. He had only named the home as a result of their arguing. In her mind, she wouldn't accept the name, she never would. As sure as she felt about Marilyn's news, there was still the slightest, teeniest bit of hope that she carried. What if it were a misunderstanding? She would find out momentarily. Holding a deep breath, she released it with a sigh and followed out her plan. Men were flocked around the door to the main floor of Anna's on the Sea. With all the bravery she contained, she threw her head up straight, shoulders back.

"Ma'am? Can I ask who invited you?" A young gentleman inquired, raising his brows at her as he took in her stunning attire. With the gentlest of winks, she motioned for the man to step to the side. Whispering softly in his ear, his eyes went wide as she chuckled in a soft,

enticing tone.

"Our little secret then?" Claiming that she was Todd Alcott's mistress and that he had asked her to be discreet seemed to do the trick. Funny, the man didn't appear at all surprised.

"I'm used to keeping plenty of secrets for Mr. Alcott, no problem." He shared, winking right back. "Oh, and be careful, the missus is with him tonight."

Her heart broke as her blood boiled. So it was true, and from the sound of it there were others! None of this was a surprise, really, she figured as much, but still needed to see it with her own eyes. Attempting her best smile, she entered the Victorian and trudged up the winding staircase. Anna's on the Sea was every bit as stunning as the place with no name. What was her plan now? To peek in, stare at him dancing with his wife and leave? That had been the original plan, but as she boldly stood in the entrance of the ballroom and spied Todd Alcott with his mousey little wife, she laughed aloud. She was dressed for the ball and she was going to the ball, dammit.

Waltzing in as if she owned the place, her head was high and she plastered the brightest smile on her face. Men turned to admire her, this felt good. She didn't need that lying louse of a man. Zeroing in on Todd, who had his wife in his arms dancing the night away, she continued to walk slowly but confidently to the center of the ballroom.

"May I ask you to dance?" Gazing up at the sound of a man's voice, she flinched. So caught up in her thoughts, the man had startled her. He was handsome in an unassuming, fresh manner, unlike the pompous ass of a man now standing a few feet away with his wife.

"I would love that," she replied, holding out her hand. The man placed a sweet kiss on her extended hand, then led her in the dance. The song was upbeat and jovial. She didn't feel uncomfortable or out of place at all here, among the upper class men and women. Strange, but the man before her held no airs of pretentiousness, he appeared quite humble as a matter of fact. Pulling the handsome man closer to where Todd danced and laughed without a care in the world, she stumbled, quite exceptionally, she might add, right into Todd Alcott. His expression at seeing her was outstanding, Todd looked as if he would vomit right there on the spot. She offered him a smug grin as she wrapped her arms tighter around her handsome stranger. It didn't go unnoticed that his eyes went wide at the sight of her daring red gown.

"Oh, how clumsy of me, I do apologize for my intrusion!" she cried out.

"It…it's fine." He turned away from her, guiding his wife across the floor. Weaving past several couples, her partner must think she was quite pushy.

Facing him again, she addressed his wife sweetly. "Oh, you must be the lovely couple responsible for this function. Mr. and Mrs. Todd Alcott, is that correct?"

"Why, yes." Mrs. Alcott ran her eyes up and down the bold dress, her mouth agape.

"If you'll excuse us," Todd mumbled, turning a noticeable deep shade of red, easy to see even in the dim lighting. As he spun his wife around, she glared at him. Although this had been a long time coming, his betrayal didn't sting any less. As if sensing that she needed attention, the handsome stranger gazed down at her as the music changed.

Dancing with an accomplished partner was everything she dreamed of. The music was beautiful, filled with soft, lingering notes. She could have cried right then and there, but she didn't wish for him to have the pleasure of seeing the damage that had been done. She had already removed her diamond ring earlier when Marilyn had first shared the news. She would keep it. Unfortunately it was her only ticket out of the house with no name. The ring must be worth enough to give her a head start on her new life. Starting fresh, perhaps in a new town, would be best. Now might be the time to even seriously consider looking into teaching.

"Penny for your thoughts." The handsome man held her close, she breathed in the fresh smell of soap, wishing she could just float away from all of her troubles.

Lifting her head to gaze into his gentle brown eyes, she chuckled a bit too bitterly. "I believe I would cause you to go poor."

"Now, now. It can't be all that horrible." He soothed her with his kind words.

"What is your name, sir?" She needed to know more about this considerate man who was easing her loneliness.

"Chad." The tall man was certainly easy on the eyes, she thought. What she didn't need right now was to jump into courting another man. Chad held her close. She would have this dance with him and at least feel carefree for the length of the soft music. She told herself not to even glance in Todd Alcott's direction. Interestingly enough it wasn't Todd who was peering back at her, but his wife. Mrs. Alcott's stare bore into her, making her feel uneasy. She couldn't possibly know, could she? Besides, she was through with the trash the woman was married to. Pity for Mrs. Alcott was all she had. Thank goodness she and Todd had never wed; this would have been her future.

Breaking free from the delightful Chad, she was spent. The stress of the evening had finally caught up to her and all she craved was sleep. Tomorrow was another day, another day to plan her future and mourn the loss of the man she once believed to be her one true love.

"What is it? Do you wish to rest? We could sit a while," Chad offered.

"That's very kind of you, Chad, but I'm exhausted. I'm going to head home. Pardon me."

He held her hand steady as he led her from the dance floor. "But you just got here, I saw you walking in."

"Yes, yes I did but I'm not feeling up to staying. It's been a pleasure meeting you and thank you for the dances." She felt his hand on hers, still holding tight.

"I hope you feel better, may I please see you back? A woman as beautiful as you should not be going home alone," he offered.

She wanted to decline, but his eyes held what seemed to be genuine warmth. She could use some caring and warmth right now. "Fine, and thank you."

Her eyes wandered one last time to the Alcotts, still dancing the night away. Mrs. Todd Alcott's gaze remained pinned to her and that feeling of uneasiness remained. Clutching onto Chad's arm, she broke the stare and headed downstairs.

"I walked, I only live a few blocks over, in one of the properties the Alcotts own." She had considered making up a story so that he wouldn't know she was in a home for poor women, but she was tired, tired of the lies and deceit. Besides, let's face it, she was a poor woman, and she would no longer feel embarrassed to live in an establishment with such wonderful women, women she would dearly miss. Chad had stared down at her, holding her hand tighter.

"It's fine, really. I'd love to know more about you, tell me your story," Chad stated, leaning down to brush her hair from her eyes.

Her story flowed from the time they walked to her street and beyond, to the beach that stretched out near the house, where she told this handsome stranger the story of her life.

CHAPTER

Twenty-Two

"I'M GETTING SO CLOSE, I have to see more," Jackson shared. Emily remained quiet, pensive. "Do you understand why I need to solve this for her?"

"I get it Jackson, it's a commendable thing you're doing," Emily offered, running her hands through her hair.

"But?" He knew her hesitation meant she felt more.

"But, it's dangerous. I worry about you."

"I worry about you, too. But it's not fair to her, Millie, I mean. I know this is going to sound unbelievable but I feel a certain closeness to her, as if somehow we're connected."

He was fearful she would run in the other direction when he spoke of this bond he felt with Millie. Instead, she reached for his hand. "It does sound unbelievable, but not in a negative way. I think it's amazing what you're doing for her, just tread carefully, that's all I'm saying."

"I love the way you get me, understand me." She was like an old soul, serious and wise about the world. He supposed that was from years of hard lessons to be learned, but she was an outstanding woman, nonetheless.

"Want to go out on the beach?" He had stopped asking if she would go back to his house with him.

"No, I'm warm and cozy right here with you, Jackson. Tell me more about how you wish to have a family one day."

He told her of his hopes for having at least three children. It didn't much matter what sex they were as long as they were happy and healthy. He remembered that she wasn't able to have children and was about to backtrack and tell her she could adopt and be a wonderful mother, but the moment didn't seem right.

"I have a feeling you would make a good, kind father. That's refreshing to hear," she stated softly.

Placing his hands on her face, he kissed her until they were lost in each other. Emily cried out at the closeness he knew she felt every bit as strongly as he did. He wouldn't push her anymore. He would be patient and wait her out until she was ready to share more of her life with him. Right now he was content to be in her arms.

"Do you feel this, right now?" Breaking free from her kiss, he waited, but then she seemed to disappear from his sights, shrinking into the background of the pub.

He was asking her if she felt the intensity between them, then she was gone, in her place were the stark visions, they were back. He was back, wandering on those lonely streets until the man, Todd Alcott, he was sure, was back, holding him. He felt Millie's emotions so strongly, she was relieved, then he couldn't quite make out the words, she was upset again, more than ever, then loneliness as he was in an old fashioned room, perhaps something out of a boarding room. His head might split with the pain, he cried out for it to cease and then finally it did. There was joy again as he felt her embracing another woman, tears of joy spilled from his very own eyes as she taught the woman to read. Images of her reading from a book he couldn't quite make out and eager women listening to him as he told story after story.

He jolted forward, gasping for air. The headache was still pounding but she had shown him more than pain, she had shown him friendship, exposed emotions, and a sense of camaraderie amongst the group of women. Millie had been a tortured soul, still was, but at one time she had also been loved by a great many people. This soul had plenty of good in it. Whatever happened to change her to this bitter spirit must have been heart wrenching, but he was determined to solve this enigma and help Millie find the compassionate girl she used to be.

Emily's hand was on his shoulder, her eyes misting with concern. "What is it, Jackson? I lost you there for a bit."

143

"Emily, she's amazing. I saw the visions again, she's admired, a woman who was a mentor, she was so loved…"

"Wait, slow down, Jackson."

"I can't, she taught those women to read, there was heartache but there was also so much joy, I could feel it." Glancing at Emily's face, a tear rolled down her cheek.

"Are you okay? What is it?"

"It's just so… sad." She frowned, turning away. Emily's tears fell freely now as her shoulders shook. Did she see connections with her own life, which was also so filled with pain?

"Oh Emily, I'm sorry. I didn't mean to make you sad, it's just that our Millie here, she was a beautiful person, she's a beautiful soul."

"I just wish it had turned out different for her, she was cheated out of life," Emily sobbed.

"I'm going to make it better for her, I promise you that."

"You will? You promise with all your heart?" Emily looked hopeful as she grasped his hands in her tiny palms.

"I promise, with all of my heart."

Millie

How could such a loving and gentle man exist? Chad had sat for the entire evening, until the sun came up, just listening to her speak, as if she were the most interesting woman alive. She held back nothing for there was nothing to be afraid of any more. She was at the bottom of her existence but more determined than ever to climb out until she saw the sunlight. He had held her close, placing soft kisses on the top of her head when she got to the awful part about Todd Alcott and his odd little wife. The woman had practically seethed, looked through her as if she knew her dirty secret, and intended to expose her. Chad had assured her that she was not to blame and that Mrs. Alcott knew nothing, but was most likely used to beautiful women eyeing up her husband. He had not offered much when it came to Todd, but she could sense that Chad disliked the man, probably with good reason. Chad was a humble man, one of the workers who had assisted with the sales of the properties, he was also a kind, good man, she was sure of it, more sure of it than anything. With merely a kiss on her cheek, he smoothed her face with his hand, asking if he could come to see her that evening, as the morning sun had risen in the sky.

It was hours later and she waited for him. Chad was taking her out properly. They would grab supper out at an actual restaurant, without the fear of being caught by a wife. It felt good, so good to be alive. Much of her day had been spent planning her immediate future. She would find another place to stay, in town for now. The money from the ring would get her in the door of another room, one which was not owned by Todd and his wife. She would see about that teaching job, yes, she could envision herself reading and writing with the youth of the town. To her surprise, Todd had not come by yet, perhaps he would stay away for good. She supposed she might be able to sit tight in this house with her friends until he said otherwise, but she wanted out, out of this place without a name, for now she absolutely refused to accept the new name of this building, it was a flat out insult. She did, however, need some time to think, to plan properly. Deciding that she would stay, perhaps just a few weeks longer, to get herself in order, she waited for Chad.

It was early, but she heard heavy footsteps approaching her door. Better early than late, right? Before she had a chance to open the door, he barged in. Todd stood before her, red faced and out of breath. Stepping back, she gasped at the sight of him. He looked downright wild.

"Who do you think you are, coming to the ball, exposing yourself right there in front of my wife?" Todd was breathless, moving closer. Exposing herself? By wearing a stunning gown? The choice of words seemed particularly harsh.

Backing toward the window, her eyes fixed on the door. If Chad could just kindly choose this moment to walk through that door it would be wonderful.

"Who do I think I am? Look who's speaking here! You're married, Todd, Married!" Yelling out, she felt her own anger resurface.

"I explicitly told you not to go to that ball, and what do you do? You show up dressed like a tramp, dancing with another man, and flaunting yourself in that awful red gown in front of my wife!" Todd boomed, closing in on her space.

She moved forward now, causing him to step back this time. "How was I to know you were a liar, a cheat? I heard through the town gossip you were married, what were you thinking, Todd? Were you planning on leaving her?"

He backed up, cornered now. "Of course not! I would have never left her. Yes, I wished to bed you and use you at my discretion, is that what you wanted to hear? The truth?"

Her hand connected with his face. At first his eyes went wide, then he grabbed her, shaking. "Don't you ever! How dare a low life tramp like you lay hands on me!" As he raised his hand, she flinched and moved away, his hand missing her by mere inches. Turning to run to the door, she noticed it was already open.

"Don't you dare lay a finger on her, Todd Alcott or I will personally see to it that your name is tarnished all over this town. Your wife will leave you and take all of her money with her," Chad threatened, pulling her close. So he didn't come from money, it was all his wife's money.

"This is none of your business, Chad. You have no idea what this lying woman is capable of. She's scheming to take my money, pretending that she will go to my wife saying we had an affair," Todd bluffed.

Chad closed the space between them. "I'll tell you what we're going to do here. First off, you will apologize for calling this wonderful woman here a liar and breaking her heart. Then you will leave her be, without paying another visit, without saying another word, to anyone. You will give her time and space to get out of this house, this house you have trapped her in, and you will never contact her again, you hear?"

"Who do you think you are, Chad? I will ruin your name around this town, don't you dare threaten me!" Wincing, she wondered how many of the women on this floor were overhearing this conversation.

"Who am I? Who am I? I am the man who will go straight to Mary and tell her exactly what you've been doing to this innocent woman. Now do yourself a favor and get lost!" Chad pointed to the door, his finger shaking.

She was wondering one last thing, so his wife's name was Mary, that made sense. What she wanted to know now was burning from her tongue. "Who is Anna, Beatrice?"

His look said it all "You're pathetic, you piece of garbage," she cried out.

"He's not worth, it, sweetheart, he'll leave you alone now." Chad pulled her tight against his chest, muffling her sobs. Peeking out from her spot in Chad's shirt, she sighed a breath of relief as Todd slammed

her door shut.

"Oh thank you." She faced Chad, wiping at her eyes. "You showed up just in time."

"You had him, you would have handled him with no problem. Let's get out of here, what do you say. I know the best little restaurant in town." Chad smoothed her hair. His suggestion sounded like music to her ears.

An hour or so later they were seated at an outdoor table, with a fantastic view of the ocean, right out in the open. Raising a glass to drink, she thought about her past with Todd, all of the waiting around, hiding around town and losing her childhood home. She had been so very naïve but now she was ready to put her past behind her. She was sure many of Todd's women would happily carry on an affair behind his wife's back in exchange for a nice room to live in and plenty of expensive gifts. Not her, no way. Thank goodness she had never slept with the slimy man. What kind of man could do that to his wife and look her in the eye each and every day? No thank you, she was glad to be free of him.

"Penny for your thoughts?" Chad's eyes lit up as he smiled at her.

"I already told you, I'll cause you to become poor." But then again, she had released so much of her past on Chad's shoulders already, there wasn't much more to tell. "Tell you what, I'll tell you what's on my mind. One last thing, good riddance to a difficult past and a horrible man."

"And hello to a bright future." Leaning over, he kissed her. This man just might be the man she had hoped for, searched for. Mother, she thought, it's been a long, hard road but I think this girl finally found what she's been looking for.

CHAPTER
Twenty-Three

KRISTEN SIPPED AT HER wine. He had hours before he was to meet up with Emily, so on a rare night off he offered to take Kristen to dinner. She was dressed all in black, a long classy skirt, and a top that hugged her curves. Now that Kristen was feeling better, he had expected her to start dating again, but so far she remained single, a thought that troubled him somehow.

"There's got to be more to this than what meets the eye. Why you?"

"Maybe I'm just that handsome?" His lame attempt at a joke got a response from her.

Laughter erupted from her mouth as she glanced around at the other diners who were now staring. "You're good, you know that? But seriously, it's as if she has this connection to you, *only* you."

"Now how do you know that? She's been around since 1871, for God's sake, she could have played with hundreds of men and more." But Kristen's words held value. He did feel a special connection with her, a bond that couldn't be denied.

"It's you, she's been waiting for *you,* and the only way we're getting any more information is through you."

"True, we could attempt to go back to Shelby's, but yeah…" Jackson laughed as he remembered how they had worn out their welcome at Shelby's Books.

Kristen's mouth dropped. "That is not funny, Jackson, not at all."

"Well, it's maybe a little funny?" He held his fingers together to give her a visual.

Despite his awful sense of humor, she laughed. "No, not even a little, you jerk. We could have caused that poor Shelby to have a nervous breakdown or worse. Besides breaking in the shop in the middle of the night, we don't have a shot at getting through the front door."

"I don't think she's going to tell us much more than she's already told us and I'm not a big fan of being arrested for breaking and entering, you know?" Jackson smiled as he grabbed a piece of bread from the table. Reaching for the butter, he felt the silence.

"Even if it meant spending the night in jail with me?" It was meant to be funny on her part, but the awkward silence that followed ruined the effect. "It was a joke, Jackson."

"I know. Hey, how about we take a break talking about Millie for an evening. What's going on in your life?" Another awkward silence.

"Kristen, I have to say something here. You and I share a unique friendship, wouldn't you say?"

Her head lifted as she locked eyes with him, nodding her head for him to continue. "I love you and cherish you. I want us to be able to feel comfortable with each other. I want it to be the way it used to be." He was referring to their times before the kiss that almost came to be and before Emily had come into the picture.

"Okay, I miss you too." Kristen sighed, clearing the air. He could remain friends with this very attractive woman and keep his head straight. Emily would have to deal with it. This was one area where he wouldn't give in.

"How is she anyway?"

"Millie?" He ventured, a smile forming.

"No, you fool, Emily. How are things going between the two of you?"

He chose his words carefully as he considered there were some areas that even good friends such as the two of them needed to be cautious about.

"Good, I suppose. Status quo."

"She still won't go anywhere else? Meet any of us?"

"No, Kris, she won't. If you met her, which hopefully you will soon, I think you'll really like her. She's beautiful, pensive, sad, at times, a bit of an attitude even at moments, but at other times she's amazing to be around."

Lifting her brow, Kristen grimaced. "Hmm. Sounds an awful lot like Millie. What is it with your taste in females?"

She was kidding, of course, but it hit him that both women seemed so intense and often melancholy. So he attracted women with unsettled problems, that was no secret. "What can I say? I guess I have a knack for attracting women with issues."

"You think?" Kristen quipped. Playfully smacking her shoulder, he signaled the waiter to bring another glass of wine for both of them.

Millie

*"*WHERE WOULD YOU LIKE *to go today, name the place and we're there," Chad offered generously, swiping the air with his hands. He was the sweetest man she had ever met and she felt sweeter just being beside him, being his girl. Several weeks had passed since that infamous night at the ball. But the evening surely couldn't be remembered as being all bad, for it was the night she had first met Chad.*

"Let's see, we could stroll through town, have some lunch, we could take even take a romantic walk along the beach. What would you like to do, Chad?" He was too kind, spoiling her all the time. They had yet to proclaim their love for one another. She knew he was fearful of hurting her. She wanted to run to the top of the nearest roof and shout it for all to hear. This was no naïve, youthful, passing fancy; she and Chad had been inseparable from the night they met. She couldn't wait to hear the words come out of his mouth. As a matter of fact, if he didn't say something soon, she might even be brazen enough to say the words first. Giggling at her daring idea, she covered her mouth with her hands.

"How about we just stay here and hold one another? How does that

sound?" He nibbled at her ear, resulting in an uproar of laughter. They were at his place, which he had inherited from his family. It was plenty big for more than one person. Chad had made a pest of himself, offering to move her in a thousand times a day it seemed. Once she explained that she was to do this the right way, he understood. Unlike Todd, this man of hers was a gentleman through and through. She wouldn't move in with him unless they were married, and they had plenty of time. There was no rush, as a matter of fact, she hadn't seen or heard from Todd Alcott since the night that Chad had admonished him. She knew she should really hurry out of the house with no name but she loved her friends so much, and each time she considered moving, she thought of another reason she should wait just one day more. Chad had admitted that he worried about her safety in that house, with Todd being so angry that day. She told him he was acting foolish, promising that she would find another place just as soon as she was sure the women at the house didn't need her anymore. It was more that she needed them, but he didn't argue.

"Listen, I have some work to do, how about I drop you off at your place, and you get some rest. In a bit, say around suppertime, I'll be back to pick you up. We'll get some dinner, take a walk?"

"Sure, and thank you, Chad, for everything." Snuggling against him, she felt happy to just be.

Her happiness was threatened hours later when there was a knock at her door. "I'll be right there." Skipping to the door, she smiled upon seeing Marilyn.

"Hi! Come on in." Holding the door open, she let her friend in. Marilyn offered her half a smile as she gazed at her.

"What's wrong?"

"I... how should I say this? I know about what happened, with er..."

"You do?" But how?

"Yes, I mean my room is directly across the hallways from yours so..."

"You know." Wonderful. She should have been more careful, they had all raised their voices that evening.

"I'm surprised you waited so long to tell me. Why now?"

"There's been talk on the streets, I don't know how much is actually true, but rumor has it that Todd Alcott had a lover."

"But that's crazy, I didn't do anything with him, I mean besides kiss him, but I had no idea he was married. That night, when you told me, the night of the ball? That was it, I ended it." Her friend couldn't think she would even begin to carry on with a married man.

"I know, I heard you all that night, and I believe you. From what I gather, Todd has had plenty of lovers and I'm sure he's already on to the next. I just don't want to see you hurt. As much as I hate to say this, I believe the time has come for you to go."

"Wait, what?"

"I feel like something is going to happen, something bad if you don't leave. I love you, honey, we'll stay in touch, just think about leaving soon," Marilyn pleaded.

"Do the other girls know?"

"I don't know, if they do they haven't mentioned it to me, but they know you and I are close so I'm not sure they would confide in me."

"My goodness, I promise you I didn't intend to cause any trouble. He made promises to me, gave me a ring, I feel awful even though I had no idea. I wish there was a way to take it all back," she cried out. "What will everyone think if it gets out?"

"They'll think you're wonderful, just like I do, and they'll believe every word you say because you are a trustworthy person, a good girl." Marilyn stood, grasping her shoulders.

"Thank you, Marilyn, thank you." Her head was spinning. She should heed her friend's advice. It was best to leave; she should have never stayed so long to begin with. Tonight she would discuss the matter with Chad and compose a plan of action. Rummaging through her dresser drawer, she searched for a pen. She needed to add this recent turn of events to her novel. Although her love story with Todd was over, a new romance had just begun. This wasn't her story with Todd after all. It was the story of her life. Her finger came upon something small and smooth. Her diamond ring. Her intention had been to take the ring and use the money to start her new life. This ring symbolized an ugly man and, therefore, she decided she would leave it behind, sending Todd the message that she had pride. She could make it without his help. Taking the ring out and placing it atop her dresser, she was sure Todd would discover it when she was gone.

When at last she had finished writing the new events of her life into her story, she got to thinking that her story would never quite end, that is, until she had fulfilled all of her dreams, true love, marriage, children, teaching, even if meant having sessions at her own house. Then and only then would her story be complete. With a sigh of satisfaction, she held her thickening stack of papers in her hand tightly. This was what it felt like to be passionate about something. These papers were more important to her than any diamond ring would ever be.

A soft rapping at the door disturbed her thoughts. *Oh Mother, you are so right, I am quite the daydreamer.* "Coming," she called out, rushing to the door.

"Ah, did you forget that we were to go to supper tonight?" Chad scanned his eyes from her toes to her head. *She was a sloppy mess; whenever she got to writing she would wrinkle her clothing and play with her hair.*

"Not that you don't look adorable." Chad offered up a bright smile. *She must be quite the sight.*

"Oh! I got carried away, I'll explain later." *She had yet to tell Chad about her writing and intended to fill him in on her pastime this evening.* "Shoo! Wait for me downstairs while I freshen up a bit."

"Don't be long, my darling. I don't think my heart could stand it."

Rising to her tiptoes, she met him with a kiss. *This man was everything she could ever hope for, he made her heart and soul sing.* "Now go!"

"Yes, ma'am," he said as he bowed.

Choosing a simple yet tasteful hoop, she fixed her hair and applied some light makeup. *Her appearance was quite different from the evening she had first met him at the ball.* With a spring in her step, she reached the staircase and hurried down the winding steps.

Waiting at the bottom of the stairs was Chad, his eyes taking her in. "You've never looked more beautiful than you do right now." He kissed her hand.

"Really? Not even when I was decked out for the ball?"

"You were stunning that night, don't take it the wrong way, but this is you, the real you. Pure, beautiful, and perfect."

"Well thank you, I'm not even wearing my fanciest attire, you know."

"It's not the attire, it's you. I'm so thankful that I met you that night." *Chad's eyes didn't leave her face. To think how she had almost missed having this man in her life. It was fate, it was destined to be. If she hadn't gone to the dance, this man would have been absent from her life. The night of the ball had sealed their fate.*

Darkness was upon them as they walked outside. She gazed up and wished upon a star. Chad glanced at her, his eyes crinkled. "What are you thinking about?"

"I'm just making a wish is all." *Her wish would stay with her until it came true and then she would write about it in her book. Even if she needed to wait until she was sixty years old.* Giggling at the delightful *thought of turning sixty with Chad, she relished in a warm feeling. She was happy, so very happy for the first time in ages.*

"I suppose you're not going to tell me what you wished for?"

"Only when it comes true, Chad, then I'll share it with you." Her chest flip- flopped as she gazed up at his kind, brown eyes.

"Promise?"

"Oh I promise." This was one promise that she vowed to never break.

CHAPTER

"I HAVE TO SAY goodbye." Emily sighed, her eyes on the wall ahead of her. He couldn't believe his ears. Why would she be leaving?

"No, Emily." Shaking his head, he was determined to get her to open up to him. "No matter what the reason, it can't be worth destroying what we have here."

"Under normal circumstances I would agree, however, he's left me no choice." Emily turned away from him, but remained seated.

"He? Arthur?" Emily nodded as she tried to make sense of what she was saying. "Is he here? Did he figure out you're here?"

Emily stared ahead once more, not speaking. Silence was driving him mad. "Speak to me, Emily! What's happening?"

"Strange things have been happening. I've seen a car following me, the same one in the past few days. I think he's hired someone to find me. I won't be found. I need to leave today."

"That's crazy, it could be anyone, it could be a coincidence. Let me help you." He was grasping at anything he could to try to make her agree to stay. He even had another idea if she would hear him out.

"I'm not taking any chances; this is my life and yours we're talking about."

"Okay, so if you must leave, I'll come along." Without considering what that entailed, he spoke impulsively.

"I can't let you do that, Jackson, besides, I'm a loner, that's who I am now. Please don't fight me on this, there's no other way, believe me, I've considered the possibilities." Picking at her fingernails, she took one last glance at Jackson before standing.

"Emily, just hear me out, listen to me." He grabbed her hand, but she was firm, maintaining her stance, she shook her head.

"Goodbye."

Jumping to his feet, he grabbed her for a kiss. One last kiss before she left, maybe it would even show her where she belonged. His heart broke as he felt her sadness seep through their embrace. This kiss wasn't full of passion, it was wrapped in heartache. Feeling a tingle, he steadied himself as Millie's visions intruded upon his farewell kiss. She was cooking something, soup perhaps, when one of the women she was teaching to read started speaking to her. He felt unspeakable shock as the muffled words came through his aching head. "He's married, he's married", boomed over and over. The ball, he glanced down at an elaborate red gown, running down the stairs, tears streaking down his face. He was at the ball now, laughter and music filtering through his mind. There was Todd Alcott again, arms wrapped around a scowling woman, the woman's eyes followed his every move. Then she was wrapped in the arms of another man, he looked kind, those brown eyes, she was in his arms, dancing...

Rubbing at his head, he came out of the foggy vision. Glancing at Emily, she had tears in her eyes. "Help her, Jackson, just promise me you'll help her." Before he could speak, Emily flew out the door, into the dark night. So she had also been in Millie's head. How could he pull himself together after this woman he had grown to love had just deserted him, out of the blue, without any warning? Had he seen this coming, he could have tried to stop her. Emily was stubborn, though, and she was used to being on the run. He would have followed her if she'd allowed him to do so, he was that invested in her. Kristen would say he was foolish, that he barely knew the furtive woman. He would also agree that he was blinded by her, but it didn't take away that feeling of loss when he glanced at the booth they had just occupied moments ago.

"*I* CAN'T SAY I'M disappointed she's gone, but I do feel bad for you."

"Gee, thanks," Jackson mumbled into his hands. He should have waited before spilling his heartache to Kristen.

"No, I mean it. I think she did a number on you. I'm just not sure if she was filling her time with you or if there was more to it. I'm sorry you're hurting, but you barely knew her, she wouldn't allow you to know her."

It was true but his heart ached for her anyway. Emily had scarred him but he couldn't be angry at her for doing so. She would always occupy space in his heart. Kristen pried his hands apart. "Listen, how about we talk about something else, Millie even?" She giggled softly.

"Ugh, Millie." She was always there, wasn't she? "I had another vision."

"I'm all ears." A smile lit her face. It wasn't hard to see why Kristen was in a good mood today. Speaking of the vision again did serve to occupy his mind, steering it away from Emily.

Drumming her fingers rapidly on the kitchen table, Kristen opened her mouth to speak and then hesitated. "Why is she telling you her story in bits and pieces?"

"I can't say other than when I'm experiencing her world through my own eyes, it hurts, Kristen, there's so much pain. I've called out for her to stop more than once, maybe she doesn't want to overload me." It made sense since each time his head felt as if it would explode.

"I suppose. Listen, Jackson, I feel you're getting close. I just wish there was something I can do, I feel so removed from her now, which isn't a bad thing, mind you, but I feel as if I'm doing nothing to help."

He reached over to hug her and allowed for a moment to pass. "You've been so much help, you still are. I don't want to see you hurt again, so just be here for me right now when I want to talk, and brainstorm. How does that sound?"

"That sounds fine and, Jackson, I'm sorry, I really am." He believed that she was sorry for his pain and it helped to have a friend right now.

Millie

You go all out when you want to show a lady a good time, Chad." Winking at him, her heart soared. The evening couldn't be better, they sat for a while, just talking and enjoying each other. She didn't wish to break the spell with her sour news.

"I have something I need to talk to you about," she began. "It's about the house. My friend Marilyn is worried that it's time I leave. She's been speaking of rumors of Todd's affairs."

"I wouldn't classify you as one of the women he's had an affair with, really. You were a young, innocent girl tricked by a cruel con-man."

"I agree, but she's worried, and feels like it's best I leave, sooner rather than later, before something happens. She's a smart girl."

"I think our friend Todd has learned that he shouldn't cross either one of us, but I have to agree. I don't like you living there either, and I've spoken of this many times." Chad reminded her.

"I know, I know. It's just the girls, I love them so."

"And they love you, I'm sure of it. This brings me to something I've wished to discuss with you for a while now, actually since that evening when you came into my life dressed as a vixen." He laughed as her mouth fell open.

"Well!" But she was well aware that he was joking with her.

"I hope you don't find this too forward, and I know we haven't the pleasure of knowing each other very long…"

"What is it? Spit it out, I don't think I can wait," she blurted out, covering her mouth with her palms as she watched him getting down on

one knee.

"Will you fulfill my dreams and make the happiest man alive? Will you marry me?" Chad gazed up at her with glistening eyes.

"Oh yes, Chad, I will, I will!" She wrapped her arms around him before he had a chance to stand to his full height. Grabbing her, he scooped her in his arms and placed a kiss on her lips. Clapping could be heard from the other diners as she laughed aloud. How could she have forgotten they were in a public place? It was of no matter, she was so happy she wanted to shout out. Kissing him this time, she didn't stop until she needed to take a breath.

"We're making quite the spectacle of ourselves, sweetheart." Chad smiled as he placed her on the ground. This was amazing, but it still didn't solve her immediate dilemma. Unhappy that she had to call reality back, she knew the topic must be broached.

"Chad, I feel that it is my time to go. Maybe it's Marilyn's words that have spooked me, but I'm leaving, within the week. I'll start looking for a room tomorrow; any property that isn't owned by that man will be a good place to start.

"That's nonsense, you don't have money for housing and food."

It was true, the supplies her mother had given her were long gone, and she hadn't needed to worry about money at the house because everything had been paid for, including the food supply that was brought to the house by donations.

"I...I can see about teaching."

"I think that's wonderful, I truly can see you as a teacher of young minds but that will take time, and we'll need to be sure that you will be hired in your soon to be married state. You and I are betrothed now, I have an idea," he began. She listened carefully as Chad unfolded his plan. They were to be wed soon, as he hadn't been more sure of the fact they were meant to be together forever. Until they married, she could live in one of the extra bedrooms with her own bath. Promising to be the perfect gentleman, he assured her his plan made sense.

It was a lot to think over but it did make sense to her, and she trusted that he wouldn't make her feel uncomfortable.

Grabbing his hands and leaning across the small table, she kissed him full on the lips, not caring if people stared.

"It's a plan, and I can't wait to become your wife!"

"Wonderful, now when shall we move you? I feel that we should make the move as soon as possible." Chad suggested, wringing his hands on the tablecloth. It was a smart idea.

"Yes, I agree. Does tomorrow bright and early work for you?" She would go home, get some rest, and start packing her few belongings. Oh, yes, she would ensure time for a proper goodbye with the women. "No, make that around noon. That will work better."

"Whatever you say, beautiful lady." Chad placed a kiss on her hands.

CHAPTER
Twenty-Five

*H*E WAITED FOR HER anyway, as he usually did, but he knew she wouldn't show. It had been two weeks since she had left. Two weeks full of missing her and two weeks since he had experienced any more visions. The pain from losing Emily didn't fade, not yet and he had a feeling that it never quite would. Over and over again in his mind, he thought of how things could have turned out differently if only she had allowed him to help her. If he knew where she had gone, he would have followed her, but he didn't even know where to begin. Where had she lived? What had her real name even been? He worried he would never uncover the answers to these burning questions. But he had known her workplace. An idea started to take shape in his mind. Maybe, just maybe somebody from The Jetty would know something about her. It was worth a shot.

With a new sense of purpose he hadn't felt in weeks, he grabbed his jacket and headed out the door. The fresh air filled his senses as he jumped into his truck and made his way to The Jetty. If he could find some possible clue to her whereabouts, he would move heaven and earth to find her. Knowing Emily the way he had, though, he figured any clues were long gone. The woman probably had the skills of an experienced criminal trying to cover up a crime scene.

The restaurant was fairly quiet, as he figured it would be

during off-season. It was lunchtime, though, so there were a few customers lingering about, particularly around the coffee counter. Fred, the owner of the establishment, nodded in acknowledgment and then to the elderly hostess, alerting her there was a customer.

"Oh no, I'm just here to speak with Fred, thank you." Walking over to the man, he introduced himself, explaining that he worked over at Millie's. Although he had met the man a handful of times over the years, Fred didn't appear to remember him.

"What can I do for you? You looking for a job?" Fred eyed him warily. Millie's Pub was no doubt considered to be stiff competition in town.

"Oh no, I'm here on personal business." Perhaps he shouldn't have said no so easily as his employment status currently hinged on whether or not he could appease the resident ghost.

"What kind of personal business?" Fred wiped the counter, mopping up a tiny puddle of spilled milk.

"What do you know about Emily?" There was no other way than to come right out and say it.

"Excuse me?" Fred leaned closer, as if he were hard of hearing.

"Emily, the woman who worked here, the one who just quit to move away."

"Am I hearing you correctly? There's no Emily, nobody left recently either." Fred eyed him as if he had a communicable disease.

"But… maybe she went by another name? She was blonde, quite stunning, early twenties? Any of that ringing a bell?"

"I've been here practically every day for the past five years, lunch and dinner." An older man sitting at the counter piped up. "Fred here hasn't hired anyone new since before then and certainly not anyone fitting that description."

Glancing back and forth between the two men, Jackson frowned. So she had lied to him. What else had she lied about? Recalling that she had stammered when he had first asked her where she worked, he reached back in time, trying to recall the name of the restaurant she had given that he had never heard of. Could that be a clue? "I'm sorry to have taken up your time, Fred, good day." With a nod of his head, he could make out chuckling behind him. The men most likely assumed he was losing his mind; it wasn't far from the truth.

162

Helplessly in love with a woman who was a stranger to him, he turned when he saw his truck and walked until he hit the beach. He was missing something, even the best of them leave some type of clue behind, no matter how perfect they believed their cover ups to be, he figured. The name of the restaurant she had mentioned first? Try as he might, Emily stumped him. The walk helped to clear his mind and by the time he headed back to his truck he thought about that old adage stating that if something was yours, set it free, if it's meant to be it will come back to you. Somehow he hoped it was true in this case. Suddenly it hit him that the restaurant she had named was Audrey's.

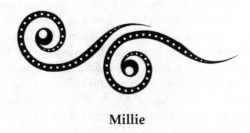

Millie

$\mathcal{I}$F SHE WERE TO put a stop to her plan, her story must end here, but then again, her mind still hadn't been made up. It had been difficult, but she had given him a break for the past couple of weeks. After all, he was mourning the loss of his girlfriend. See, she did have a heart. Giggling softly, she cried out until her voice carried through the desolate ballroom. What had started as laughter now closed with tears of heartache. Could she actually go through with this? Just because she wasn't connecting with him didn't mean she couldn't watch him. Time was running out with him, she knew it in her heart. A man like Jackson wouldn't stay alone forever. If she truly wished to end this suffering, she would need to act soon, while he was still receptive to her.

Sitting in the back of the pub, she wasn't visible to him or anyone else. It was tough watching him work when she longed to wrap him in her embrace. She couldn't stand this much longer, the past days without touching him, the loss of connection with him had caused her to wilt, and like a flower, she needed her energy.

"I HAVE TO GET going," John called as he grabbed his jacket from the back. That would mean he would be alone. Funny thing, he wasn't scared, not anymore. He kind of missed Millie in a weird way, so if the woman decided to grab him when he was alone, so be it. Not much mattered as Emily was far away; even the ghost seemed to have dumped him. The fact that Kristen was there for him brought him a small sense of relief. He couldn't even begin to imagine sharing his recent experiences with anyone else. Laughing, he figured John would call the hospital to have him committed for a full mental exam. Would Gary have believed him? It didn't matter, not anymore. Trust, it all came back to trust. Call him a fool, but he had trusted Emily, hell, he still did, as foolish as that made him seem. Worlds away from Maria, Emily had bailed because she had no other choice. He wasn't angry, but devastated. Now his trust lay solely with Kristen, and there it would most likely stay for a very long time if not indefinitely. He had traveled a long, hard road, and he was tired, Emily's absence had drained him both physically and emotionally.

An ice cold beer sounded good. Reaching over, he stared at the booth he used to occupy with Emily. Still, he waited for her each night. Pulling back his beer, he sat for a long while, reviewing everything that had happened since he and Kristen had begun their ghost hunting adventure. From Shelby's Books, the clerk's office, the museum and everything in between. They made quite the team, and he missed her banter here at the pub. The pub wasn't the same without her, customers constantly inquired as to her whereabouts every single night. John still held out hope of her return, making excuse after excuse as customers questioned him. Each time, John would glance at him from across the room and shake his head in irritation. It wasn't his fault that Millie wanted to murder Kristen, don't shoot the messenger. In all of his memories of Millie, nothing popped out at him, leading him to solve the mystery. She would tell him in her own time, though, he was sure of it. It was what happened after the truth was revealed that scared the life out of him. More and more, he suffered an unnamed anxiety when he thought of Millie's tale being complete. She was close, very close, so close he could feel it. It was driving him nuts.

"God, Millie! Just tell me, please. I can't imagine that you are this horrible, spiteful woman you show to others. There's more to you, Millie, there's good, there's so much kindness, compassion, love," Jackson called out to the empty pub. Something stirred across the room, where he and Emily would sit night after night. He felt the floor vibrate at first, the windows shook with fury, glasses from behind the bar crashed to the floor. She was an emotional wreck right now, a basket case. He was driving her to it by telling her how good she was.

"I'm not afraid, you're not fooling anyone, Millie, do you hear me? He yelled, arms spread wide. "Bring it, bring it on, and tell me why you're so angry, why you can't love anymore!"

The shaking ceased, the room cloaked in silence. "Millie, please, I promised Emily I would see this through. I don't break my promises," he whispered, his emotions raw. He was hanging by a thread here, something had to give. Closing his eyes, he breathed in as the familiar sensations began. There she was. "Good girl, Millie, you can do this."

He was in her room, her friend talking about being afraid, she must leave, she had to go before she was found out. The handsome stranger was at her door, waiting to take her somewhere special. Where would they go? Excitement built as his head was free from pain. This was good, he could see clearly this way, without the pain clouding the images. They were at a cozy restaurant; he felt the pure joy radiating from her very being. This wasn't like it had been with Todd Alcott, this other man was what she had been searching for, he was the one, he was sure of it. His eyes opened wide as excitement and surprise hit him. He had a ring; this man had a spectacular diamond ring. He was proposing to her. Chad! This was the first he had heard the man's name spoken. He had seen the man once before in Millie's visions, while they danced. Those eyes. Trying to zero in on the man's face, it was hazy, but something about the image of Chad felt strangely familiar, his brown eyes so warm. So it was Chad that made her heart sing, he thought. He wondered how this beautiful story could possibly end in destruction, his heart opened for her, she was a young woman, so young, it was too sad to bear. The headache threatened, right on the horizon, but he focused on her happiness as he was now jumping up, in Chad's arms, safe and carefree. What was that in the distance? Straining to focus more intensely, he saw it again, a sign of sorts, with large old fashioned print, hanging from the door of the restaurant... *Audrey's.*

He couldn't breathe. "Oh my God!" Sucking in a choking breath, his heart hammered wildly. Audrey's, but it couldn't be. How did any of this make sense? How could Emily have known about Audrey's?

Raking a hand through his wild hair as he came back to the presen; he pointed a finger around the room. "I'm not done with you, sweetheart, you and I have unsettled business, but for now it can wait. Hang in there, girl, we're almost there." From the distance came the most sorrowful sound that had ever touched his ears.

CHAPTER

Twenty-Six

"WHAT DOES IT MEAN? What could it possibly mean?" He was going mad from the suspense. Kristen's mouth was open wide, shaking her head.

"I don't know, Jackson, but it's got to mean something, it's got to. Let me think this through. Even I have never known of this restaurant, and you know how I feel about the history of this town."

"Let's check it out at the clerk's office, we're not banned there," Jackson suggested.

"Yet," Kristen added, causing them both to laugh.

"Behave yourself then, no trouble from you, you hear?" He rubbed the top of her head as he grabbed her hand. It was still early enough on a Saturday that it should be open.

"What are you hoping to find out from a blueprint?" Kristen cocked her head to the side, her eyes on him.

"I want to get a feel for the layout of the place, who knows, anything might trigger a clue."

The answer seemed to satisfy her for now. Racing to his truck, they hopped in and headed toward town. His mind was on one thing only, he wouldn't rest until he set Millie free, he had made a promise. Kristen seemed to accept his silence as they drove to the clerk's office. Only when they got out of his truck did she speak.

"I don't know, I'm afraid to admit this but I'm kind of jealous of the connection you have with her. What is it like to have such a strong bond with her?"

Mulling it over, he chose his words carefully. "It's like we're kindred spirits, like I would do anything to help her out."

"I can't even imagine," Kristen mumbled, reaching for his hand. They found themselves at the door of the clerk's office once again. He got to thinking how much had transpired since their last visit and how his own bond with Kristen had grown.

There was another woman working the desk today, but she was equally kind and helpful as they told her the short version of their purpose for being there. The woman, Olivia, clasped her hands together as if settling in to see a favorite movie. "How interesting! Have at it and be sure to tell me if you find anything exciting."

"Of course," they responded together.

Once more, they worked in the dusty back room, hunting through files, but this time they knew exactly where to find the files with the date they were looking for, so it saved them some time. Jackson was intrigued as he found file after file noting different establishments.

"I could sit here all day just looking at the documents of different buildings in town." But wait, time and again the same name was written as owner of properties: homes, stores, restaurants, you name it. "Hey, look at this."

Torn papers were displayed on the table, he pointed out the recurring theme, Todd Alcott's name. "Seems like our friend, Todd Alcott was quite the proprietor." Kristen whistled softly. "But we kind of knew that already from the museum."

"True," Jackson agreed. But it did put things in perspective. "If they were having some type of affair, which was clear to me from the visions, although I'm not actually sure how far they took things..." He sensed that Millie had held back, that she was the type of girl who would have waited until marriage. But if he were already married to someone else? "Imagine how much Todd here would stand to lose if his relationship with Millie became public knowledge," he finished.

"But you saw her with someone else, getting engaged..." Kristen interrupted.

"I didn't say any of this made sense, I'm not even certain she's got her timeline correct, but I'm sure if we figure it out, everything will fall in line." Jackson felt it was only a matter of time before he knew the full story.

"If I wait around for her to tell me, the story will be over soon. I can't explain why but I equate hearing the end of the story with something sinister."

"How much more sinister could it get?" Kristen asked with a sarcastic laugh.

"You weren't there; you had to have felt her fury when I asked to hear more, when I screamed at her that she was a good soul. She's experiencing a lot of internal conflict, Kris, it's eating away at her."

"Look, here it is, Audrey's." Kristen pointed at a yellowed sheet of paper. The diagrams showed a main room with an outdoor plan as well.

"That's it, that's what I saw." Jackson's heart sped up. The papers didn't bring forth any new information but he felt this trip hadn't been wasted, for it had pieced together Todd Alcott's true status in Cape Florence, 1871. The man had surely been an informal mayor of sorts, quite high on the social status.

Sneezing from the dust, Kristen shook her head. "Seen enough?"

"Yeah, sure." He supposed there was nothing else to do now but play the waiting game, but he was growing impatient and wanted to figure out this ever changing conundrum. Work at Millie's was on the schedule for this evening, after hours he would wait for a woman whom he knew would never arrive, but he would also instigate from Millie more of her story, maybe even the final chapter.

ANOTHER BLOCKED NUMBER. He wasn't being baited this time. With all that had been going on with Emily and Millie and the busy shift at the pub last night, he had nearly forgotten his troubles with his ex-wife. And he had almost forgotten that to-morrow was his scheduled court date. A missed message signaled as Jackson sighed. He could listen to it or he could erase it. Listen or erase? Hell, he felt compelled to listen; otherwise he would wonder what he had missed hearing. It could be important, related to the case tomorrow, but then wouldn't his lawyer, Tom, have called? Oh hell.

Maria rambled on about last chances to settle this out of court. Stating that she would like to meet with him, tonight if possible, to discuss matters and hopefully avoid an embarrassing fight in the courtroom. She only wanted what was due to her so that she and Gary could move on. *I am a fair woman after all, Jackson.* He felt his rage building as he tightened his grip on his cell. Take a breath, man, calm down. Emily's face popped into his mind, he remembered when she had suggested he bring Maria to the pub to discuss matters on his territory. That actually wasn't a bad idea, he figured with a growing smirk. If he figured correctly, Millie would despise Maria, therefore having his back and causing God only knows what kind of trouble for his ex. Shaking his head with a bitter laugh, the opportunity was tempting but he couldn't live with himself if Millie caused serious harm to another person, even one as lowly as Maria. It didn't stop his imagination from running wild with possibilities, however.

Like hell he would meet with Maria. Tom would have his head if he were as foolish as to attempt a meeting with Maria the day before court. Biting into his turkey and cheese sandwich, he swallowed some water to wash it down. He would have to hunt down his boss before his lunch hour was over to tell him that he would be taking a rare day off tomorrow for court. Dave would understand and he would wish him the best.

"Hey man, some of the guys are heading over to Millie's after work to have a drink if you're interested in joining us, that is, if you're not working there tonight," Billy offered, patting his back. Billy was a good guy and understood what Jackson had been going through with his recent divorce. Billy had recently divorced and was presently engaged to a new woman. He hoped he had better luck this time and wondered why he was jumping back into the institution so quickly.

"Yeah, man, I'm off tonight, so I'll meet you guys over there. Right after work?"

"Yup, all sweaty and everything, the chicks love it."

The chicks, he had to laugh. Millie's wasn't particularly famous for its selection of singles during off-season; it was more of a man's pub this time of year.

"Deal, but I have to run home to make some calls before I meet you guys." He needed to speak with Tom on some last minute details before heading to the courtroom in the morning. Standing up, he brushed the dirt off his workpants and headed to find his boss.

OTHING FROM MILLIE IN days, and it wasn't from lack of trying to connect with her. He had yelled, teased, shouted, you name it, but she remained silent. Still, he went to the pub each night regardless if he was scheduled to work, hoping for Emily to come back or an attempt at communication from Millie. Last night at the pub with the guys had been a much needed night out, it had helped him to unwind and take his mind off his troubles for this morning.

Sweating it out with his lawyer beside him, he braced himself for whether or not she would come alone or bring Gary. Surely she had better sense than that, right? He didn't know what the woman was capable of nowadays. "Excuse me for a moment, will you?" Was it hot in the courtroom or was it just him? On the way to the bathroom he saw her walk through the door, arm and arm with Gary. It felt like the air had been sucked from him, it was warm, so warm, he needed water.

"Well, well, too good to call me back yesterday?" Maria's voice was like nails on a chalkboard. He would not engage.

"She's talking to you, man," Gary intruded. "At least have the decency to respond."

Okay, that comment he would not be able to ignore. "Don't take this the wrong way or anything, *man*, but you have no busi-

171

ness being here, and I don't need to speak to that woman ever again, one of the perks of being divorced from that witch."

Gary's fist flew toward him, ducking just in time, his fist connected with the wall behind him. Jackson had some limited experience with self-defense and kick-boxing under his belt from many years ago. It was good to know that the knowledge had come in handy. Before he could even consider striking the man back, which felt like the best option in the world to him at that moment, a police officer grabbed Gary from behind, dragging him out of the building.

Facing the open-mouthed woman he once called his wife, he chuckled loudly. "Looks like you have to be a big girl here, Maria, and stand on your own two feet for once in your life."

"Go to hell!"

"Hey Maria? You'd best be careful or you'll be the next one escorted from the courthouse." Turning to go back to the courtroom without stopping to get water, he didn't feel quite as warm right now. A new air of confidence came over him. Maria and Gary were two selfish, conniving fools, it should be easy for the judge to see right through them.

"What the hell happened back there?" Tom leaned over, a faint sheen of sweat covering his upper lip.

"Oh, you have no idea." The judge walked in as everyone in the courtroom stood in respect. It appeared as if they were ready to begin. "Let's just say that Gary won't be a problem here today," he whispered, attempting to contain his grin.

Their case was presented and it seemed to have gone smoothly enough. The lawyers both presented their client's side of the situation and now they needed to wait for the decision. Maria glared at him from across the room, appearing as if she had aged ten years in the course of an hour. She was surely pissed about Gary, about how lame her lawyer's case sounded, and most likely a few other reasons he couldn't even begin to care about.

"Okay, let's go," Tom shuffled some papers and placed them in his briefcase.

"That's it? We're done?"

"For now, but we need to wait for the decision, it could take a few weeks, it's always different," Tom explained.

So that was it. Without another glance at Maria or her lawyer, he followed Tom out of the courtroom and to the parking lot.

Gary was nowhere to be seen, which was a good thing. He wondered what his consequences would be for fighting in a courtroom. Heck, who even cared at this point. Good riddance to them both.

CHAPTER
Twenty-Seven

"**A**NYBODY BEEN AROUND LOOKING for me?" He doubted Emily would stop by during daylight hours or when others were in the pub, but he had to ask.

John's head lifted from counting out bills in the cash register. "Like who? Your ghost?"

John could be a real wise ass when he wanted to be. "Fine," Jackson responded, taking a drink order from John's niece. He was counting the minutes till closing when he got a thought in his head. Why hadn't he thought of it before? If John wasn't so uptight, he would run up to the attic this minute. The attic. The attic, why hadn't he thought to look there? But he couldn't go sneaking around up there without Mike's permission, and, much as he was chomping at the bit, the thought of a dark attic in this house frightened the heck out of him. Tomorrow, he would swing by tomorrow after work, when Mike was still open for business. Like everything else in his life right now, he would wait.

"Staying for a drink?" he asked a somber Andrew.

"Nope, heading home."

"Like *you* should be," John interjected with a smirk set on his mouth.

"What's with you guys lately? Nobody wants to stay and hang out?"

"Well, considering that since you won't permit Kristen to come back to work, I have to run out to take my niece home nearly every night."

Sarcasm dripped from his voice as Jackson's eyes went to Andrew. "And you?"

Andrew mumbled something about missing Kristen with his head dropped toward the floor. "Great!" So they were both pouting like little boys because Kristen wasn't here. They didn't get it, couldn't possibly understand his reasons for keeping her far away from here.

"What's the difference anyway?" John called out again. "You seem to enjoy ghost hunting on your own, we wouldn't want to spoil your fun."

It was the first time he had really seen Andrew laugh. "You guys can be real idiots when you want to be, you know that?"

More laughter erupted as a rare moment of John having a sense of humor showed, at his expense nonetheless. "Nothing like a little support after my court case from my buddies, right?" That's right; he would make them feel guilty.

John's face froze then he glanced at Andrew. "Sorry, man, tough break, I forgot to ask how it went."

"I don't know, and thanks. I feel that if the judge has any sense, it would be clear what the decision will be since Maria came across as being a bit of a gold digger, but hey, you never know."

"It'll all work out, man, hang in there." Andrew slapped his shoulder, nodding. "Hey, if you want company…"

"Nah, but thanks. You have a wife to go home to, I'm okay." He was looking forward to some down time, and, of course, he hoped that Emily would come to her senses.

"You sure?" Andrew asked, scratching his head.

"Absolutely." Jackson poured himself a cold draft, careful not to let the head get too thick. It was a skill he had mastered and was quite proud of.

Alone. He was alone in the pub, just waiting for either one of his complicated women to show. Minutes ticked by painfully, this time he wouldn't yell, threaten or beg. He would wait patiently. Still nothing. Two beers later, he raised his hand and gestured goodbye. "I'm not giving up on you, you know," he called to Millie.

Millie

She HAD THE POWER to hurt him, take him down, to capture him forever, but she considered that she also had the power to let him go. Jackson could live his life, even with that woman he seemed so fond of if he chose. They could have children, he could fulfill his dreams, something she hadn't been able to do since her own life had been cut short. It was a spell of sorts, being trapped here. She'd always known it, from spirits who roamed the area to spirits who were now free. The thing that was holding her back was the thing that most upset her. True love, her dream of true love had never been fulfilled, her wish upon the star that night so long ago. Thinking back to Chad, she knew she had been well on her way to finding love, until he was taken from her, when he married another. Chad, she knew, did fall in love again, so how could it be true that he was her one destined love? She also knew that Chad had a very good reason never to set foot in Millie's again, not that she didn't spend decades waiting for him. When he had passed of natural causes, well into his older years, he and his wife, their souls were connected and at peace. She couldn't fault him for choosing a wife, now could she? It wasn't as if he hadn't properly mourned her. But she did blame him. He could have waited for her, come searching, but no. Had the tables been turned, would she have abstained from love in life, waiting to find love in afterlife? Yes, she believed she would have, and that made him a traitor of sorts.

Still undecided about her course of action where Jackson was concerned, she picked at her fingernails and gave it some more time.

The ring was missing but the door had been locked when she entered her room after supper with Chad. That was odd, but it wasn't as if she cared about the ridiculous ring anyway. It could have fallen off the dresser, she supposed, but it wasn't anywhere obvious. No matter. Her papers were strewn in her dresser drawer, but they were all accounted for. Perhaps she had been in a mad rush when she left earlier and didn't take the time to properly put her belongings away. A fleeting possibility was that Todd himself had been in her room, searching through her things. She wondered if he would have taken the time to read her story, highly doubtful, she supposed. None of it mattered, really, because tomorrow marked the day that her new life began.

Diving right into her writing, she held her papers clutched to her chest. She wrote until it was very late, every single detail, every single moment of happiness lay written in her story. This was her last night occupying the house with no name, and she had one more thing to do before she settled in for the night. Twirling her new diamond around, she allowed her eyes to take a look at the spot where the old ring had sat earlier. It made her quite ill, to think of it.

Jumping up from her seat at the small writing table, she opened her closet and perused her gowns. There it was, the glorious red gown that she had worn the night of the ball, she would always be fond of the dress that had set the wheels in motion for the new and exciting road ahead of her. Quickly changing into the gown, she took a last look in the mirror before hurrying to the door with the smile of a child. One last dance in the ballroom, and she would be on her way in the morning. Closing the door behind her, she locked it, and checked it twice, then made her way to the grand ballroom where the music had always beckoned her.

She had taken great care selecting the perfect music for the last night here. It was the song that was playing as she and Chad had danced that first time. Attempting to gain closure for her past mistakes, she let her mind drift to warm memories as well, seeing Marilyn gasp as she read her first line in the Jane Austen novel, seeing herself writing her very own novel and meeting Chad. The melancholy notes dipped and soared, mirroring her emotions, finally setting her mind free from demons of her past.

CHAPTER

Twenty-Eight

$\mathcal{D}$AYS FLEW BY AND blurred together into one frustrating mess. He felt as if he were the ghost trapped somewhere between dimensions, crying for someone to help him. He couldn't rest until he had helped Millie and now she wasn't allowing him to do so. Kristen had bravely volunteered to show herself at the pub, but he firmly declined her offer. She meant too much to him to put in the line of fire. With time to put things in perspective, he was now willing to admit that his relationship with Emily had been an unusual one. He no longer felt that she would walk through the door at Millie's, and he no longer waited for her, but rather, Millie. Emily was a sad, tortured soul that he had once loved very much, and he would always treasure her memory and wish her well.

It was on a sunny but frigid Saturday morning when the news of his divorce case came through. The knock upon his door had startled him, he hadn't been expecting company. Peeking through the peephole, his body became stiff at the sight of his lawyer. Was it a good thing or a bad thing that he had personally come to share the news?

"Hi Tom, come on in." He allowed Tom to come into the foyer before shutting the door closed.

"Jackson, good to see you. I know you're probably on pins and needles here, so I might as well come right out with it."

Balling his hands into tight fists, he held his breath.

"It's over. You, my friend, are officially free of any further financial obligation to Maria," Tom stated, waiting for Jackson to respond.

"You mean...?" He needed to hear the words so that he could tell himself he wasn't imagining what he had just heard.

"We won, you're free man." Raising his hand high, Tom waited for Jackson to slap it. He was free, a free man with no obligation whatsoever to that woman. He could close that chapter of his life and move on. Sitting down, he laughed as his hands shook. It was amazing to know this was over.

"Thank you, Tom. I don't know how to thank you enough." Shaking Tom's hand, he felt more carefree than he had since this whole mess had begun.

"It's my job. It's nice to see when the good guys win, though," Tom said. "Now I don't mean to be rude, but you've got your life to get on with. No offense, but I hope you won't ever need to call me again. Have a good life, you deserve it."

He closed the door behind Tom, breathing a sigh of relief. All of that waiting had paid off, and now he felt like celebrating. The only person that came to mind to share his good mood with was already being called on speed dial. "Get your butt over here, I've got some good news I can't wait to tell you about." She hadn't even asked what he was referring to; the only sound he heard on the other end of the phone was a shriek.

While he waited for Kristen to show, he paced the living room, unable to remove the smile from his face. He paced until he heard Kristen at the door. She looked like a breath of fresh air, standing there with her red cheeks in the cold sunshine. Maybe it was the news of his divorce being finalized or the craziness of the past few months with Millie. Heck, it was a combination of all of it. It was also because standing before him was a gorgeous woman with an even better personality. A twinge of an unnamed emotion registered as he put his feelings to the side for now.

"Kris, I wanted you to be the first to know. I am officially free of Maria!" He embraced her, unable to hide his emotions.

"You won? It's over?" Her eyes were wide with astonishment.

"Yup!" He grabbed her again and enjoyed the peaceful feeling that was settling in around him.

"Well, this calls for a celebration! What should we do?" Kristen asked.

They had the whole day ahead of them. A thought struck him as he pulled her hand to follow him to the couch. "Okay, how about we hold off on the celebrating, just until tonight. I had an idea." He proceeded to tell Kristen his plan. They would go to a local store, pick up some index cards and markers. They would map out all the facts regarding Mille, clues and all. Always a visual learner, Jackson didn't know why he hadn't thought of it before. Why wait around for Millie to share when he could try himself?

"*That's* what you want to do to celebrate?"

"I told you, we'll go to dinner tonight, right now, this is it."

"Fine, let's go to the store and pick up some fresh coffee and bagels on the way back. This actually sounds like a smart idea, I just wished I had thought of it," Kristen said.

"Don't kill yourself over it, that's why I'm the brains of the operation," he chided.

"Oh fine, so if you're the brains, then what does that make me?" Standing with her hand on her hip, he blurted out the first thought that popped into his head.

"The beauty."

The silence that ensued got him thinking again. Crazy, but part of him wanted to go back in time and try again for another attempt at the kiss that Millie had so rudely interrupted. Instead, he gathered his keys and jacket.

"Let's go."

"So ALL OF THIS adds up to what?" Scratching his head, he strained his eyes to read the print on the index cards. "And why do you have to write so small?"

They had been at it for hours and he was getting a slight headache, most likely from eyestrain.

"You're just cranky because all of this got us nowhere. Nobody was stopping you from writing, you know."

Index cards were strewn in every direction, Millie's name, their names, Emily's name, you name it, it was there. "Yeah, yeah, you offered to take the role of the writer, I figured you could handle it." Glancing at Kristen, he could see her hands crossed over her chest. "Sorry, I didn't mean that. It's just so frustrating."

"Tell me something I don't know. I feel we're at a standstill with Millie, she tells you what she wants to tell you, and all of the other clues have gone cold."

"You mean frozen?"

That got a laugh out of both of them. They looked like something out of a crime detective show, both of them stumped by the criminal. "Okay, I'm done for the day." Glancing at his watch, he stretched his neck. "How about we think about celebrating in a proper way? What do you think if I pick you up around seven and we head out for some Italian food?"

"Done, I thought you'd never ask." Rising to her tiptoes, she placed a sweet kiss on his cheek. "See you then."

*D*INNER WAS JUST WHAT he had needed. Sitting there across from her at a cozy, isolated table tucked away in the corner, he admired her navy blue blouse. "I like that color on you, it brings out the blue in your eyes."

"Why thank you, I bought it a few weeks ago. It's very sweet of you to notice."

He was noticing more and more of her lately but he was clueless as to what it meant, and what he should do about it, if anything. He was thinking about Kristen in a way that no friend should be doing. The hours before picking her up before dinner were filled with thoughts of her. Worried that he wasn't thinking rationally, that he was rushing into this plagued him. No, he and Kristen had been friends for a while, growing closer, if anything he had rushed into his relationship with Emily. Yes, that he would freely admit, and it concerned him that he had basically no self-control over his actions and emotions during that period. It just hadn't been like him, the stress had wreaked havoc on his brain functioning, that must be it.

There was a feeling in the air, and he knew instinctively that Kris felt it as well. This dinner date was different, the tension palpable. It was why they both struggled for conversation. "So, what's new?"

Kristen tilted her head to gaze up at him. "Since a few hours ago? Nothing, and you?"

"No, nothing."

Wonderful. He could bring up the subject of Millie, but he figured they were both on Millie overload tonight. "I'm sorry I was irritable with you earlier."

"Oh, that? It's okay." She swiped her hand in front of her and laughed.

"There's nothing wrong with your handwriting, not really."

Placing her fork down with a clang, she gazed directly into his eyes. "Okay, I've had enough. This is ridiculous, this stilted conversation. What gives?"

"You tell me." He had no clue how to voice his feelings at this moment. Was this all one-sided or did she feel it too?

"I...I don't know." She fumbled over her words, flushing in the candlelight.

"Well that's great, that leaves two of us." He placed his own fork down and glanced out the window at the dark street outside. They were friends, best of friends, and he couldn't formulate a simple sentence. The rest of the night carried on this way, awkward conversation and gaps of silence. In a moment of desperation, he had even brought up Millie's name but the conversation had ceased after a few exchanges.

"You're...you're not upset with me anymore, are you?" Kristen looked at him from across the table, her brows creased with concern.

"Upset? With you? God no," he exclaimed, reaching for her hand. They were getting somewhere here, at last. "Why would I be upset with you?"

Kristen glanced around the dark restaurant, her eyes finally settling back to him. "You know, I gave you a hard time with Emily and everything."

"Oh, that. Well, yes, you did. I see your point now, I guess. Looking back I suppose I was moving way too fast and, yes, Emily certainly had some issues, has some issues, rather."

"That's for sure," she mumbled under her breath.

"Hey, that's not fair. Say what you want about me moving too fast, but that woman only did what she needed to in order to survive."

"Huh." Kristen blew out a puff of air. "So you still have feelings for her?"

She was getting under his skin, attacking Emily again. He didn't like it at all. Choosing his words carefully, he leaned closer from across the table. "Why don't you tell me the truth, for once. Tell me why you disliked her so much." Maintaining direct eye contact, there was nowhere for her to go. He waited, but she didn't speak.

"I thought so."

Raw emotions took over as he grabbed her neck, pulling her closer. He was kissing his best friend and, yes, it was absolutely crazy. From her sexy southern twang to her beautiful smile, he liked everything about her. He didn't stop it from continuing and neither did she. Had Millie not intervened that night, he could have experienced this amazing chemical attraction many times before today. Damn, he and Millie were going to have a little talk, that ghost knew exactly what she was doing and why. Even Emily's kiss paled in comparison. It was mysterious and intriguing, but it had always felt as if he had no choice in the matter, like he was under a spell with the woman. This was attraction and friendship, melding into one to make him feel the most amazing emotions in his entire adult life.

"Jackson, I thought…" Her swollen lips tugged at him, he wanted more. Silencing her with another kiss, an even deeper one, he finally released her.

"I was a fool. Forgive me, Kristen, but I should be knocked over with a two by four. Where have you been?"

"I've been right here beside you, all along."

"Why don't we go see the gang? I really miss them, you know?" Kristen scrunched her nose in the most adorable manner. It had been days since that kiss at dinner and he still couldn't stop the moment from replaying in his mind. He wanted to take her and squeeze her right here and now, in the middle of the lunch crowd at The Jetty. As anxious as he was to spend every second with his best friend sitting across from him, he wanted to take it slow so their relationship didn't end up in the proverbial garbage pile with the rest of his failed relationships. What he and Kristen had felt so different than anything he had ever experienced and, although he wanted to take it slow, he was also prepared to hold it tight, if that made any sense at all.

"No way," he said it again, just as he had the past several times she had asked. "You of all people should be running in the opposite direction."

"I know, you're right. I miss the place though."

"Yes, that I understand, but give it some time, I think old Millie is going to come around yet. She's got to. She couldn't have exposed this much to me and then nothing. She wants her story to end, I know it."

"But then why hasn't she been around the past few weeks? It doesn't make sense for her to share so much and then pull back."

"You're right, she's pulled back for a reason, maybe she's biding her time, all I know is that she's making me nuts. All this waiting around," Jackson explained as he reached for her hand from across the table.

"How about we take a day off? Forget about Millie, take a road trip, something," Kristen suggested, biting at her lip in a most sexy way.

"A day trip? That doesn't sound half bad but what's there to do around here off-season besides heading to a casino?"

"The casino you say?" A spark of mischief filled her blue eyes.

There were plenty of casinos within twenty minutes from here. He wasn't the gambling kind, but there were shows, fancy restaurants, and plenty of shops at the casino. The idea wasn't half bad.

"The casino it is. Hey, would you like to stay there overnight? I promise to ask for double beds, even adjoining rooms if you'd feel better about it?" It would be great to get away from here for the night but being that it was a Saturday, he hoped he could get a decent room.

Kristen lifted her face, her eyes narrowing. "I don't know, Jackson, it's so soon," she stated, twirling her hair.

"Tell you what, we'll get adjoining rooms or we'll just make it a day trip. Let me make a few phone calls and see what I can do. What do you say?" He hoped she would be game, when he promised he'd be a gentleman he meant it. Perhaps it was Millie's virtuous ways rubbing off on him, but he needed to be smart when it came to Kristen, even though he'd spent the last week seeing her every day, each day had been harder than the next trying to keep his hands to himself.

"Sure, why not?" Kristen agreed, taking a bite of her pizza.

They finished their lunch and headed to his truck while he was already conducting an internet search on his cell for some of the nicer casinos in the area. "Here, this one looks good, indoor pool, ten restaurants." Kristen peeked over his shoulder as they walked, nodding her approval.

"Hold up." Jackson stopped on the sidewalk and made the call. After a few moments, his smile grew as he secured two adjoining rooms. "How do you like that? We got the rooms; let me get you back home so you can pack a bag."

"You know, you don't have to do this, any of this," Kristen mumbled softly, her gaze on the sidewalk beneath her.

"Stop right there," Jackson ordered, taking hold of her shoulders. "I am doing this because I want to, because I'm a stupid fool who couldn't see what was right in front of my face. Now that you and I are together, I'm not letting you go." He kissed her right there on the sidewalk in broad daylight, just to prove he meant business.

"It's just that I can't believe we're here, I feel like I'm dreaming this. I'm also a bit worried, Jackson."

It wasn't like Kristen to dampen the mood. She must have been doing a lot of thinking about them. "What? What's on your mind?

"It's Emily again. You seemed so in love with her." She shuffled her feet, then gazed into his eyes.

"I'll admit you're right, what can I say except I don't think I was in my right frame of mind with Emily. I realize how strange that sounds, even to my own ears, but it's true. Now that I've gained perspective, it's almost like I was a bug, trapped in a spider's web." His emotions had been trapped by Emily for certain. Either the woman had been a master manipulator or he had just been carried away by his life at that time. Millie, Maria, Gary, he had been an easy target for sure.

"You don't think she was dangerous, do you?" Her eyes locked with his, a look of confusion played over her face.

"Dangerous? No, but maybe we were just two souls who needed company at the time, finding solace in a relationship that was removed from reality."

"Because she wasn't really letting you into her world?"

"Yes, it was as if she worried we would grow closer, do normal things, and reality would settle in," he attempted, but it didn't sit right with him. "Hey." He didn't know why he had missed the possibility before.

"What?"

"Okay, so get this. The only time that I saw Emily was either at the pub, upstairs in the bed and breakfast or on the beach."

"And?"

She wasn't getting it. His partner in crime was slacking. "*And,* what if Millie had a hand in this? It makes sense, God it makes sense. Think about it, Emily was privy to some of my visions, she saw much of what I saw and felt the same way about me."

He could see her trying to make sense of it all. A small smile spread as she nodded in agreement. "Maybe, maybe…"

"Forget maybe, I think I'm on to something. You and I were about to kiss that night, and what did Millie do? She put distance between us, she caused you physical harm. She never wanted us together but she sure as hell wanted me with Emily for some reason." It was like a door was opening, his ideas came flooding in.

"But why? Why would she approve of Emily and disapprove of me? She doesn't even know me."

"And even if she did, she would have no reason not to like you unless you were a threat of some kind…"

"Or if I was in the way of something she was planning." Kristen filled in, her eyes opening wider with possibility.

"Yes! And it's weird you know, whenever Emily was out of sight, I felt for her but not nearly as strong as when I had her beside me."

"It was Millie pushing you and Emily together," Kristen gushed.

"But where is she now?" They stated in unison. It was so good to be with Kristen again, that conniving Millie had wrapped his brain entirely around Emily with the sheer purpose of keeping him from Kristen. It had to be the answer. It was the only explanation that made sense, now he just had to figure out why.

"And did Emily have any knowledge of what Millie was up to or was she just an innocent bystander like you?" Kristen wondered aloud.

"*That* is an interesting question," he admitted. "Come on, let's go, we've got plenty of time to talk about this on the way there."

"Wait a minute, I thought the purpose of this night away was to take a break from all of this." She laughed.

"Yeah, well, we'll talk about it on the way there, that's it." He couldn't hide his smile.

"Okay, Jackson." Leaning over, she kissed him.

THE TRIP WAS LOADS of fun so far, but he knew it was because of the company. Hours were spent roaming the casino; they had strolled along the nearly deserted boardwalk and even had some fun in the local tourist shops. Now, they were seated face to face at one of the top steak restaurants in the area, housed right in their own casino.

"Did you have a good time today?" He didn't need to ask, he

could see it written all over her face, but to hear the words spoken would be nice.

"Yes I did, I had a great time. I think it's doing us both good to step away from everything."

"I agree. Hey, I just realized that we went hours here without discussing *you know who,* I can 't believe it," he exclaimed as he raised his glass of wine to toast.

Raising her own glass, she grinned. "To forgetting about her."

Now that she was on his mind again he couldn't believe that he had forgotten. "Kristen, I can't believe I forgot to check the attic, it completely slipped my mind."

"The attic?" She scrunched her brows.

"Yes, we never searched the attic. Who knows what's up there? I have to ask Mike if he's ever searched up there."

"That's a great idea, I'm surprised I never thought of it my-self," Kristen stated.

"Okay, no more Millie now," Jackson suggested. He rather enjoyed getting the woman off his mind and wondered if this is what it would feel like if he just left Millie's and never looked back. Could he live with himself? Definitely not.

"That works for me. Let's make a pact, no more talking about her until we enter Cape Florence."

"Deal," he agreed, diving into his gigantic steak.

"I have to find work, Jackson," Kristen mumbled through bites of her own steak.

"I thought we weren't going to talk about it." Jackson smiled.

"Well, we're not, not really. I need to find another job and Mil-lie's is the best place around to waitress, especially off-season." Kristen's attempt at finding a job near the pedestrian mall hadn't panned out. None of the restaurants were hiring at this time of year.

"How about *temporarily* finding some work in a completely different area, maybe office work?"

Wrinkling her nose, she shook her head. "No way, I hate of-fice work."

"You know, we've been using temps at the construction com-pany, it's easy work, decent pay, you should think about it." He scooped some mashed potatoes onto his fork.

"Hmm, I don't know," Kristen muttered, placing her fork down. "Are you happy with your work? I mean, do you love it?

"What do you mean?" He wouldn't say he *loved* the strenuous work and worried about keeping up on the job when he grew older. He liked the guys on the crew, though, so he supposed he was happy. He hadn't intended upon talking about all of this, but her question put him in the mood to share.

"I never told anyone about this before but let me start by saying I do like my job but when I'm older? I can't see myself doing all the heavy lifting and manual labor like some of these guys on the crew."

"And?" A spark of mischief caught her eye.

"And… I've recently started putting some money aside so that in the future, I can keep my options open."

"Hmm. What do you see yourself doing?"

"I kind of like the idea of owning my own bed and breakfast one day. Who knows, maybe if old Mike ever retires and sells, he'd think of giving me a shot at it." Knowing that he would also need to solve this Millie mystery, he figured there were a lot of factors that would need to be in place.

Nodding her head appreciatively, she waited for him to continue. "I know it's a lot of money we're talking about here, but if I start saving now, who knows?"

"I like that idea, you know, I could see you doing that. No offense to Mike or anything, but the house is a bit humdrum, I think the place could use some spark."

He laughed at her comment. "Oh, give the guy a break; he's got to be pushing seventy-five at least."

"Yeah, I just feel that there's so much potential there. Millie's truly is a beautiful, vast property. Did Mike inherit the house from family?"

Thinking it over, he never thought to ask. "I don't know, but I could ask, if that's the case, he would most likely want it to remain with family after he retires."

"Well, no worries, there's plenty of other Victorians around," Kristen stated, wiping her mouth with her napkin. That was true, but Millie's was special.

"What about you? What is it that you really want to accomplish?" Jackson studied her.

"Let's start by saying that I regret not going to college, or rather staying in college."

"Oh? What was your major?" He had no idea she had gone

down that path.

"I hadn't declared anything yet, I was just taking a few courses. I took several writing classes and actually got some decent grades," she admitted.

"School wasn't your thing in high school?"

Waving her fork through the air, she waited until she had stopped chewing. "Not really, nothing held my interest. I kind of just skated by on the skin of my teeth to graduate."

"But the writing?"

"It's funny, I caught right on, it just seemed to come naturally." She smiled, rehashing the memory.

"You could always go back to school, it's not too late," Jackson suggested. Sipping his wine, he watched her expression change.

"Nah, I'd miss you guys too much." She dismissed the topic. "Let's just hope I can go back to work one day soon."

He picked up on the way she changed the topic. Something told him she would have loved to have finished college, but didn't have the confidence in herself right now.

"Hey, I thought we weren't going to discuss you know who, and besides, if you ever wish to go back to school, I'm sure you'd do great."

"Well thank you, I appreciate that." Holding up her glass, they toasted.

"Not to change the subject, but any chance you and I can hang out in one of our rooms tonight, maybe with a nice bottle of wine? I promise I'll behave." Jackson placed his hands up in the air.

That got a chuckle out of her. "I never said I want you completely on your best behavior."

"Check!" Jackson called out, joking.

"You are so naughty, Jackson, did I ever tell you that?"

"Only about a hundred times," he recalled, smoothing his napkin on his lap.

"I like this," Kristen shared. "I've always liked you, you know?" She was growing serious, her voice lowered as she flushed. It could have been from the wine, but he was pretty sure it was from her admitted feelings.

"I like you, too." He wanted to kiss her right here, but practiced every bit of self- control he possessed.

Dinner was finished in a hurry as Jackson couldn't wait to be alone with her. They walked back to the elevator in silence, if it hadn't been so crowded he would have grabbed her right there. Instead he kept his eyes on her until the doors opened. They were the only ones to get out on the seventh floor.

"Come here." He pulled her toward him and then backed her against the wall. Kissing her like they were alone in a hotel room, he got lost in his feelings. The physical attraction was like a magnet, he couldn't keep his hands off her.

"You're going to be in big trouble, sweetheart, if you don't stop me now." He breathed into her neck, placing soft kisses on every inch of it.

"Jackson," she cried out. "You're killing me. Come on." Taking him by the hand, she led him to her room. Fumbling with her key card, he kissed her, disturbing her concentration. "Jackson!"

Laughing, he grabbed the card from her hands and opened the door effortlessly. Their kisses continued through the doorway and they spilled onto the large bed in the center of the room.

"So much for taking it slow," Kristen exclaimed through their kisses.

"Kris, you know how much I love your southern drawl?" Her smoky eyes met his. She nodded.

"But, shut up, you... you talk too much." He silenced her with his mouth.

CHAPTER

Twenty-Nine

ᗷACK TO REALITY. The night away had been just what he had
needed to clear his head. He and Kristen had grown closer,
and, despite breaking their promise to try to slow things down, he
couldn't be happier with the outcome.

Parking his truck outside of Millie's, he squinted at the third
floor window. *Where are you, Millie and why have you been avoiding
me?* He would speak with Mike first before trudging up to the
attic. An elderly woman held the front door of the Bed and Breakfast open for him on her way out. Smiling politely and thanking
her, he headed toward the front desk. She was the first person he
had seen come out of Millie's in quite some time.

"Hey Jackson, what brings you here? Let me guess, more
ghost hunting?" A smile lit Mike's lined face.

"You got it. Figured I'd come in a bit early before my shift
downstairs begins. Do you mind if I head up to the attic, kind of
look around?"

"Have a blast, not sure what's up there, though. I'm embarrassed to admit I haven't been up there is ages, since I first bought
the place. There were some boxes and such lying around, that
much I remember," Mike shared. That was kind of odd, to own
a place but not make use of the storage, to each his own, he supposed.

"Great, I'm going to head up, thanks."

"Jackson, I like your perseverance. You seem like a nice fellow."

"Thank you, Mike. See you later, okay?"

"Sure, go ahead up to the third floor and the attic is located off the largest bedroom, there's a doorway that looks like a closet. Just follow it right up, and, good luck, hope you find what you're looking for."

"Thanks, Mike, I hope I find something too." He had the feeling Mike would have liked to chat a while longer. As a matter of fact, he had been feeling it for a while. He liked talking to Mike, with his wife passed away many years earlier; the man was probably keen for company. He would make a point of stopping by more often, when things settled down around here. *If things settle down around here,* bounced around in his head.

No longer was he worried about encountering Millie on the third floor. As a matter of fact, he was actively seeking her out now so that he could close this cold case and free Millie from her dark past. From the last few times he had been up here, he knew exactly where the largest bedroom was. The echo of his footsteps slapping on the hardwood floors and the door creaking were the only sounds that filled the top floor. Here it was; the attic door. Okay, so maybe he was a little spooked, he would have to admit, as he walked up the creepy dark stairs. Where was the light? Surely there must be a light here somewhere. Coughing from all of the dust, he figured Kristen would have a sneezing fit if she were here.

There it was. A string attached to a light bulb, far in the corner of the entrance. What would the chances be that the bulb would even work? Pulling on the string, he was disappointed to see that the bulb wasn't working. Fine, no problem. He had recently installed his own flashlight app on his cell, one similar to Kristen's. It did the trick, but an actual light would have been better. Boxes were neatly placed, some in the front of the attic and others pushed way in the back. Let's see, if he were to buy this place and wished to store items, he would imagine the previous owners would have just kept pushing boxes toward the back to allow room for storage. He nearly tripped as he made his way through the boxes to the far wall.

"Where to start, where to start?" He mumbled, pointing his cell toward the boxes. Some of these boxes could barely contain the items, they were weathered and sunken. He tore them open, sneezing as the dust covered his nose and mouth. "Come on, come on."

Several boxes were neatly labeled with faded writing. *Alcott*, among other names. "Crap!" His heart raced as he looked around. He needed to get these boxes down where there was light. Starting with the largest one, he pushed the box and scooped it up, paying careful attention not to break it. With both hands on the bottom of the box, he made the first of several trips up and down the attic stairs. Once five or six of the boxes were safely resting in the third floor bedroom, he sat down and caught his breath. Rummaging through box after box, he found items of intrigue, such as old combs and photographs, but nothing to help him as far as clues went. One photograph showed old Alcott himself, presumably with his wife, a frumpy looking grim faced, old-fashioned woman. No wonder he had affairs, Jackson laughed out loud at the thought. Why didn't the town house some of these items at the museum? He made a mental note to ask Mike if he wanted him to take some things there. Besides knick-knacks of a time gone by, there was nothing useful. All the sweat and coughing for nothing. He sat for a few minutes just catching his breath and thinking. He had come this far, he might as well continue searching the attic for a few minutes longer. Glancing at his watch, he figured he could spare at least another fifteen minutes before heading to work at the pub.

"Okay, last shot, Millie." Sighing, he climbed the stairs once more, this time his flashlight app was ready to go. Chuckling, he glanced at the light bulb on the string. Stupid light, what good is it if it doesn't work? Out of irritation, he pulled on the string, surprised to see the light bulb turn on.

"What the?" Glancing around the attic, a chill swept over his body. She was here, hidden away somewhere, out of sight. Careful not to piss her off, he nodded his thanks and noticed how much easier it was to search the attic with some light. Maybe this time he would go the front of the attic, you never knew. Banging sounded in the back of the attic as a box fell over, causing its contents to spill on the floor. She wanted him to find something; either that or she was baiting him.

"Millie, let's make this clear. You do remember that I'm here to help you, don't you?" A chill coursed through his body.

Nothing, but he didn't really expect a response. Treading though the boxes, he found himself in the back of the attic once more. He would have never discovered this box in the short time he was here. It had been contained in a tiny corner of the attic, squashed against an alcove, another box pressed in front of it. He stooped down to collect the items to place back in the box. It would still be more comfortable for him to search the contents of the box down in the bedroom. This box was small in comparison to the others, but there had to be a good reason why she wanted him to see its contents.

"Okay, Millie," he mumbled as he sat looking through the items in the box labeled with nothing but a large uppercase E. Fishing his hand through the ancient box, he found some turquoise earrings. Recalling the turquoise items from the museum, he figured this had matched her comb and brush set. She must have really liked the color. Some quill pens and other combs were scattered on the bottom of the box. "Millie, Millie, what are you trying to tell me here?" Frustration compounded with impatience as he fished through the box. This didn't make any sense. If the original house had burned down, why would this box still be in the attic? Unless… somebody took her belongings *before* the house burned down and kept them safe, only to store them here after the new building was rebuilt. Why, though? There was something tiny and hard that was stuck in the folds of the box. It was a ring. Actually there were two of them. Picking the first one up, he studied it. It held a tiny but tasteful diamond in its band. Was this what she wanted me to find? The next ring was larger and quite stunning in appearance, diamonds swirled together like a carefree ribbon. They didn't make rings like this anymore, this ring was something else. Recalling his vision of her engagement with Chad, he recognized the ring to be the same. "Wow, old Chad there certainly had good taste," he whispered as he turned the unique ring around in his hand, admiring the clear diamond that he knew some polishing would brighten up and shine like new. Placing both rings in his pocket, he intended to tell Mike of the rings, but not quite yet. Millie had wanted him to find them, and he wasn't sure of the reason yet. Mike could have them back when this was all over. Most likely, they probably belonged to the town, but that could be sorted out later. Shaking his head, he was stunned to discover that a treasure trove of antiques and history had been hiding up here all along, right under Mike's nose.

"Thank you, Millie, I'll be sure to hang on to these." Crouching to put all of the contents of the box back together, he spied a tiny piece of faded paper. It, too, had been wedged in the corner of the box, hidden by the folds. At first he felt one sheet of paper, but then there was more, there had to be a stack of paper close to an inch thick here. Faded with time, but otherwise in decent condition, he gathered the stack and held it pressed together in his hands. Pages were out of order; he would need to make sense of them later. One sheet, about ten pages in, was mostly blank, but it held what appeared to be a title. What was this, a book?

A Tale as Old as Time was written in perfect handwriting, that would be the title of this book it seemed. Glancing further down the page, he spied a name, the author's. Written by Emily Summers. Emily Summers? Emily? He didn't feel steady, why would the name Emily be written as the author of this story? Sweat clung to his shirt as he struggled to catch his breath. Turning the box, he stopped when the uppercase E came to sight. What does this even mean? He sat trying to piece together this latest clue, one he was positive to be the most telling. Ruffling through the papers, he read pages that were out of order, but he was getting the gist of the story, it was a tale of a very innocent young woman courting a man named Todd Alcott. This was Millie's story! This was what she had wanted him to find, he was sure if it. Millie must be a nickname for Emily, of course! But then how did that fit in with *his* Emily? Was it a coincidence or was there more to it? In his heart, he already knew the answer. As he got to the middle of the stack, his fingers brushed upon a different texture, it was smoother than the other papers and smaller by comparison.

Pulling the paper up to eye level, he discovered it wasn't a paper from the story at all, but a faded old black and white photograph. Unlike the other photo he had discovered, this one displayed a woman, so unearthly beautiful, smiling widely for the camera. Recognition came slowly, but it came. It was so unreal, this feeling that possessed his body. His heart stilled and he couldn't draw a breath, he was going to be sick, it must be a mistake. But no, looking at him from the worn photograph was Emily, *his* own beautiful Emily.

"**W**HERE HAVE YOU BEEN? I've been calling you for the past hour, Jackson! Let's go, we've got a full house here to-night," John yelled from his spot at the bar. "You pick some time to be late my friend."

He couldn't wrap his brain around all of it; it was too much for him to bear. How long had he lain on the floor of the third floor bedroom? It was a miracle that he had been able to even walk down here to show his face, and John was lecturing him for being tardy to work.

"I'm sorry, man! I can't..." Feeling faint again, he sat on a barstool his head in his hands.

"What the hell is the matter with you? You got the flu or something? Get your act together and get to work!"

Tough love, yeah, that was exactly what he needed right now with this headache that was growing, and a ghost that had tricked him in the worst possible way. He had so many things to think about. Was it possible that Emily was a descendant of Millie's? No way, the two women had looked like identical twins. Emily was Millie and Millie was Emily, but how and why? Dammit! How could he have been so naïve? Wait until he told Kristen, would she even believe him, would she think he had gone over the deep end? And wait until he received his next visit from Millie, he would give her a piece of his mind alright. Here he was, helping her and doing something kind and she had returned the favor by messing with his head, making him fall in love. God, when he thought of all the secrets he had shared with that woman. He had kissed her, the ghost, or whatever she was. He had told her things about Maria and Gary and his feelings that no other person had been privy to. She pissed him off like nobody's business, hell, she was even more calculating and manipulative than Maria and Gary combined. She was quite the actress, quite the little liar, spinning her tales of spousal abuse and being infertile.

John was still mumbling under his breath, and Jackson could see the crowd at the bar was growing impatient and thirsty. Damn, this would all have to wait. He fully intended on staying after hours tonight, and heck, this time he figured there was a very good chance Emily just might show her face.

Working through the next couple of hours occupied his mind for the most part. Busy, it was always good to keep busy when his mind was raging with unanswered questions. During a short lull in the crowd, Jackson had texted Kristen, telling her they needed to talk, but not to worry and that he would see her tomorrow. Tonight, he had things to do.

When the last customer had paid their tab, Jackson tried to hurry John and Andrew out the door.

"What is with you today? First you show up late and now you're practically throwing us out of here. Cassie's friend is picking her up, so I figured I'd have a drink, keep you company," John explained.

"I'll have a beer, too. Tammy won't mind, she's sleeping anyway," Andrew added.

Great. Wonderful. The one night he needed to be alone, these two picked to stay and keep him company. "Fine, fine." He would be polite and then wait until they left. Something told him that Millie or Emily, whoever she was, would grace his presence tonight. Making small talk to the best of his ability, he bit his lip as he gazed at the clock for at least the tenth time.

"Well, it looks like our friend isn't too fond of our company tonight," John exclaimed, rinsing his glass in the sink and heading to grab his jacket.

"Nope, he's sure not," Andrew agreed, following along to rinse his own glass. Both men were on his nerves right now, hell, everyone was on his nerves. Moping along like Eeyore from his old favorite childhood series, Andrew nodded goodnight, closing the door, leaving him alone.

CHAPTER
Thirty

$\mathcal{I}$T HAD HAPPENED, FINALLY. He was now sitting alone, staring at the pub where he and Emily had sat for hours, kissing. God, he had kissed the spirit of a dead woman! Next, he gazed at the door, willing it to open. Nothing, the witch was waiting him out. "That's okay, Millie, I'll stay all night if I have to!" He slammed his fist down on the bar, cursing. No wonder he and Emily could never go any further than the beach here, no wonder she didn't have a phone, didn't invite him to her apartment, it was because she lived right here, under his nose the entire time.

"Emily." His voice came across as creepy, fitting for his mood and this place. "Emily, show your face. I know you're here, damn, show your face!" He dropped his head as tears of frustration and anger welled up inside of him. How could he experience all of these crazy emotions and survive?

He thought he heard a faint sound. There it was again, the door was creaking, opening, but nobody was there. It was her; he knew it as well as he knew his own name. As angry as he was, part of him wished to see her, Emily, in the flesh, one last time. Would her beauty cause him to calm down or become angrier?

Her beauty stilled his racing heart; it hit him to the core and nearly knocked him over. There she stood, in a glamorous modern red gown. She was utterly breathtaking, more beautiful than ever now. "Emily," he whispered, lifting his head slowly from the damp bar.

She went to him and took him in her arms, sobbing, with him clutched close to her chest. There he was, caught up in her spell once more. She had caused his anger to subside. When he could finally manage, he gazed into her shockingly green eyes. "Emily, why didn't you tell me?" he managed. "And, Kristen, my God, you almost killed her! What do you have against her?" He recalled the first night he had met "Emily" and her disgusted face at his suggestion for a gin and tonic, her offbeat comments about Kristen…

She smirked, a look of mischief in her eyes he had never seen before. "She was in the way."

"In the way of what? Don't hurt her, I love that woman. I'm in love with Kristen, and there's not a damn thing you can do about it." There. He said it. He was in love with Kristen, if he didn't know it before, he knew it now. A feeling of protectiveness over Kristen took hold.

"Don't be upset, please. This isn't how I wanted it to end, forgive me, Jackson, for what I've planned, for what I still must do."

"Don't hurt her! Promise me you won't hurt her!"

"She's nothing, she's of little consequence to us," she stated, using her hands to swipe at the air. He should have picked up on her diction, realized that she didn't fit in by today's standards. He was such as fool.

"What are you talking about?"

"Did you read my story?"

"Huh? No, I haven't had time yet, what happened to you? You are such a liar and manipulator. My God, Emily, you were so kind, you still are, I know you are, somewhere deep inside, I can feel it."

"Kind?" She laughed eerily. "I think not. Kindness will only serve to get in the way of what I need to do. But my story, it's no matter that you didn't read it. You know the most important parts of my life anyway."

"It was your life story, you were writing a novel, you could read and write. That's wonderful, did it ever get published?" He was baiting her and she was smart enough not to be fooled by his stalling tactics.

Again, the eerie laughter. "Hardly, Jackson. I couldn't even finish it."

"But… what happened? Tell me, please."

"Jackson, I don't think you really want to hear the end of my story, because if I show you, it will be too much pain to bear, you might not survive," she explained in her soft, enchanting voice.

"What do you mean? It will give you closure, you can be at rest then. I've done all of this for you, Emily, to set you free so that you can finally be happy.

"I'm afraid it doesn't work that way," she stated in a sad voice, sounding so very young. "Come with me and see?" She batted her incredibly long lashes and held her palm open, waiting for him to take it.

"And if I don't?"

"I think you and I know that at this point, neither of us has much choice. We fell in love and that set the wheels in motion." It was such as simple statement, but the words couldn't have been more true. He thought he had fallen in love with her once; she had helped him deal with his emotions regarding Maria. Conflicting feelings of love and hatred battled inside of his head. It was such a fine line, now he understood the famous expression about what love could do to someone's head. Somewhere in the back of his foggy mind, registered the fact that he was caught up in her spell again, but she was too strong to fight, it was of no use. Helpless to making any other decision, he reached slowly for the palm of her hand; he had always known there was no other way. The moment his hand was within her grasp, she cackled loudly and grabbed it tight. Did he say that he wasn't frightened of her anymore? He took it back, but realized too late, he was a goner.

"I've been waiting so many years for this, Chad." She sighed a breath of relief.

Chad? She must be confused, he wanted to correct her but knew it didn't matter. "This time, you'll see it through your own eyes. You'll see me clearly and know exactly how I came to be trapped in a lonely soul. But that's okay, Chad, we're in it together now."

She was talking nonsense, but his head was too clouded with the vision she had just slammed into him. "Maybe it won't hurt so much this time with you beside me. Hold onto my hand, Chad Tomkins, and don't let go. You and I have some unfinished business to take care of."

She was mad, but what had she just called him? He knew who

Chad was but this was the first she had referred to him by his full name. Tomkins was his own last name. His head split with pain as he wished he could make sense of what she was trying to tell him. She must have read his mind, for she laughed. "All in good time, you'll see how it all comes around. Hold on tight."

Jolting back, he was in her room. He saw her writing her book while she hummed and stopped to admire and spin the gorgeous antique diamond ring around her finger. It went in fast motion as she was now at her closet, reaching for a gown. Now, she was dancing gracefully in the center of the grand ballroom. She was in a red gown, but this one was different from the modern one she now wore, this was the vintage dress she had worn the night she had met Chad at the ball. She was twirling, leaping, and swaying to the melancholy notes. The music pumped the blood through his head, he tried escaping from her grasp but she held so much strength.

The music came to a screeching halt as she looked up. Todd Alcott's wife stood before her, her old ring and papers from her novel clutched in her plump, shaking fist. Spittle had formed at the woman's mouth. She strained to understand her ranting; she drew closer so that she could communicate with her.

"What are you doing? Those are my things." Why had this woman been snooping through her room?

"You're done, sweetheart, done. Do you think I'm going to continue to turn a blind eye when my husband flaunts his tramps around? You make me sick, women like you, going after another man's wife! What's the matter, you can't snag a classy man like Todd so you play the tramp for him to get free room and board, fancy gifts?"

"I... I didn't know, Mrs. Alcott, we never did anything, you must believe me." The woman was in an uncontrollable rage, sweating, fists pumping.

"Oh please, I'm not a fool! I've seen it time and again with him, and now I'm going to put a stop to it! You're telling me this isn't the ring he gave you?" Holding up the small diamond, Emily knew it looked bad, really bad.

"Well yes, but I had no idea he was married, I gave it back as soon as I found out, I swear," Emily stammered, clutching at her ball gown, her heart pumping furiously.

"Silence! Look at you, a tramp in that red gown, the same gown you wore the night at the ball, stirring up trouble, trying to make my hus-

band jealous, in the arms of another man," she shrieked, drawing closer. "And what is that?" Mrs. Alcott's eyes were peeled on her new sparkling diamond. Emily covered it up instantly, protecting it dearly.

"It's mine. You can have the other one. Just give me back my papers!" Rushing at the woman, her feeble attempt was interrupted by the sight of a shotgun that Mrs. Alcott had whipped out from under her coat. Oh my God, this woman was mad. How could she stop her? Breaking out into a cold sweat, she cried and begged for Mrs. Alcott to understand.

"I'm speaking to you as one woman to another. I never slept with him, never even came close. As a matter of fact, I haven't slept with anyone. I'm to be married to Chad Tomkins, you know him, please, I'm not lying. If you read everything in your hand there, you'll know I'm telling the truth." Hysteria rose in her throat as she saw the woman raise the shotgun.

Emily was on her knees, pulling at the woman's dress. She was too young, she had her whole life ahead of her. "Please, I'm to be married, I want to be a mother, a teacher..." Images of Chad and Marilyn, her sister, Sammy, and her parents swam through her head. She couldn't breathe, this couldn't be happening.

Fear unlike anything she had ever known before consumed her. Maintaining eye contact with Mrs. Alcott, she begged for her life again and again.

"Oh, you're good, I'll give you that. But honey, I know a tramp when I see one." Mrs. Alcott aimed her shotgun down at her, still clinging to her skirt, she closed her eyes and prayed for Chad to save her.

He never did. Oh, how could one woman endure so much pain? He felt her pain as strongly as she, and he sobbed with her. His head throbbed with so much blackness and agony. He didn't try to let go, not now when she needed him. Chad had failed to rescue her, not that he had even known what had happened until it was too late, but *he* couldn't fail her and leave her alone with all this pain, he had gone this far and he wasn't leaving her now.

As if viewing from the distance, they both watched the past flash back as Mrs. Alcott reached down and stole the diamond from the dead woman's finger. He opened his eyes, seeing Emily's eyes squeezed shut, sobbing so quietly, it broke his heart.

Closing his eyes once more, he squeezed her hand tighter, ignoring the worsening pain in his head. Mrs. Alcott placed her head in her hands, gasping, as if surprised by her actions. Glancing around the ballroom, she held the two diamonds and the papers tight. Mrs. Alcott ran from the room, but she wasn't finished yet. Moments later, she returned with a lit candelabra, glancing all around. Placing it on the floor beside Emily's lifeless body, she lifted the red gown and placed it directly in the flames. In sheer terror, Jackson held Emily's hand tighter as they rode it out together. He dared to open his eyes and his breathing stopped when he faced Millie. That beautiful face, what was happening? She shrieked, turning grotesque. He wasn't afraid, he could stand it. What he couldn't tolerate was the intense pain in his head, and the heat, growing worse with each second. When would it be over? He shut his eyes tight. Mrs. Alcott's screams of warning to the other sleeping girls sounded as he watched every single soul escape the house with no name. He knew her entire story now as sure as he knew his own life story, their connection was otherworldly. Todd had named the house Millie to appease her just before she discovered he was married. He saw it all, her whole life now flashing before him. She had never accepted the name, all this time she hated the name of the Victorian. There was so much he didn't know. The house had burned down to the ground, taking several other homes with it, Emily the only casualty.

Sobbing, he still held her hand, daring to look at her. Her horrifying face was twisted with agony. She screamed at such a pitch that all of the windows of the pub shattered. They were connected. He knew instinctively what she wanted. My God, he should have seen it before. Emily's thoughts came across clearly. Chad's eyes, he looked familiar to Jackson because he was his descendant, his great, great grandfather. The resemblance was uncanny. What had begun as revenge turned complicated as Emily fell in love... in love with Jackson.

The boiling rage that took over Emily still made her unrecognizable. He wasn't going to turn from her. He would grasp every bit of courage and face this monstrous looking creature eye to eye. If she didn't stop, he wouldn't survive though, the pain was already unbearable.

"Emily, you don't frighten me. I'm here for you. I love you and always will." Shouting, he grabbed her shoulders firmly. He would love her, in a way that no other person could even begin to understand. Still, she raged, screaming over and over until he could take it no more. "Chad loved you, but he moved on, just like you need to do! Kill me, take me with you… I made a promise to you that I would always protect you. I never break my promises. I'll do whatever stops your pain. I love you, Emily… that much." With wracking sobs, he shut his eyes tight, preparing for the worst. He would die for this woman, if it helped her reach peace. He knew her plan entailed a lifetime trapped in this other dimension with her. He would do it… for her.

The pain stopped suddenly and he could breathe again. Opening his eyes slowly, he saw *her*, Emily, the beautiful woman she once was. Emily's tears flowed freely as she placed a hand on his cheek.

"Don't cry, sweetheart, don't cry."

"I can't do this… I have to let you go."

"And what will happen to you?" He couldn't bear the thought of her tortured soul suffering for all eternity.

"I'll die a slow death until I'm nothing but anger and resentment, but I'll suffer even more if I take you. Jackson, I don't know if you can understand this, but all my life, I've been searching for true love. I had thought I had found it with Chad, but nothing touches what we share. For another soul to offer up their life for *me,* that's something I'll never find again, *that's* true love. It's you, Jackson Tomkins, not Chad Tomkins that has captured my heart. After all these years of searching, in you I've finally found my one true love."

He couldn't bear the heartache, part of him wanted to stay with her still but an even bigger part of him wanted to be with Kristen. "Go to her, and don't worry, I can't help but like her, she's perfect for you, I guess that's why I felt so threatened by her right from the start. I won't cause her any harm because you love her so."

Never did he believe that he could be in love with two women at the same time, his heart tore for this unearthly spirit he had come to know of as Millie and the girl that had become his best friend, Kristen. "Emily," he began, only to be hushed by her. Placing a gentle finger on his lips, she silenced him.

"Can I just ask for one more thing before you go?" Emily cocked her beautiful face to the side.

"Anything."

"One last kiss…"

They melted together as he savored every bit of love and affection from her. To her, he gave himself in a way he never would again. He would remain forever grateful for Emily, she had allowed him to trust in the human race again, love again, and have faith again during a time he had needed love the most. They had given to each other as well as received, the kiss continued, wrapped in so many emotions until she pulled away.

"Don't ever forget me. I'll always love you." Emily closed her eyes and she was gone.

"I'll always love you, too." He sobbed openly, reeling from the events of the evening. Watching, he saw her reappear, crying tears of joy as a light shone around her. She was leaving this house, this world, he could feel it, and now she would be in a place where she would finally experience the happiness she deserved.

He didn't even notice she was standing there until it was too late. "Kristen!" he called out, but then she was gone.

CHAPTER
Thirty-One

Millie

*H*ER ONE TRUE LOVE stood, holding her hand, bearing every ounce of her pain as she relived the entire experience, from start to finish. She had met Chad Tomkins for a reason, but not the one she had always believed. Sometimes two souls are destined to be, in a way that is truly amazing and uniquely beautiful. She had met Chad so that he could bring her to Jackson. It was Jackson she was meant to find, all along. Kindred spirits in a way that even lovers could never understand. She would take eternity now holding onto her memories of Jackson. He would always be close to her, sealed right there in that special place in her heart made just for him. Finding herself in the ballroom, she grabbed and twisted at her hair until it was styled up off of her neck. Letting go of past hurt was all part of letting go. No longer would she shy away from the color turquoise, either. She was in the mood to dance.

At first it was a feeling of lightness, then warmth. As the warmth flowed through her body from head to toe, she gulped. The last time she had felt such pure happiness and innocence had been when she had played with Sammy, cooked with Mother, taught Marilyn to read, met Chad, experienced all the pleasures of her young life. It was gone, the bitterness, the anger, the need for vengeance, all swept away. He had set her free anyway, and she had set him free, too. Together, they had done it. Dancing what she knew would be her very last dance in the Victorian, she squeezed her palms together, and a sound of pure joy escaped. She was saying goodbye to the house with no name. Forever.

KRISTEN. HE COULD ONLY imagine how it had appeared, him and Emily wrapped together in an embrace. Kristen had no idea that Emily was Millie, what must she be thinking? Why had she even been at Millie's? She knew better than to arrive at a place where a ghost had tried to kill her. Several times. But now it was safe for her, he needed to tell her everything that had occurred that night, starting with the attic and building up to Emily's novel. The novel, there was so much he needed to do, he would read it from start to finish, even though he knew the entire story already. Emily had stated that she hadn't finished writing it. An idea formed in his mind, one that he would place on hold for now. Now that Millie, or Emily, rather, was at peace, he discovered his job was not quite over, not yet. He knew Emily was counting on him to take care of her unfinished business, and he knew just where to start, but he would need Kristen's assistance, and her company.

Rapping on her door, he waited, knowing that she would make this as difficult as possible. What would he think, though, if the situation were reversed? Counting to ten, he knocked again and was met with the same result, nothing.

"Oh, heck, Kristen! I see your car in the driveway, open up!" Because of the late hour, all was silent in the neighborhood except the sound of his voice. The dog from next door barked wildly. He was going to get himself in trouble with the neighbors if he continued on like this.

Fine, so she needed time, he could give her that. Heading back to his truck, he grumbled to himself. What if she didn't understand? Even after he explained that Millie was actually Emily, would she be okay with everything then? Was kissing a ghost actually cheating? If that ghost was amazingly gorgeous, it could be problematic, he supposed. The good news was that Millie wouldn't bother her anymore; she could come back to work. If she wouldn't speak to him, at least he could text her the information. Keeping it as simple as possible, he told her that she was safe to come back to work and that he needed to speak with her, it wasn't what it appeared back there at Millie's. Heck, he wouldn't believe it either. She must have gotten his other text earlier and worried when he didn't answer her calls.

Waiting for a response from her, his cell remained silent. It hit him suddenly that he was dead tired, after the otherworldly experience he had just participated in, he needed his bed but seriously doubted that sleep would come. His mind was on overdrive, whirling in so many directions. Instead of heading for his house, he headed for the beach. Chuckling to himself, he now understood why going to the beach in cold temperatures never bothered Emily. He also realized why she never ate or drank while they sat together at Millie's Pub. Bundling his jacket around him, he chuckled as he figured he would appear homeless if spotted on a cold beach in the middle of the night. Grabbing Millie's story and his cell with the flashlight app, he made his way to the sandy beach. It was so peaceful out here, no matter the temperature or the driving wind. He was at the beach in front of Millie's, no other beach would do. Glancing back at the third floor window, he became emotional. There was nobody looking back at him, the window would forever be empty of Emily Summers. He would miss that girl so much it hurt, but she was very close to getting her happy ending and he was glad to be a part of it. Realizing how much of the story involved him gave him pause. Through his ancestor, he and old Millie had a connection that pulled them together, they were destined to meet and become kindred spirits. He knew that she would be in his heart forever and he was just fine with it.

"Oh, Emily..." he sighed as the wind whipped the pages of her life. Sitting there with his eyes peeled to the papers, he held them tight, not realizing until the sun rose that it was morning.

MIRACLE OF ALL MIRACLES, after he had finished reading Emily's story, he drove home and actually got some sleep. He had known her story, yes, but what he didn't know were some of the fine details, very important details that were essential to closure for both him and her. She got her happiness, now it was up to him to give her complete closure. Other things he didn't know about Emily Summers included her love of reading, what a sweet daughter and sister she had been, her sense of the romantic and her outstanding writing abilities. Had she lived, he was certain she would have been a role model, an author, and a mentor of women of her time. Thinking back to Marilyn and the other women in the house with no name, he figured she had been well on her way. It was a damn shame that she was taken so early, at such a pivotal part of her life.

Millie's would never feel the same to him again, there would be no sense of the supernatural, but he would always have the memories, and Emily's breathtaking photograph. Although he was on the schedule at Millie's that evening, he couldn't wait to speak with Mike. It was the first item he needed to tend to on his growing list of things to do.

"Hey Mike, how are things going today?"

Mike spread his arms, taking in the empty lobby. "Quiet, things are obviously very quiet around here. How are you?"

"I'm fine, better than I have been in quite a while, thank you. I'm here, well I'm here to discuss something with you that might seem a bit out there…"

"Go on, please. I'll let you in on a little secret, Jackson, nothing seems out there to me anymore, not when I own a haunted Victorian." Mike chuckled, glancing around.

"Well, that's just it. It's not haunted anymore." He let the comment sit with Mike for a moment before continuing. "Millie is gone, she's off to a place of peace and happiness."

"Huh? Wait, how on earth would you possibly know this?" His eyebrows knit together in confusion.

"Let's just say that Millie and I had some unfinished business that has been taken care of, almost, that is. That's what brings me here."

"Do tell, I'm listening." Mike tilted his head, his weary brown eyes glued to Jackson's face.

Jackson told the short version of the story, emphasizing the part about "the house with no name."

"And you know this how?" Even Mike appeared skeptical, with a firm line set to his mouth.

"She told me and I read her story." He proceeded to tell Mike about Emily's story, how he had found it in the attic.

"Whoa, her story should probably be given to the proper people, the Museum by the Shore most likely, and I'd like to read it too."

"Trust me on this, Emily and I share a bond, I need to hold onto her belongings right now, but it's all part of the plan to hand everything over to the town, the museum." He was already imagining her turquoise earrings that she hid away for so long and her diamond rings in their proper place by the comb and brush set at the museum.

"So what is it that you need me to do? I have to tell you, though, I kind of liked having her around, I think she was good for business," Mike exclaimed, shaking his head.

"I kind of liked having her around, too. But she's happy now and that's what's important. Here's what we need to do. Her nickname, Millie, was given to her by Todd Alcott, whom she grew to despise. He only named this place after her, and then only her secret nickname, because she was pissed at his lack of attention. She had no idea he was married, and all of his other houses had women's names, one after his wife and others named after his mistresses. This house was never named, so he did it only to appease her."

Following the story, Mike nodded, a smile setting in. "I see where you're going with this and I like it, I like it."

Interjecting, Jackson continued. "She never accepted the name and abhorred it, period. To this day, she still referred to this house as the house with no name. In Emily's honor, I'd like to change that. I'd like to call this house Jane's Ending. She wouldn't want it named after her. She had tremendous respect for Jane Austen, the author, and I think it's perfect, she finally came to the end of a long, hard road, and now she's at peace. It was her house, like it or not, she deserves this title."

"Jane's Ending? I kind of like that? Let me think about it. What would the pub be called?"

"Jane's Pub, and please; you know it's the right thing to do."

Waving his hand through the air, he sighed. "Oh, all right. I don't know what your buddy John will think of all this, but fine, I kind of like it."

"I had a feeling you would, and don't worry about John, his bark is worse than his bite." Mike owned the entire property, so it didn't much matter what John felt anyway. He figured he'd complain and then get over it, as usual.

Jackson thanked Mike and turned to leave, but then stopped as he felt the old man's gaze upon him. Sure enough, Mike's brown eyes seemed to look through him. A strange feeling swept over Jackson, but as quickly as it came it was gone. Mike lifted a hand to wave goodbye.

CHAPTER
Thirty-Two

SHE STILL WOULDN'T ANSWER his calls. Nor did she stop by the pub as he had expected. If she had gotten his numerous texts, basically begging for her to give him a chance to explain, she had ignored them all. He needed a new plan of action; he had to speak with her. His last text had even explained that Emily was actually Millie. She probably thought he belonged in a mental facility.

John whistled as he poured a beer for a man at the other end of the bar. Apparently Mike hadn't told him about the name change yet. He had been thinking all day of changing the sign out front, once he got Mike's okay. He could offer to collaborate to come up with a design. Maybe Jane's Ending with a tasteful book or an etching of the ocean. He had time, but the idea was growing on him, Emily would have been pleased.

"Hey, have you seen or heard from Kristen lately?" He called over to John.

His friend smirked. "As a matter of fact I have. I have no idea what's going on with the two of you and quite frankly I really don't care to know at this point, just leave me and work out of it."

"What did she say?"

"She asked for her job back, that's it."

Good, that was good. So she had received his messages.

"That's it?" He had a feeling there was more.

"Oh, yeah. And she doesn't want to work any shifts when you're here." John nodded as he spoke.

Bad, that was bad. "Fine, when is she working next?"

"Figure it out, when's the next night you're off?"

John was such a smart ass, he couldn't stand it. He would stop by tomorrow night and attempt to see her, speak with her.

*H*USTLING TO HER TABLES, he sat at his favorite booth. She had been so busy she hadn't seen him walk through the door. He figured it was just a matter of time before she spotted him, slouched in the corner, hiding behind a menu.

"Hi there," she drawled. He had missed that southern twang of hers. "What can I get for you tonight?"

"A minute of your time," he said, slowly revealing his face. She was furious; he could see it in her stormy eyes. "Kris, we need to talk, you can't hide from me forever, work different shifts, come on."

"I have nothing to say to you. If you want something, serve yourself." She strutted off in a huff. Adorable, even when angry, he waited her out. Each time she sprinted by, he attempted to make eye contact. She was one stubborn woman.

He couldn't take much more of being ignored, not by her. The next time she walked by, he gently placed his hand on her arm. "Kindly remove your hand or I'll scream." She hissed through clenched teeth.

"Kindly sit with me or I'll scream. I will, I'll make a scene, I'll tell everyone all about that cute little birthmark on your thigh." He winked at her.

"You wouldn't!" She seethed, sliding into the booth across from him.

Of course he wouldn't, but she didn't need to know that. "I am working, I have customers, what is it that you want?" Her eyes rolled to the ceiling. God, she was adorable.

"I want you to listen to me very carefully. Emily is Millie." Her eyebrows rose in displeasure. "Millie is Emily, oh, you know what I'm saying."

"And *I* think you've finally lost it. I don't care if the woman is the soul of Amelia Earhart, reincarnated, we're done!" Kristen spat, swiping a stray hair from her face.

"Amelia Earhart?" Where the heck did that come from?

"Whatever. I don't care who she is, ghost, human, you can have her. I hope the both of you are very happy together, because I won't be a part of this sick paranormal love triangle any longer."

"So you believe me."

"That's neither here nor there, but yes, I believe you." She sighed heavily, glancing at the table. "But it doesn't change what you did, Jackson, especially after the weekend we had. God, you hurt me." Her eyes misted over.

Grabbing her hand from across the table, he was secretly thrilled she allowed him to hold on. "I'm sorry, you have to know that, but it isn't what it seems."

Blowing a deep breath through her mouth, she choked back a sob. "Oh, I've heard *that* before, but from you, Jackson? *You?* I thought you were different, I trusted you!"

"And you can *still* trust me!" He was losing his patience, he figured if she believed Emily was Millie she would understand.

"Tell me one good reason why I can trust you!" She managed through her tears.

"Because I love you, dammit, I'm in love with you."

"What did you say?" she whispered.

"I *said* I love you, it was you, your face that I saw when she started sucking me under, taking me with her. I wanted to stay here, so I could be with you." His eyes watered and he stifled back a sob.

"You love me?"

"I do, from the top of your blonde head to your tiny feet, and that southern accent? Ugh… you kill me."

She was by his side, kissing him through her tears. "I love you, too." He placed his mouth on hers, gently kissing her.

"Hey! What the heck is going on here? This is a place of business!" John shouted across the booth, startling them both. He couldn't help but laugh as Andrew slunk by, his face as red as a tomato.

"Go, I'll be here waiting for you, and I really am hungry. How about a burger and a salad?" he asked as Kristen stooped to kiss him once more. He could now breathe again, now that she was back where she belonged.

Watching Kristen sashay around Millie's Pub, correct that, soon to be Jane's Pub wasn't a bad way to pass the time, she was so darn sexy. With dinner in his stomach and Kristen finishing up her shift, he got to his feet to help her clean up.

"What's this? Now you're hanging out here when you're not on the schedule? The lady said she didn't want to work here when you're around," John barked from across the room.

Was the man kidding? Prepared to give John a piece of his mind, he opened his mouth to speak when he saw John's smirk spread into a full blown smile. "Seriously, I'm glad you guys seemed to have finally worked through your *many* issues. You guys look good together."

"Ah, he does have a heart!" Jackson quipped, getting a reaction from Andrew who was standing beside him.

"I always knew it was somewhere in there," Andrew added, giving Jackson a rare high five.

"Who wants a beer?" For once, in a long while, everyone's hand shot up. Placing the beer glasses down, he turned to prepare a gin and tonic for Kristen first. The men gathered around, and they sat and talked for hours. Jackson still felt that John was nowhere near ready to open his mind to the tale of Emily, or a tale as old as time, as he was now also referring to her own title describing her life. Maybe another time, who knew, but for now he was content to sit and enjoy the company of good friends.

Only when they were alone did he go out to his truck to retrieve Emily's partial novel. He wanted to read it again, this time in Kristen's company. After grabbing another drink for both of them, they settled into his favorite booth. Taking out the old black and white photo, he placed it beside him on the table, along with both rings and the earrings. "Wow." Kristen fingered the stunning diamond ring that had been from Chad. "This is freaking amazing!" He allowed her to twirl it around, catching the light, it created a hundred different colors. He didn't have the heart to take it from her hands, so he let her admire it until she placed it down.

He began reading the story aloud, stopping to make comments here and there.

"Can you just read and then we'll talk about it? You're breaking the flow of her story," Kristen asked, kissing him gently on the cheek.

"Fine," he stated, feigning that she had hurt his feelings. He was well into the story when she gently took the papers from his hands.

"Here, let me have a turn." Her voice was silk as it flowed from one page to the next. It didn't take a detective to tell him that Kristen was now falling for Emily as well, in her own way, that is.

"Listen here." Kristen pointed at the page she had been reading. "It's so, so sad. I wonder what her wish had been?"

"Huh?" He hadn't been listening, he had been caught zoning out, staring at Kristen. He loved her compassionate side, heck, he loved everything about her.

"I *said*, the wish upon the star, she never got her wish and Chad never knew what she had wished for." A lone tear slid down Kristen's face as he kissed it away.

Emily had gotten her wish, it had taken a while, but she, or rather they, had found their own strange twist on true love. "I believe she did get her wish after all."

She tilted her head, gazing up at him. "She did? How do you know?"

"It's complicated, but let's just say she found what she had been looking for," Jackson mumbled.

Kristen averted her glance and pouted ever so slightly before turning to face him once more. "You know what? I don't want to know."

"Good, now continue reading." He kissed the top of her head as she snuggled into his chest and read the rest of Emily's tale. By the time she had finished reading, they were both in tears.

"Look at us, a bunch of fools," Kristen sobbed, wiping at her eyes. "It's just so heartbreaking and so very sad that she never got to finish her story."

Swiping at his own tears, he couldn't agree more. "Isn't it though?"

"And to think, justice was never served, you said Mrs. Alcott was never apprehended or even suspected of committing the crime?" Kristen asked.

"Oh, I think justice was served, Emily claimed to have haunted this house and Mrs. Alcott when it was rebuilt and they resided here. Remember, it was much fancier after it had been rebuilt. Mrs. Alcott was said to have had a nervous breakdown. If I know anything, Emily was quite capable of spooking people. She got her justice there."

"I suppose so, and Mr. Alcott, too. I figure the way he ran off and never even sold this place, he must have been scared out of his mind. I bet he never took advantage of young women ever again," Kristen mused.

"The box in the attic, though? How do you suppose it got there?" Kristen gazed up at him.

"I would venture to guess that when Mrs. Alcott took Emily's things, she gathered them all up to shove in her husband's face, after the fact." Jackson figured Mary Alcott had threatened the man, bringing back evidence of the crime she had committed. This way, he would know what she was capable of and he probably kept her secret and never ran around on her again. The box had most likely been stashed away, hidden from prying eyes.

They sat for a moment, wrapped in each other's arms, neither in the mood to speak. If only there was some way to make this grim situation better. It felt so wrong to have her book left unfinished.

"She was so talented. I love to read, I've even read many books by Jane Austen. This girl, Emily, she had a real talent."

"I know." He had read more than a few good books himself, so he wasn't just saying it. He knew what he must do, within seconds it had hit him. "Hey, how would you like to help me finish writing her story?"

"What? Really? I mean, could we actually do that?" She shot out of his arms and pressed her shoulders back.

"I think between the two of us, we just might be able to." He would definitely need help in the writing department and Kris seemed to fit the bill. "Kris, no pun intended, but will you be my ghostwriter?"

Her eyebrows shot up and she doubled over. "That was good, you know that? Very funny." Through his own laughter, he was glad that they could find some humor in the otherwise grim situation. He supposed that's why they worked, why they clicked together as a team.

"But seriously, would you?"

"Me? Seriously?"

"Sure, I know the end of the story because I was basically there. Are you game?"

Placing her hands on the table, she drummed her fingers. "I kind of liked being your partner and now that our search for clues has ended…"

"Kris, I think it's safe to say we make a good team, what do you say?" Leaning up to look in his eyes, she kissed him.

"I say it sounds like a spectacular idea, what do you say, partner?" With a wink, she kissed him again.

"What do you say we spend the night here? It's late and I'm sure Mike wouldn't mind. We can even go up to the third floor if you're daring enough," Jackson challenged with mischief in his eyes.

"Ah, no." Kristen laughed. "I'm not that adventurous, not yet anyhow. Let's make it the first floor and it's a deal."

"Deal." Jackson stated as he grabbed her hand.

CHAPTER
Thirty-Three

T HEY HAD AGREED TO meet up as soon as Jackson had finished work on the construction site. It had been a long day with very little sleep the night before. He was getting too old for this staying up half the night, but he had found it difficult to sleep once he and Kristen had settled themselves into one of the first floor rooms. At one point he could have sworn he heard footsteps outside their room, and, considering that Mike was fast asleep on the other side of the house, it did get him wondering, especially since Mike had shared that all of the guests had checked out earlier in the afternoon. He had even woken Kristen asking if she had heard anything. Her annoyed, clipped response that ghosts had gone to his head finally allowed him to get some sleep.

"Let me speak! You can't keep interrupting with questions. How about you tape record me on your cell and then you can play it back to your heart's content?" He and Kristen had gotten little accomplished as she kept interrupting and he kept kissing her. Fine team they made today.

"*That* is actually a very good idea. Take it from the top," Kristen exclaimed, fighting back her laughter.

"Ugh! Okay, last time!" he groaned.

And so it went, he told the rest of Emily's story the best he could. Once they were finished with their banter, he found it impossible to tell the story without getting emotional.

"I don't know how you witnessed that; I can't imagine how difficult it must have been for you, even without the headache, I don't think I could have watched."

"Difficult for me? No, it was horrendous for her, and to imagine she had to go through the emotions twice, in order to find closure?"

"She needed the closure, and she wanted you there to help her through," Kristen whispered, tears flowing openly now. She was getting it. He was relieved to see that Kristen was finally coming to understand the inexplicable bond he and Emily shared. It would make the writing of the story flow smoother. Deciding to keep the partial manuscript in its original state, the last quarter of the novel would be authored by the both of them. He considered the final outcome would be a joint effort, co-writers, so to speak.

"Do you ever wonder where she got the title from?" Kristen twirled her pen in her mouth, thoughtful. He had thought about the same thing, many times and he believed he had figured it out.

"A Tale as Old as Time. I believe it's pretty clear. At first I was convinced she meant the love story, love stories are tales as old as time. But then, she was crushed and betrayed by Todd, so I figured that's also a tale as old as time, men cheating, hurting innocent women."

Kristen followed, nodding in understanding. "But there's more…"

"Yes, there is." How could he explain this last part without hurting her feelings? "In the end, after all her struggles and heartache, she gets her wish."

"Her wish upon the star… you never told me what it was," Kristen whispered.

"She finds her soul mate… Kristen, listen," he began, trying to tread carefully. "If there's anything that I learned from this entire experience, it's that people can love each other, become soul mates, in many different ways. A mother and child, best friends, the list goes on."

Although tears misted her eyes, she nodded, urging him to continue. "Kristen, a soul mate is someone who would give their life for you, someone who loves you that much. I've been lucky to find two soul mates in my lifetime." Wiping his own tears away, he smiled as he wondered how Emily had turned him into such an emotional pile of mush.

"A tale as old as time, essentially then, is about life, and all of our experiences. People have been going through all these emotions since the dawn of time and will continue to do so long after we're gone," Kristen added, her gaze on Jackson.

"Yes, and as Emily had pondered that very first night on the beach with Todd Alcott, the oceans will remain, the land…"

"It's perfect," Kristen whispered. "Absolutely perfect for her book."

"Our book," Jackson whispered, kissing her tenderly.

OH, I THINK SHE would love it, she would be so happy!" Kristen squealed in delight, clapping her hands together.

"Whoa, relax. I'm not finished yet." He placed the sign on the workbench in his garage. It was pretty cool, he had to say so himself. Jane's Ending, it read. The large oval displayed a vintage font and a simple sketch of a beach and a closed book. It was exactly as he had pictured it in his mind, weeks earlier.

"Why the closed book? Why not open?" Kristen studied the sign, moving closer.

"It was a simple choice. Did you consider Millie to be an open book or a closed book?"

"Oh, yes, definitely closed, that woman held so many secrets, and for so long. Ooh, and her book was closed, finally finished."

"I like it," Jackson agreed, pulling her close. Holding onto her waist, he kissed her.

"Hey, you've got work to do and I've got to get to work." She laughed, smacking him playfully.

"Fine, just leave me here, all alone." Laughing, he kissed her goodbye and prepared to put the sealant on the sign, then it would just need to dry. It turned out Kristen was more than just talented in writing; she was a pretty good artist, too. Her representation of the beach and book were spot on. Now all he had to do was go and show Mike the sign for his final approval, then he would take the awful "Millie's" sign down and give Emily a bit more closure.

KRISTEN REALLY WASN'T A half bad writer, the final project was finished. Kristen had retyped Emily's part of the novel on her computer and then added the rest of Jackson's own experience with Emily. Kristen and he had spent nearly every moment of her free time on the project and it showed. It did help that the novel was more than three quarters finished. The last chapters of the story included the fateful night in the ballroom and closure. Kristen had even added some interesting facts from the Victorian era as well as a copy of Emily's black and white picture and some modern photos of Jane's Ending and Cape Florence. He was very proud of her efforts, it made for a spectacular book.

"What genre do you think?"

"Non-fiction memoir," Kristen answered.

"You know we have to place the original partial manuscript right beside it in the museum." Jackson reminded Kristen as she flipped through the printed copies of their manuscript. "Hello? Earth to Kristen?"

Looking up at him from behind her messy blonde hair, she spoke. "You know, I just had a thought."

"I'm listening…" He loved it when she got like this, she had some amazing ideas, he was coming to find, by working with her on this book.

"We *could* try to get it published."

"Really?" She shocked him with that one for sure. "How?"

"What do you mean, how? Like anyone else does. We'd have to read up and do some research, but I would certainly be interested in reading a book like this, especially if I lived in the area."

She might be on to something there and what better way to honor Emily? "Where would we submit to? Large publishing houses?"

"Large, small, and anything in between." Kristen scrunched her nose and continued. "I'm getting on this, right away. Oh, and I need a picture of the Victorian with her new name, so call Mike already."

"I've been calling him for the last few days, he's not picking up. As a matter of fact, I went there before work the other day and he wasn't around."

"The place was just empty? That had to have been creepy," Kristen commented, looking up from her laptop. Look at her go; she was already researching publishing houses, no doubt.

"Yeah, it kind of was. Maybe he took off for a day trip or something since it's so slow." He hoped the man was okay. He had let himself in the back way, through the stairs leading up to the bed and breakfast but there was no sign of the man anywhere.

"I hope he's not ill," Kristen said, her eyes focused on her computer. "Maybe you should check on him again today."

"Yeah, not a bad idea. Want to come with me?"

"Sure, just give me an hour or so, I think I'm getting some useful information about submitting Emily's book."

"Our book," he reminded her. But he thought of it the same way, honestly, it was Emily's book, her story to tell, hopefully now to many people.

CHAPTER
Thirty-Four

"COME ON." JACKSON TOOK her hand and they walked up to the front entrance, leaving the sign behind in his truck in case Mike was still out.

"I don't know, Jackson. It doesn't look like anyone's here." There was no movement coming from the windows of the lobby and it looked dark inside. They approached the front door, but it was still locked.

"I don't like this. I hope everything is okay with him." Jackson rapped on the door, but he got no response.

Taking her hand again, he led her around the pub entrance. Walking in, he winced as he noted how crowded the pub was. When, oh when would the man hire some more help? Attempting to sneak past John, they looked like children tiptoeing past their parents, sneaking in late at night. "This is ridiculous," Jackson whispered, poking Kristen's side.

"I know!" She laughed out loud. Too loud, John turned at the sound of her voice.

"Oh good, you're both early, we're swamped. Jackson, I need you behind the bar, pronto!" John ordered. Geez, he needed this like he needed a hole in the head.

"John, man. Kris and I have an hour before we start work. We're trying to get upstairs to see Mike, we're worried, he hasn't been there in a few days, and the place has been closed." Hoping

John would understand, he glanced at Kristen, but she too looked defeated.

"Andrew! Table three, hustle, for God's sake, move! Jackson, what the hell are you babbling about? Give me a hand over here." Shrugging at Kristen, they both took their places and got to work. It would have to wait, as usual.

His feet hurt, after hours of pouring beer and attempting to talk to John as if he were human. He finally sat down and took a breath. It was off-season, for heaven's sake, where did all these people come from? He shouldn't complain, he had an extra job that paid him good money.

"You guys hanging around?" John inquired as Andrew had already made his way to the door to leave.

"Actually, we wanted to talk to you for a minute," Kristen piped up. It was better the question came from her, John tended to listen more when she spoke.

"Yeah, I can hang around for a minute, what's up?" John took a seat next to her. "Jackson, can you grab me a beer?"

"Sure thing," Jackson said, reaching for a beer and a glass. "Kristen?"

"I'll have a diet cola tonight." He poured her soda and passed it over.

Grabbing John's beer and one for himself, he took a seat on the other side of Kristen.

"What's up with Mike? We've been trying to talk with him but there hasn't been any activity up there in a few days," Kristen announced.

"We're concerned now and wonder if you've heard from him," Jackson added.

"Pardon me?" John's eyes went wide. "Are you two on something?"

Jackson turned to Kristen who appeared every bit confused as he was. Shaking her head, Kristen spoke up. "Excuse me?"

"You guys *are* joking, right?" John leaned in, a smirk on his face. "I mean, it's not even a funny joke."

"Okay, stop. Let's try this again. Have you seen Mike lately?" Jackson attempted once more.

Glancing back and forth between the two of them, John's mouth was agape. Jackson had never seen the man at a loss for words.

"You… you're kidding, please tell me you two are kidding with me."

It was beyond frustrating how difficult it was to speak with his friend. "You know what? Just forget it, it was a simple question. Come on, Kris, let's go." Standing up, he pushed his barstool in. John grabbed his wrist, stopping him.

"You're serious, aren't you?"

Pulling his wrist from John's grip, he sighed, "Why wouldn't we be?"

"Because," John began, his eyes on Jackson. "Mike died a couple of months ago. How is it possible that you didn't know that?"

The world went still, he felt unsteady on his feet. The sound of Kristen's cry was distant to his ears. He couldn't process what John had been saying, it was too much, way too much to deal with. But, could John be joking?

"Man." Jackson found his words, hopeful that this was all part of a prank. "You're the one who's joking now; please tell me this is all a prank."

"I do have a sense of humor, believe it or not, but I would never joke about Mike's death. Come on, man," John responded.

Kristen's hands were on Jackson's lap. "Oh my God, my head is reeling, Jackson, what does this mean?"

What did this mean? How was it even possible? "Wait a minute here," Jackson addressed John. "Why didn't you tell us? How was this place open for business? Who's been running it?"

"Wow, this is what happens when you run around chasing ghosts. Your sense of reality has been compromised. Man, I wish Andrew was here to witness this," John exclaimed, shaking his head firmly.

"Okay, Kristen, come on. John, for once could you just open your mind to the possibility that there is definitely something going on around this place. This place attracts ghosts like nobody's business."

That comment seemed to give John pause. "Hey, Kristen, are you buying into all this, too?"

"Not only am I buying into it, but I wrote the book," she commented, shaking her head up and down. "Let's go, Jackson, we've got some things to check out upstairs."

John's mouth was open again, glancing at the two of them. "Fine, goodnight. Just for the record, I'm starting to get worried about the both of you. You might need some help, just saying."

Jackson ignored the man's comments, focusing on heading upstairs to the lobby of the bed and breakfast. If he had never been witness to this ghost business here, would he also be a firm disbeliever? It was hard to say, he would like to think he could listen to someone's account of events without acting like a total jackass.

"Why us, Jackson?" Kristen's question had been on his mind, seconds earlier.

"I don't know, sweetheart, I don't know." Jackson had heard that only certain people were open to perceiving otherworldly events. He and Kristen apparently, were among those who could see beyond what was right in front of them. Others, like John, were perhaps too closed minded to bear witness to these souls.

Darkness enveloped them as they made their way to the top of the old, musty staircase. It hadn't been this dusty the last time he was here, only days ago. Kristen cleared her throat as they opened the door.

"Where's the light switch?" Jackson grumbled. Whipping out her cell with the flashlight app, she shone some light on the surrounding wall.

"Here it is." Jackson spun around, glancing at the room beyond. "Come on."

The lobby was desolate, dust covered every surface as far as the eye could see. "What the hell?" Even the front desk was covered, papers strewn all around. Mike had kept this front area spotless, what had happened here?

"Jackson." Kristen came from behind, clutching the back of his shirt. "I've gotta tell you, this is really freaking me out."

It hadn't been all that long ago when he and Kristen had stayed the night. Recalling the sound of footsteps he heard that night, outside their door, he shivered. Mike had seemed so comfortable with the mention of Millie and all of the ghost talk. Even when Jackson had discussed changing the name of this place, it had been way too easy a conversation, Jackson recalled. Mike seemed to be giving him free reign of important decisions around here. And the attic? No wonder he seemed so calm about the mention of Emily's found novel. Jackson just figured he had been an easygoing man, now it was clear there was so much more.

"Kris, let's get out of here. We'll come back later."

"That's fine with me." Holding her arms across her chest, she shivered. It was late, but there was no way his mind was shutting down, he doubted sleep would find Kris either.

"You want to grab a cup of coffee? I think the Cape Diner should be open twenty-four hours."

"I thought you'd never ask." Kristen laughed. "There is no way I'm sleeping tonight."

There was no need for chatter on the way over, he didn't know about Kristen, but he required this silence to help him make sense of the recent events. So now he had been completely blindsided when it came to ghosts. The idea of Millie was one thing, but to discover Emily was Millie and then to find this out? Who the heck had been running the bed and breakfast, paying the bills?

The diner was empty, save for one man eating an omelet at the counter. He would never be able to fully believe what was right in front of his face again. For all he knew, the man eating his early breakfast could be a damn ghost.

"We'd just like some coffee, please." Jackson addressed the waitress once they were seated.

"And maybe some cheesecake?" Kristen added.

Jackson rolled his eyes. "And some cheesecake."

The waitress smiled and was off to grab their coffee. "What? I'm hungry," Kristen whined adorably.

"So, you tell me what you're thinking right now. I can tell you, my head feels as if it's ready to explode."

"I'm floored, Jackson, but I guess after everything we've been through, nothing should surprise me anymore," Kristen shared. She had deep circles etched beneath her eyes. Recent events had no doubt kept Kristen awake many nights, too.

"You're not sleeping much either?" He asked, hoping she wouldn't be offended.

"It shows?"

"Yeah. What do we do with all this? I hate to say it, but the thing on my mind right now is wondering how we're going to change the name of the place to Jane's Ending and how to get that sign up. It's really important to Emily that we see this through."

Kristen nodded as the waitress set their coffees and milk on the table. They remained quiet until she returned with a large slice of cheesecake. Digging in with her fork, Kristen rolled her eyes in delight as she scooped a bite in her mouth.

"This is *so* good."

Leaning over, he grabbed his own fork and took a taste. "Mmm, this is good. So what do you think?"

"I think we should find out who's in charge of the estate. There has to be a relative that he left the property to, right? And if he didn't leave it to anyone, the town would get it. We can ask John if he knows tomorrow."

"I can't believe it, poor Mike. First his wife passes away and now him." His wife. "Hey, Kris, how many people have you seen coming in and out of there in the past few months?"

She appeared thoughtful as she sipped at her coffee. "Well, let's see. It is off-season... come to think of it, nobody recently. Have you seen anyone?"

"Just one woman, she was older, around Mike's age," he shared. Taking a sip of his own coffee, he smiled. "You don't suppose that she was the missus, do you?"

"I have no idea. I only met her a handful of times over the years. What did she look like, this guest you saw?"

Jackson thought back to the last time he had seen Mike's wife. A vague image of a sweet elderly woman, very tiny, appeared in his mind. "I don't know, it didn't register before, but she kind of looked similar to Mike's wife I suppose, or it could have been a completely different person." Raking his hands through his hair, he sighed. "I don't know anymore, I don't know what to think."

"Listen, why wouldn't Millie have shared that another ghost or more occupied the house?"

That was something he hadn't considered until now. Numerous possibilities crossed his mind. Discounting a few, he shook his head. "I don't know, Kris, but think about what we do know about Millie." Holding up a hand, he displayed a finger. "One, she was distraught. Two, she kind of had a one track mind." Counting down the reasons on his fingers, he continued. "And three, she really wasn't much of a communicator, up until the very end, and, I'm sure Mike wasn't on the top of her list of items to discuss."

"That makes sense," Kristen commented, gazing out the window into the dark night. She grew uncharacteristically quiet.

"Penny for your thoughts?" It was one of their lines now, after reading Emily's book.

"Do you ever miss her?"

"Emily?" He wasn't sure where this was headed.

"Yes, Emily, Millie…"

How could he answer this question honestly without hurting her feelings? He did miss her, every single day, in an odd way. "Yes, I do. Emily was all-consuming; you have to admit it's true. She was good, she was kind, she was a terror, she was a force to be reckoned with."

"Sounds like most women." Kristen actually laughed. This was good, she was cracking jokes.

"Yes, Kris, as a matter of fact, it does," he quipped. "But, seriously, deep down, for all she had been though, it's a miracle she came so far. I'm glad we both had something to do with that. I'm glad to have met her."

"I guess I can understand that. After reading her book and helping to finish her story, I kind of like to believe I, too, share a special bond with her."

It was one of the things he loved best about her, her kindness and empathy for others.

"So tomorrow we'll ask John about the house and we'll take it from there. Tonight, we try to get some rest. Come on, I think it's time I get you home," Jackson suggested.

Gulping down one last sip of coffee, she grinned at him. "I'm ready."

CHAPTER

Thirty-Five

"SPEAK WITH HIS SON. His name is Ted Mansfield. I have to tell you, since Mike passed away, I think I've seen him around here only once or twice. It doesn't seem like he holds too much interest in the property," John informed Jackson. "As a matter of fact, rumors are swirling around that he may not keep it in his family, that he's looking for a buyer."

"A buyer?" Damn, if he sold the place, God only knows what will become of it. A new owner could do a number of things to Millie's, including keeping the name the same.

"I'm not sure if it's even true, look the guy up, and talk to him. I've got his number in my office."

"Sure, I'll do that. Mind if we get that number now?"

"Oh, sure, let me just drop everything and get it for you," John responded in his usual sarcastic manner.

"If you tell me where it is, I'll grab it. This is important, John, otherwise I wouldn't ask."

"Okay, give me a sec and I'll run back. Can you bring those beers over to table five?"

He waited until John had the chance to give him the number. He couldn't relax until he spoke with the man. Hoping that he would be as goodhearted as his old man, Jackson thanked John and headed upstairs to the empty bed and breakfast. He hadn't seen anything out of line last night as far as additional signs of hauntings and he encountered the same now. It had to make sense that if the place no longer appeared open for business, if Mike's ghost was absent, then perhaps the man was at rest. He certainly hoped so, Millie had been a lot to handle, and he needed a break, a permanent break from otherworldly spirits.

Holding his cell to his ear, Jackson waited for Ted to pick up. *Pick up, please…* more ringing. He had been about to disconnect when he heard a man's voice. It was Ted himself, and he had agreed to meet with Jackson in a few days to discuss his plans for the property. From what Jackson could gather, Ted was undecided about Millie's. He decided to wait until he met Ted in person to discuss changing the name and hanging the new sign. The man just might run in the opposite direction if he blurted out his real reason for the meeting. But what would he actually say to Mike's son when they were face to face? This place is haunted, and I'm soul mates with spirit who used to haunt the property, and she doesn't like the name? Oh boy, he had some thinking to do. It would probably be best to make up a feasible reason for the name change, one that excluded ghosts. Why would Ted even listen to him? Who was he, in the man's eyes, besides a bartender that works downstairs at the pub.

Taking a last look around before he took off, he tried his best to listen for any evidence of the supernatural. Nothing.

That night, while he lay in bed, he allowed Emily's face to take center stage in his mind. Would she be pleased with everything he and Kristen were trying to do for her? He knew instinctively that she would be. It felt right and that was good enough for him. Kristen and he were both exhausted and he needed to be up early for work the next morning, so they planned on meeting up after work at his place for dinner. He found himself thinking about Kris more and more lately, their dreams, their future. He could see himself and her growing old together, as corny as it sounded, it made sense. He couldn't consider anyone else for the job title of his partner in crime.

*I*T HAD BEEN HARD to concentrate on anything else except his meeting with Ted. He still hadn't come up with a plan for the delivery of his speech. Kristen wasn't able to join him as she was filling in downstairs for John at the pub. He felt like a nervous schoolboy as he sat in the old fashioned lobby of Millie's Pub and Bed and Breakfast. The name of the place had always seemed so long, too many cumbersome words. Jane's Ending flowed much smoother. Glancing around the lobby, he half expected Mike to come out, pat his back, and have a talk. He had never gotten around to spending more time with the man, it was no wonder he had appeared lonely, he supposed being a ghost could do that to you. *Help me out, man. You know the deal around here, you liked the idea, too.*

Ted was more than fifteen minutes late, he had no choice but to wait around for him. Flipping through some of Mike's papers that still littered his desk, a business license, and such. Yawning, he covered his mouth with his hand as he spotted an old driver's license. It looked as if Mike kept most of his personal items here instead of at home. He had the room here, why not? Who was this? Drawing his eyes closer to the license, he squinted. This wasn't Mike, but the license had his name printed right on it; Michael Mansfield. Clearly the man who had been running the place was not the same man, but then who the hell was he? His head felt full, he couldn't comprehend the meaning of the license in his hand. A door creaked open, causing Jackson to jump nearly out of his skin.

"Hi there, Jackson?" The man extended his hand and firmly met him in a handshake.

"Oh, Ted, yes. Nice to meet you, thanks for coming by." He could process what that photograph on the license meant later.

"So I'm assuming that you're a potential buyer?" Ted inquired, taking in the dusty room.

"Well, no… maybe." He had no idea where he was going with this conversation. Ted continued glancing around the room.

"Sorry about all the dust and everything. I have it on my to-do list to hire a cleaning crew and give this place a thorough top to bottom cleaning. It really does clean up well."

"Oh, yes, it does. I work downstairs part-time bartending so

I'm pretty familiar with the place."

Ted smiled widely. "I figured as much when I walked in and you were already seated here. Did John let you in?"

"Yes, I hope you don't mind," Jackson commented. The last thing he needed was to get off on the wrong foot with Ted.

"No, of course not. You must have known my father then?"

"Sure, as a matter of fact, I found some old things of his. Holding up the driver's license, Jackson looked at Ted. "That's your dad, huh?"

Ted took a step back and cleared his throat. "Ah, yes. Yes it is. Mind if I take that?"

Great, the man now thought something was wrong with him, wait until the next part of the conversation.

"Sure, here. I was wondering about something your dad and I were recently discussing," Jackson began. So he wasn't being completely honest here with Ted, but he figured the situation called for drastic measures. "The name of this place, Millie's, I don't think your dad like it much."

Ted narrowed his eyes, staring at Jackson. "That's kind of odd, my dad never shared that with me, as a matter of fact, he seemed to like the history and wasn't the type of guy to go changing things that have been working for years."

"Well, that's just it. Your dad and I had been kind of researching the history of this place and we found some interesting evidence pointing to the fact that old Millie herself despised the name, she couldn't stand it." He was sure the heat wasn't turned on up here, but he felt warm suddenly.

"Excuse me, but what did you say your full name was?"

"Jackson, Jackson Tomkins. Anyway, your dad and I had just decided that we'd like to rename it, to Jane's Ending, your father was completely invested in the name."

"Jane's Ending? How the heck did you come up with that name?"

"It's from Jane Austen the author..."

"I know who Jane Austen is," Ted interjected. Impatience was evident from the tone of his voice.

"Yes, and then ending, well, Millie loved Jane Austen, and she was an author herself and had been writing..."

Ted swiped his hands through the air. "Enough, enough! Listen, Jackson, with all due respect, I have no idea what you're talking about, but I will tell you that as the owner of the property, I'm not changing the name. Millie's works for me, and why would I change the name if I'm not even sure I'm keeping it?"

"Because... it's what she wanted," Jackson stated slowly. Realizing that he sounded like a rambling lunatic, he deflated. There was no way Ted was going to agree to the name change, not unless he sold the house and even then...

"Who? It's because *who* wanted it?"

"Millie, listen I know you think I'm crazy here, but just bear with me," Jackson stated, raking his hands through his hair.

"*Think?* Listen, I have another appointment so unless you're interested in buying the property, my time is up here." Ted shook his head and made his way for the door.

"Stop! What's your asking price?" The words slipped out before he could even think it through. What was he considering? He didn't have that kind of money.

Ted edged closer to him, a wary expression on his face. "Are you serious?"

Swallowing loudly, Jackson felt the sweat running down his back. "Yes, I believe I am."

CHAPTER
Thirty-Six

HE KNEW WHO THE man was, the one who had been impersonating Mike, it had to be him. Now, all he needed to do was prove it. Around here, there were no such things as coincidences.

"Now hold on, you're telling me you're going to buy the place? How?" Kristen paced the floor; she had that adorable expression written all over her face, the one where she scrunched her face, deep in concentration.

Fixing himself a cup of coffee, she glanced at him. "Milk..."

"And sugar," he finished. "I never forget, you should know that. They had come so far since that day when he made her first cup of coffee. Now he knew all of her moods, expressions, and dreams.

Chuckling slightly, she took the coffee mug from his hand. "Thank you. Now, how do you suppose you're going to come up with the money, and are you sure this is even what you want? Isn't this more about the name change?"

"At first it was, but now? I can't imagine somebody new coming in to take over, with all of the history, with everything we've both been through." He hadn't told her yet about his suspicions regarding the man who had been "running the place" for the past few months.

"Sure, I get it, but can you see yourself running a bed and

237

breakfast?" Kristen inquired. "Me, I would love to…"

"And you would help me. Listen, there's something I've been waiting to tell you. The man who was running the place?"

"Mike?"

"Well, come to find out, he wasn't Mike after all," he shared. That got her attention.

"What do you mean?"

"To make a long story short, I found Mike's driver's license, the *real* Mike Mansfield." Watching the expression on her face change, he continued. "It was a different man we saw and I think I know exactly who he was." It made sense, it was the only explanation. Even the way the man wished to spend time with him, getting to know him.

"I think…" Pausing for effect, he studied her closely. "I think he was Chad Tomkins, my great-great-grandfather."

Rarely did he stump Kristen, but he was pretty sure he did just that.

"I DON'T SEE HOW we're going to find anything here," Kristen sighed. They had been at it for hours, searching through records at the clerk's office. This time when they entered, Olivia humorously inquired as to whether either of them would like a job there.

He was at a loss as well. It wasn't as if they *had* to prove his theory, but it would make him feel happy knowing, that years later, after his own death, Chad had come to watch over her. The logistics were hazy, but if it were true and Chad had come back, what did that mean? Had he also been in a state of unrest? Doubting that, he figured that if any of this ghost business were true, which he now knew for a fact, that the rules might not be so rigid. He would like to imagine that old Chad had been very happy, but had sensed Emily's state of unrest. Maybe he had been there trying to help her, or an even more interesting theory was perhaps great-great-grandfather Chad had been there trying to protect Jackson himself from the fact that Emily had once wished to take his soul with her, which was why Chad was now gone. He'd like to think it was a combination of both theories. Maybe that elderly woman he had seen had even been Chad's wife, coming to take him home.

"What about one of those old ancestry websites, you know, where you find your family tree?" Kristen suggested.

Grabbing hold of her face, he kissed her right on her lips. "Yes! Now why didn't I think of that myself? Come on, let's look."

Sitting down at a computer they had signed on to, he searched the internet until he came upon one of the sites that allowed him to search his ancestors. The basic functions were free, but as he got more into it, he discovered he's have to pay in order to go back further into his family's history. "Come on, a great-great grandfather shouldn't be that difficult to find."

They perused the site together, Jackson typing in his pertinent family information. "Father, Eric, grandfather, Mark, come on." It would have been much easier had his parents been local, he could have just popped by, but they lived in Florida and were presently cruising the Alaskan wilderness.

"Bingo!" He yelled, jumping up from his seat. Every eye in the place was on him. Kristen laughed, placing a hand on his shoulder.

"Settle down, cowboy. What did you find?"

"It's him! It's Chad Tomkins, aged seventy-nine. I knew it!" More stares from the other guests around the room.

"I'm glad it was him, Jackson, I was hoping it was, for you and for her." Kristen leaned over to kiss his head. He glanced at her, and she was misty eyed.

"What I can't figure out is why she didn't know, couldn't sense him," Jackson wondered aloud.

"I bet she was so wrapped up in her anger and her revenge that she couldn't see what was right in front of her face," Kristen suggested. "So true love has many forms, I suppose, and it crosses many different boundaries."

A slight shiver coursed through his body as he pondered over her words. The human spirit is quite amazing. It's a force to be reckoned with.

"I suppose it does," he agreed, tousling the top of her hair. "One last stop, let's hurry, before they close."

Kristen scrunched her brows together. "Where are we going now?"

"To the bank to see about a loan, now move it, before I change my mind."

It was certainly a busy day. They had been to the clerk's office earlier to share their news with the ladies and thank them once more for their time and assistance with Emily's story.

Shelby's Books was the next stop and despite the look of sheer terror when she spotted them, Shelby eventually had calmed down enough for them to tell her Emily's tale.

"I don't even know what to say. In my years, I've seen and heard many things, but this takes the cake. You two should be proud of yourselves, you did a good thing."

"Thank you, Shelby, and we're sorry it had to be so rough on you," Kristen added. Shelby swiped her hand through the air, dismissing the comment.

"Nah, it was all worth it. I'm not saying I'd do it again, but I'm very happy that Mille got her closure."

"Emily." They both corrected Shelby.

"Yes, Emily. Hey, I'd love to read Emily's story, you wouldn't happen to have it on you, would you?" Shelby inquired, peering at Kristen's large bag.

"I do, but we're heading to the museum next, to place the story in its proper hands, along with some other items. You're welcome to take a look now, we have the time," Kristen stated, glancing at Jackson.

Nodding in agreement, Jackson watched the two women from different generations admiring Emily's vintage belongings. Shelby shed a tear as she admired the old diamond ring. It was the small one, the one that had once belonged to Todd Alcott.

"You two have made my day, heck my year. I mean it, thank you for sharing this with me."

"You're very welcome, it's been our pleasure." Jackson smiled at her.

"You know, the two of you should write a story about all this, you have so much information here to work with," Shelby suggested, turning to face them both.

"Ah, we already have. We finished Emily's tale and added some of our own experiences and such," Kristen explained. Jackson watched as Shelby's face lit up.

"Why didn't you mention it before?" Shelby nearly shouted, causing Jackson and Kristen to laugh. "We need to talk. I have a friend in the publishing business, it's a small press, but no matter, I could ask, see if I can get her to look at it."

Kristen's eyes glazed over. "What do you say, Jackson?" He reached for her hand and smiled at Shelby.

"Sure, that would be wonderful, thank you."

Jackson held onto Kristen's hand as she chattered endlessly about the possibility of having Emily's story published. Her enthusiasm was contagious, by the time they reached the museum, he was in the best mood he had been in for quite some time. He recognized Bill, the museum employee who had been working the day that now seemed like ages ago.

"Hi there," Bill greeted them with a warm smile. "Glad to see you guys back."

"Hi! You remember us?" Kristen grinned, looking up at Jackson.

"Of course I do, you two make such a nice couple, how could I forget?" Scratching his head, he gazed at the both of them. "Ah, sorry. You're not a couple, just friends, right?"

Jackson looked down at Kristen, whose face was flushed a faint pink. "Actually… we are, we are a couple." Kristen smiled at Jackson, then turned to face Bill.

"Yes, I guess you could say we are."

"Well, what took you so long? I could see it when I first met the two of you." Bill laughed openly. "Now, what brings you here?"

Kristen pulled the items out of her bag and laid them on the glass countertop, carefully explaining the significance of each one. Jackson let her take over and delighted in seeing her elated expression as she told each piece of Emily's story. Once she was finished, she scrunched her brows, rooting through the bottom of her bag.

"Hey, Jackson, where's the other diamond?" She asked, still searching.

"I have a special place I'd like to deliver it," he stated.

"Oh, well, okay." She turned to face Bill once more.

Bill rubbed his hands together, asking them to follow him to the display case on the far end of the room. They all seemed to notice Todd Alcott's photograph at once. With an angry growl, Bill reached down and removed the photograph and article pertaining to the man. "Rubbish!" Bill muttered. "I'm guessing we'll find a new place for him in this museum once your story gets out. Until then, he goes in the back."

Bill began to place the items in the showcase from the behind the counter. Stopping to glance at Jackson and Kristen, he spoke, "Hey, why don't the both of you come back here?"

Kristen peered up at Jackson and he nodded for her to go ahead. It would give him joy to watch Kristen place Emily's belongings in their proper place. Gingerly, she placed the delicate items down. The turquoise earrings complimented the brush and comb set perfectly. The original partial manuscript found a home beside them. Once they had placed every item in the showcase, Kristen and Jackson thanked Bill for his time and help.

The cold ocean breeze blew strands of Kristen's hair in her face. Jackson turned to face her, placing the strands behind her ears. She looked up at him, but no words came. His own tears matched hers as he held her tight. "I know," he breathed into her embrace.

Six Months Later

STANDING BEFORE THE GRAND Victorian, Jackson wiped his hands across his jeans. "That does it, what do you think?" She wrapped her arms around him. "I *think* it's amazing."

It hadn't been an easy feat, but between his minimal savings, a small inheritance he cashed in on from his grandfather and the business loan he was approved for, he had made it happen. *They* had made it happen. Nothing in his own story could have been accomplished without her, his partner in crime.

The sign for Jane's Ending was hanging up in the spot where Millie's Pub and Bed and Breakfast once been. The place was his and he had so many plans. The first one he wished to set in motion immediately.

"Do you have a few moments to come inside? I want to show you something," Jackson asked.

"Sure, I have a few minutes before I have to head to work, but that's it, we wouldn't want John to have a conniption."

Their day had already been so full, earlier they had taken another trip to the museum to place the published paperback copy of A Tale as Old as Time in the showcase, resting right beside the partial manuscript. Shelby had taken several to place for sale at the bookstore and predicted the book would be a favorite among locals. The small publishing company had provided formatting, editing, and a spectacular cover image, a blonde woman with her hair swept up, dressed in a stunning red gown. The woman faced a grand old haunted house, the setting of her turmoil and release.

It was perfect.

Now, Jackson had one more loose end to tie up. "Come on." He pulled her hand as they climbed the endless staircase together.

"Jackson, where are we going?" She huffed.

Once they reached the top floor, the third floor, they walked into the middle of the hallway and stood. "What do you think?"

Kristen glanced around, laughing. "What do I think? I don't know, I think it looks like a hallway."

"Oh, come on. I know you have more imagination than that. Picture it, the walls knocked down, a grand ballroom in its place..." He took her hands in his and began a slow dance.

Gazing up at him, she paused. "You're serious, aren't you? You want to make this top floor a ballroom again?"

"A ballroom, a banquet hall, it could have many purposes, even a conference center. What do you think?"

"I think it's a spectacular idea and I love you, you crazy man!"

He leaned down to kiss her for a moment. "There's one more thing that would make this place perfect and as a matter of fact, I don't think I could run this place without it." He leaned down further, until he was on one knee.

Gazing down at him was the most beautiful girl in the world, the woman who was perfect for his soul. "Kristen, will you help me run Jane's Ending? And will you be my partner in crime for life?" Tears flowed down her cheeks as she waited, hands covering her mouth. "Will you marry me?"

She sank down to the floor beside him as he placed the twinkling, ribbon, diamond ring on her finger. He had seen the light in her eyes each time she looked at that ring, and he figured he was the rightful owner, since Chad was his great-great grandfather. Besides, it didn't take a rocket scientist to know how much both Emily and Chad would have loved the idea.

"Yes, oh Jackson, yes!"

"I love you, Kristen, and always will."

She buried her face in his shoulder, gazing up at him. "I love you, too."

Leaning over, he closed in for a kiss. A soft, sweet melody from off in the distance grew louder. "What is that?" Jackson paused, glancing around. He distinctly heard what sounded like a young man's voice chuckle in mischief.

"Did you hear that?" Kristen's body went stiff as she strained to listen. Grabbing her neck gently, he pulled her close once more. "Something tells me we're going to have our hands full here." She laughed out loud in delight.

"Right now, though? I don't care about any of these ghosts that keep popping up, just kiss me." Jackson placed his lips on hers and forgot all about the resident spirits. This was the place he now called home. He was finally at peace.

ABOUT THE

Author

MYA O'MALLEY was born and raised in the suburbs of New York City, where she currently lives with her husband, daughter and three step-daughters. The family also consists of a boxer, Destiny and a ragdoll cat named Colby. Mya earned an undergraduate degree in special education and a graduate degree in reading and literacy. She works as a special education teacher and enjoys making a difference in the lives of her students.

Mya's passion is writing; she has been creating stories and poetry since she was a child. Mya spends her free time reading just about anything she can get her hands on. She is a romantic at heart and loves to create stories with unforgettable characters. Mya likes to travel; she has visited several Caribbean Islands, Mexico and Costa Rica. Mya is currently working on her eighth novel.

Acknowledgements

*J*GREW UP VACATIONING down at the Jersey Shore each summer. Thanks to my grandmother, Cape May has always held a special place in my heart. From the sprawling bed and breakfasts to the vast beaches, this town's beauty inspired me in so many ways, which is why the setting of this story is loosely based in Cape May. Alexandra, I think your love for the paranormal has rubbed off on me, no kidding. I wanted to thank my friends and family for their love and support. Alan, thanks once again for reading my stories. I value your input and opinions. Mom and Dad, I know you have read so many of my stories, starting from when I was a child. Thank you for encouraging me to dream. I'd like to thank my PA, Sara, for your support and for beta reading. Also, thanks for being there for me whenever I need advice or just to chat. Lastly, I'd like to thank my street team for everything they do, from beta reading to supporting me and just having fun interacting together. Writing A Tale as Old as Time brought forth so many different emotions; it's been a wonderful adventure.

ALSO FROM
Blue Tulip Publishing

BY A.M. KURYLAK
Just a Bump

BY KRISTEN LUCIANI
Nothing Ventured

BY KELLY MARTIN
Betraying Ever After
The Beast of Ravenston

BY NADINE MILLARD
An Unlikely Duchess
Seeking Scandal
The Mysterious Miss Channing
Highway Revenge

BY MYA O'MALLEY
Wasted Time
A Tale as Old as Time

BY LINDA OAKS
Chasing Rainbows
Finding Forever

BY C.C. RAVANERA
Dreamweavers

BY GINA SEVANI
Beautifully Damaged

BY ANGELA SCHROEDER
The Second Life of Magnolia Mae
Jade

BY K.S. SMITH & MEGAN C. SMITH
Hourglass
Hourglass Squared
Hourglass Cubed

BY C. MERCEDES WILSON
Hawthorne Cole
Secret Dreams

BY K.D. WOOD
Unwilling
Unloved

BOX SET — MULTIPLE AUTHORS
Forbidden
Hurt
Frost: A Rendezvous Collection